"They taught me so much about ranching and just things about life in general that were priceless. Now, nine years later, I'm still here—but they aren't."

"But the Bell is yours," he reminded her. "That has to help dull the pain a little."

"Yes. The Bell is mine and I intend to see that it stays mine." She gestured to the area beyond the windshield. "We're almost at our destination."

He said, "And it looks like the snow is starting up again."

"The cows will be happy to eat, no matter about the snow." She glanced over to see he was frowning at the fat flakes that were beginning to fall thickly from the dark gray sky. "Look, Flint, if you'd rather stay in the truck, I can manage this easily. Like I said, I do it—"

"Every day," he interrupted. "I didn't come with you on this trip to sit in the truck."

"You didn't come to the Bell to go to work, either," she quipped.

"I volunteered. Remember?"

Yes, he'd volunteered. Now she was almost wishing she'd turned down his offer. Just being with him for this short trip was working on her senses, and at the moment they were all spinning way too fast and in a direction that was far too intimate.

Dear Reader,

When Flint Hollister agrees to make a trip to Bonners Ferry, Idaho, he expects to be gone from his job as a deputy sheriff for only a few days. It shouldn't take him very long to find out whether Hadley's half sister has any information regarding Lionel, the late patriarch of the Hollister family. But when Flint arrives at Bell Ranch, he learns widowed Debra, his half aunt, has recently passed away and willed the mountain property to her devoted ranch hand, Pippa Shanahan.

A petite redhead with a stubborn streak, Pippa has been running Bell Ranch all alone. She's work-weary and leery of men in general. Especially one as rugged and sexy as the Utah deputy. But for Debra's sake, she offers to help him search for his grandfather's birth history.

Flint is relieved he won't be around Pippa for more than a day or two. Something about the ranching woman stirs up all kinds of strange feelings in him. But then the unexpected happens. Pippa becomes ill, and with no one around to help, Flint decides to stay on the isolated ranch to care for her and her livestock.

Nursing lovely Pippa back to health and tending to ranch chores on the Bell quickly change Flint's view of himself and the direction of his life. She needs him. But for how long? And is Pippa more important to him than his job and home back in Utah? Meanwhile, Pippa recognizes how much she needs Flint. But would she be foolish to think he'd ever want to make a home with her on the Bell?

It isn't until they eventually uncover the truth about his grandparents' broken marriage that Flint and Pippa realize their love is the forever kind.

God bless the trails you ride,

Stella Bagwell

STONE CREEK SHERIFF

STELLA BAGWELL

H Harlequin
SPECIAL EDITION

Harlequin®
SPECIAL
EDITION™

Recycling programs for this product may not exist in your area.

ISBN-13: 978-1-335-40228-8

Stone Creek Sheriff

Copyright © 2025 by Stella Bagwell

For questions and comments about the quality of this book, please contact us at CustomerService@Harlequin.com.

TM and ® are trademarks of Harlequin Enterprises ULC.

Harlequin Enterprises ULC
22 Adelaide St. West, 41st Floor
Toronto, Ontario M5H 4E3, Canada
www.Harlequin.com

Printed in Lithuania

MIX
Paper | Supporting
responsible forestry
FSC® C021394

After writing more than one hundred books for Harlequin, **Stella Bagwell** still finds writing about two people discovering everlasting love very rewarding. She loves all things Western and has been married to her own real cowboy for fifty-one years. Living on the south Texas coast, she also enjoys being outdoors and helping her husband care for the animals on the small ranch they call home. The couple has one son, who teaches high school mathematics and coaches football and powerlifting.

Books by Stella Bagwell

Montana Mavericks: The Trail to Tenacity

The Maverick Makes the Grade

Harlequin Special Edition

Men of the West

A Ranger for Christmas
His Texas Runaway
Home to Blue Stallion Ranch
The Rancher's Best Gift
Her Man Behind the Badge
His Forever Texas Rose
The Baby That Binds Them
Sleigh Ride with the Rancher
The Wrangler Rides Again
The Other Hollister Man
Rancher to the Rescue
The Cowboy's Road Trip
Her Forgotten Cowboy
A Cowboy to Remember
Stone Creek Sheriff

Visit the Author Profile page
at Harlequin.com for more titles.

To Spider John,
I still miss you, my boy.

Chapter One

Flint Hollister steered his truck off the highway and braked to a stop in front of an iron cattle guard set between two fat cedar posts. On the left post, a small, rusty-brown metal sign read Bell Ranch.

The concierge back at the hotel where he'd stayed last night in Bonners Ferry, Idaho, along with the navigation system on Flint's truck, had managed to direct him this far. But the system was treating the gate as his final destination rather than leading him all the way to the house. So from this point on, he'd simply have to follow the road, or what he could see of it, and trust the narrow trail would lead him to the main residence.

And, of course, he'd have to hope that the road was clear enough for him to drive it at all.

From what he'd been told by a few of the locals back in town, snow had been falling off and on for the past week, especially over the mountains and foothills. Judging by the drifts and the deep blanket in his current view, they'd not been exaggerating.

Dad, why in hell did you have to send me on this wild-goose chase? Why can't you just let the past be the past and let it all stay there?

The mental questions directed at his father, Hadley, made Flint curse beneath his breath. He'd agreed to make this trip to Idaho because his father had asked him to pitch in and help with the genealogical search into the Hollister family history. But that didn't mean Flint liked anything about the situation. He didn't mind driving nearly a thousand miles from Stone Creek Ranch to here. Nor did he mind all that much taking off two weeks from his deputy sheriff's job in Beaver, Utah. What bothered him the most was coming all this way just to meet a woman who was supposedly his father's half-sister. A woman he'd never seen or talked to in his entire life. A woman who might very well shut the door in his face, making this whole trip a waste of time.

What was he supposed to do to convince her to hear him out? Walk up and say, *Nice to meet you, Mrs. O'Shea. You don't know me from Adam, but I'm your half nephew and I'm here to ask you some personal questions.* Oh hell, that ought to go over just great. She'd really want to divulge some family secrets with that kind of introduction, he thought with a grimace.

With a frustrated groan, he reached for the lever to engage the four-wheel drive on his truck. Because it was a cinch he was going to need the extra traction before he reached the Bell's headquarters. As for what he was going to say to Debra O'Shea…well, he'd just have to play it by ear. After all, he'd been a deputy sheriff for ten years now. A major part of his job was communicating with people, asking frank questions and summing up a situation in a matter of minutes. Surely he could meet one woman and sensibly explain his reason for showing up on the Bell Ranch.

Close to twenty-five minutes later, after slipping and spinning his way over the snow-packed gravel road, he spotted a spiral of smoke filtering up through the tall conifer trees at the base of a short mountain. A minute more and the narrow canyon he'd been traveling through opened up to reveal a single-story log house with a steep tin roof and a porch running around three sides. Some fifty yards off to the left, behind the house, stood a huge red barn with a similar tin roof. Next to the barn were several corrals, some made of wood railing and others from wire fencing. Off to the side of the holding pens were two smaller sheds with overhanging roofs to shelter the livestock, along with what appeared to be a storage building.

Presently, he could see a ranch hand carrying a feed bucket inside one of the corrals. Several Black Angus cows were trotting after him and Flint had to think the guy was a brave soul to be tromping through such deep snow with hungry cows on his heels.

Rather than go straight to the house, Flint decided it would be easier to speak to the ranch hand first and get the lay of the land—make sure he wasn't interrupting at a bad time. He stopped the truck several yards away from the corral and reached for the coat he'd left lying on the passenger seat. Thankfully, he'd remembered to throw in a pair of galoshes and after donning the coat, he took a moment to pull them over his boots.

As he walked toward the pen of cattle, he buttoned his coat to his throat and flipped up the collar to ward off the icy wind sweeping down from a ridge of forest-covered mountains to his left. Off to his right, behind the log house, foothills rose to meet another ridge of snowcapped mountains.

When Flint had first learned he'd be making the trip to Bonners Ferry, he'd had no idea where the town was located in Idaho. After a quick search on his PC, he'd learned he'd be driving to a place less than thirty miles away from the Canadian border. He'd noted the quickest route, but hadn't bothered to research the area. After all, he only expected to be here for one or two days at the most and he sure as heck wasn't in town to see the sights. But he had to admit that, next to his family ranch in Utah, he'd never seen a more beautiful place.

"Hello. Can I help you?"

Flint turned at the sound of the female voice and stared, somewhat fascinated by the small figure walking toward him. She was carrying an empty feed bucket and it instantly struck him that her green-plaid coat was what he'd spotted from a distance. *She* was the ranch hand with the cattle trotting after her.

"Hello." He walked forward to meet her. The snow was so deep, it very nearly spilled over the tops of his galoshes. Traipsing through this heavy sludge for any length of time would wear down a strong man much less a petite woman like her, he thought.

Once Flint was close enough for her to hear him over the wind, he said, "Maybe you can help me. I'm looking for Debra O'Shea."

She leveled a suspicious look at him. By then, Flint could see she was a young woman. At least five or six years younger than his thirty-three years. The hood of her coat hid her hair, while the furry border of the head protection framed a pale face dominated by silver-gray eyes and a pair of chapped lips.

Her gaze on him remained direct but wary and he could

tell she was trying to decide whether to respond to his inquiry or send him packing.

"Perhaps you should tell me who you are first, before I start answering your questions."

In spite of the frigid wind, Flint could feel a blush of embarrassment rush to his face. "Sorry about that." He stepped closer and, pulling out his wallet, flashed his deputy sheriff's badge and personal identification at her. "I'm Flint Hollister. From Beaver County, Utah."

"I'm Pippa Shanahan," she told him. "You say you've traveled all the way from Utah?"

"That's right. I only arrived in Bonners Ferry last night."

Her eyes squinted at the corners and he wondered what she was thinking. That he was some sort of conman impersonating a deputy sheriff, or worse?

"So why are you looking for Debra O'Shea? As far as I know, she never set foot in Beaver County. Whatever situation you're investigating, I don't see how it could have anything to do with her."

He drew in a deep breath. "You're right that I'm investigating—but it's a personal matter, not sheriff's business. She's my father's half-sister. And we—that is, my family and I—were hoping she could help us with some genealogy blanks in the Hollister tree."

If anything, the skeptical expression on her face deepened.

"I'm sorry, but your story is a bit hard for me to swallow. Debra never mentioned a brother to me. Besides, missing genealogy information can easily be found on the internet. All you have to do is put your search engine to work."

Flint was growing colder by the minute and he very much wanted to suggest they could discuss the matter more comfortably inside. If she didn't want to invite him into the house, the barn would be nearly as good. But this woman clearly wasn't going to let him in anywhere until she was convinced he was telling her the truth. So he'd have to talk fast.

"Normally, you'd be right. But my family has worn out every genealogical program that's offered. Our situation is…not the garden-variety type," he said. Sucking in another lungful of icy air, he added, "But to make things a bit clearer to you, my grandmother is Scarlett Wilson. She lives in—"

"I know where she lives," Pippa Shanahan interrupted. "In Coeur d'Alene in an assisted living complex. I think— let's step over here to the barn and get out of the wind."

Flint let out a relieved sigh. "Thank you, Ms. Shanahan. I appreciate your time."

He followed her past three corrals then on to the back end of the red barn to a small door at the corner of the building.

As they stepped inside a dimly lit corner of the barn, Flint was soothed by the familiar scents of dust, alfalfa hay, molasses-coated feed and horse manure. Unlike the barns on Stone Creek Ranch, this one was obviously not equipped with fluorescent lighting or heaters. It was very nearly as cold as the outside and the only light to be seen was that coming from a couple of bare bulbs hanging from the rafters.

She gestured to a wooden bench shoved against the wall. "Have a seat if you'd like."

"No thanks. I'd rather stand. The drive up here has worn me out with sitting."

Folding her arms against her chest, she said, "Well, I'm sorry you came all the way up here for nothing."

"What do you mean?"

As she nudged the hood back off her head, Flint was mesmerized by the sight of thick, copper-red hair falling in waves to her back.

"Debra died six—no, more like seven months ago now. So there's no way she can answer any of your questions."

In Flint's mind, he was cursing a blue streak for his bad luck, but to Pippa he did his best to remain polite.

"I'm very sorry to hear this news. I—well, all of us Hollisters—were counting on her help. Was her death sudden? When we learned her name and where she lived, there was no mention in anything we found online of her being deceased."

"Debra didn't want a funeral. So there wasn't much of an obituary. Just a small announcement of her death in the local paper."

"What about her husband? Is he anywhere around?"

She shook her head. "Yance died a few years ago from a heart attack. After that, Debra and I took care of things here on the ranch. Now, it's just me."

He stared at her as he tried to digest everything she was telling him. "Just you? Don't you have some hands working for you?"

For a moment, he thought she was going to laugh, but then her whole demeanor sobered and she looked away from him. "I'm the only hand. The Bell…well, I can't afford help right now."

I can't afford help. Did that mean she owned this ranch? That she was working it all by herself? The notion made his head spin with questions.

"Uh, I guess I'm a little confused. I assumed the O'Sheas owned the Bell Ranch. Does this mean you own it now that they've passed on?"

She nodded. "Debra willed the property to me."

"I suppose you're a relation? Her daughter?"

"Oh no. I'm no relation at all. Debra and Yance never had any children. I came to work for them several years ago to help with the ranching chores and they took me in—I guess you could say like I was their daughter. So I ended up making my home here on the Bell."

And what about Pippa's family? he wondered. Where were they? And what had they thought about her making her home with the O'Sheas? He wanted to ask her, but frankly, her personal life had nothing to do with the information he was seeking. And the last thing he wanted to do was to put her off by prying into her private affairs.

But there was one question he just couldn't help asking. "After Debra died, did you want to keep the ranch? I ask because it's obviously a big responsibility for one person. Or do you have a husband or significant other to help you?"

"I have no one but me," she answered with a scowl. "And, of course, I want to keep the ranch! The Bell is my home—my lifeblood! I'd never leave it or sell it for any reason!" she stated emphatically.

One thing for sure, Flint thought, the woman didn't quibble about what she wanted. "I see. Well, I guess by now you realize we didn't know about Debra's death. Otherwise, I would've never made the trip up here."

Her expression relaxed somewhat and Flint used the moment to let his gaze wander over her face. Her features were pretty and the sprinkle of golden freckles across her nose and cheekbones gave her otherwise pale face a lovely bit of color. Although he didn't know why, he wished he could see a full view of her hair. He wasn't interested in Pippa as a woman. So why would he want to see that bright red mane flowing around her shoulders? He could only think the thousand-mile drive he'd made from Utah had momentarily addled his brain.

"No. I don't believe you'd want to waste your time in such a way. So tell me, what kind of information were you needing from Debra?"

"We thought she might have heard her mother speak of her first husband, Lionel Hollister. We're trying to find out where and when he was born, but so far we've run into nothing but stumbling blocks. Did you ever hear Debra mention anyone by the name of Lionel? Or did she ever bring up the fact that her mother was married before she married Ode Wilson?"

Pippa thought for a moment. "A couple of times I did hear her say that her mother had been married twice. But she really never talked about Scarlett all that much, except to discuss her dementia condition. I went with Debra a few times to Coeur d'Alene to visit her mother, but by the time I'd met the woman, she was already getting confused about things."

"So she's been confused for a long while?" Flint asked.

"Oh, yes. I'm twenty-seven and I came here to live on the Bell when I was twenty. Even then, Debra talked about her mother having some sort of mental deterioration. At first she thought it was Alzheimer's disease, but turned out it was some other issue with similar symptoms."

Even though Flint had never met his grandmother and had only seen one faded photograph of her, he felt a twinge of sorrow to hear she'd been struggling for so long.

"Yes, well, I'm sure you can understand why we can't go to her for information."

He looked at her. "Did you clear out Debra's things after she died, or are any of her papers still here? There might be a chance Debra had some old papers of her mother's with information regarding her first husband. I realize it's a long shot, but at this point I'm not sure what else to do or who to turn to."

"Yes, I still have her papers—but are you sure this is the best avenue for you to try? Were you aware that Debra has a sister, Taylor?"

"Yes. But we thought her name was Ruthann, and we haven't had have any luck locating her. My sister managed to trace Debra here to the Bell. That's why I'm here."

"I see. Well, no wonder you couldn't locate her if you were using the wrong name. Ruthann was Scarlett's middle name, I think. Taylor lives in Wyoming. You might make a phone call to her. But I should warn you that she and her mother weren't all that close. I mean, they got along okay, but Debra is the one who always took care of her mother, especially after Ode passed away. That's how Scarlett ended up living in Coeur d'Alene. Debra moved her mother there in order for her to be closer."

Flint nodded that he understood. "I really appreciate what you've told me, Ms. Shanahan. As you can see, I'm sort of searching around in the dark."

She continued to look at him and Flint wondered how it would feel to have her gray eyes look at him with warmth instead of suspicion. He'd bet she had a beautiful smile. Not that he seemed likely to see one of those aimed at him.

Thankfully, the sound of a horse nickering at the opposite end of the barn interrupted Flint's straying thoughts and he gave himself a hard mental shake as he waited for her to make some sort of reply.

"Well, I'll tell you, Mr. Hollister, I still have quite a bit of feeding to do before I'll be finished with the morning chores. Once I get all the animals tended to, I'll make a search through Debra's desk and see if I can come up with anything that might help you."

Feeling a bit like a heel, Flint said, "Look, I can see you're very busy and I'm throwing a bunch of extra work at you. The least I can do is stay and help you with the chores."

"That's hardly necessary, Mr. Hollister. I'm accustomed to the work and—"

"Call me Flint," he interrupted. "And if you're worried that I'm just wearing a hat and boots because I like them, or that I'm a greenhorn around ranch work, think again. I live on a ranch that's been in existence for over sixty-five years. We raise cattle and sheep on more than a hundred thousand acres in southern Utah. I know all about taking care of livestock in all seasons."

As he'd talked, her eyes had widened and he realized she'd not been expecting him to offer his help or to learn he was a rancher.

"Okay, Flint. Then you should call me Pippa. And I would be grateful for a little help. As you can see, the weather has been especially brutal this past week. I'm trying to make the hay stretch, but God only knows if it will."

"Yes. I've noticed the weather. Is the snow usually this deep?"

She lifted the hood back over her head and tightened the drawstring beneath her chin. "Just depends. Some winters are not as bad. Some are worse. I'm hoping this one gets better. I really don't want to have to sell off any cows to make ends meet. They're all carrying calves now, so I'd be losing two ways."

"I understand," he said.

"We'll come back later to finish the last of the chores in the barn," she told him. "Right now, I need to take hay over the mountain to a herd that's been sheltering in some cedar thickets. There's a molasses lick nearby and for now they're hanging close to it."

He followed her to the opposite side of the barn to where a white heavy duty Ford truck that had to be at least twenty years old sat backed up to a pair of doors that latched in the middle.

"The hay is in the loft on this left end of the barn. I'll throw the bales down to you. If you don't mind stacking them on the truck," she said as she opened the doors to the barn wide enough for the truck to go through.

"That's fine with me," he told her.

She climbed in the driver's seat of the truck and started the engine. Flint stood to one side as she backed the vehicle into the barn. About ten yards in, she stopped the vehicle so that the bed would be directly under a large rectangular opening in the ceiling. The loft was several feet off the ground and the first thing that came to his mind was how risky it was for her to do such a chore with no one else around. If she made a misstep and fell, or the weight of one of the hay bales pulled her along with it through the opening of the loft, she'd be seriously injured or worse.

"Uh—Pippa, why don't you let me climb into the loft? Or better yet, you sit in the truck and I'll take care of the hay."

She responded with a short laugh. "No thanks. That's not the way I do business. You just stay out of the way until I finish dropping them from the loft floor. You didn't drive all the way up here to Bonners Ferry to get your neck or back broken."

Flint could hardly argue that point. Shrugging, he said, "Okay. I just thought I'd be a gentleman and offer."

She walked over to where he was standing near the passenger door of the truck. "Look, Flint, I appreciate your offer. But I'm accustomed to ranch chores. Maybe the women you know don't do such physical work, but I do this every day."

The women he knew. If she meant the women he sometimes dated, then she had a point. None of them would be caught dead behind the steering wheel of the old Ford, much less try to lift a bale of hay or wade knee-high snow with a bunch of bawling, hungry cattle on their heels. But that wasn't to say he didn't know any women who handled their share of tough, dirty ranch work.

"Actually, my sister-in-law, Clementine, who's married to my younger brother, is a sheepherder. She's more than accustomed to roughing it. Especially in the cold mountains. I'd end up looking like a wimp if I tried to follow her example."

Wry disbelief twisted her features and Flint thought how luscious her lips would look if they weren't burned and scaled from the brutal weather.

"I seriously doubt you'd fall that short in comparison," she said then turned and started up the tall wooden ladder that led up into the loft.

Flint watched her make the climb and because the hem of her coat only reached a few inches past her waist, he couldn't help but notice the strong shape of her thighs straining against the denim of her jeans and the way her little butt filled out the back pockets.

Careful Flint. You didn't come to Idaho for a literal roll in the hay. And Pippa Shanahan isn't about to offer you one.

Hell, he didn't need that reminder. He could see for himself that Pippa wasn't the playing-around type of girl. Besides, he wasn't the playing-around type of guy. Especially since the last fiasco he'd gone through with Rachel, the secretary queen of Beaver City Hall. No, he was there to check Debra's papers—there was nothing else at Bell Ranch that should hold any of his attention.

Chapter Two

For some reason when Pippa had rolled out of bed this morning, she'd felt a little off. She'd put it down to the fact that she'd sat up late last night going over her monthly budget. She'd drifted off to sleep trying to figure out how she could feed herself, four dogs and that many cats, and still pay the electricity bill. Now, she could only think that the combination of fatigue, financial stress and the fierce weather had addled her thinking. What else would have made her agree to let Flint Hollister hang around to help her with the chores?

She simply wasn't herself, she thought as she slammed a hay hook into the heavy bale of alfalfa and dragged it over to the opening in the floor. And it sure wasn't because he looked like one hot cowboy. No. She didn't care how handsome or wealthy, or nice he might be. She wasn't in the mood for a man's company and she seriously doubted she'd ever be in the mood.

"Stand back," she called down to him. "Here comes the first one."

She pushed the bale over the edge of the wood-planked floor and heard the heavy thud as it fell into the bed of the truck.

"How many are you going to get?" he yelled up to her. "These are big bales."

She leaned her head far enough over to peer down at him. "Six more. You'll probably have to stand them on their edge to make them fit."

He made a thumbs-up sign to her and she went back to the stack to fetch another bale. As she repeated the process, she thought about Flint's reason for showing up here on the Bell. He'd said Scarlett Wilson was his grandmother. The information had practically floored her, although she'd tried her best not to show the surprise she'd been feeling.

If Debra had known she had relatives in Utah, she'd never mentioned it to Pippa. Of course, Yance could've known about the Hollisters. But he'd been the type of man who'd not discussed private family matters with Pippa or anyone other than his wife. His focus had been on running the Bell and making sure Debra was happy.

Hook, drag and shove. Pippa repeated the process over six more times, until the last bale had fallen into the bed of the truck. By the time she climbed the ladder down to the ground, Flint was already in the truck bed, stacking the bales of alfalfa neatly and tightly together.

It had been a long, long time since Pippa had seen a man do any kind of work around the ranch. Yance had been dead for more than six years. Once he'd passed on, Debra and Pippa had worked the ranch alone. On a couple of occasions they'd hired a pair of day hands to help with the branding and vaccinating, but even that had stopped more than four years ago. To see Flint lifting and positioning the heavy bales of hay seemed strange.

What's strange, Pippa, is your reaction to seeing the

man flex his muscles. You're staring at him like a starving person at a plate of food.

Disgusted with the voice going off in her head, she purposely walked around the cab of the truck and climbed inside. A couple of minutes later, Flint motioned that he was finished and she drove the truck out of the barn.

Once she'd braked to a stop outside the building, Flint opened the passenger door and stuck his head inside the cab. "You stay put. I'll shut the barn doors."

"Okay," she said then quickly added, "I should let you know that the dogs always go with me. They ride on the tailgate."

He nodded. "I'd already figured that out. They're loaded."

He shut the truck door and while he dealt with the barn doors, she turned on the heater then passed a hand over her face. She didn't have to peer in a mirror to know her face was pale and looked ragged. She'd barely taken the time this morning to splash warm water on her face and run a brush through her hair. But then, the livestock and other animals didn't care what she looked like as long as they were fed. And Flint? Well, he hardly had any interest in her appearance.

The door opened and Pippa gestured to the passenger seat. "Just brush the junk onto the floor. I don't ever have company riding with me and that seat ends up being a catchall."

Instead of shoving the odds and ends to the floorboard, he pushed them to the left side of the seat until there was enough space for him to sit comfortably.

"That's what work trucks are for," he said, "to haul around the things we need while doing our jobs."

He climbed into the cab and the cold wind followed him along with the faint scent of aftershave. The smell was a mixture of saddle leather and sage and evoked the image of a cowboy riding a tumbleweed trail. And he was all cowboy, she thought, in spite of his quality clothes and the deputy's badge he was carrying.

"Yes, well, I'm always promising myself to clean up the insides," she replied. "But I never get around to it."

He latched the seat belt in place and was in the process of settling his shoulders against the back of the seat when he leaned over sideways and fished a large syringe with a covered needle from beneath his thigh.

"Been vaccinating?" he asked as he placed the syringe aside.

"No. Unfortunately, I've had a few sick cows. The ones you probably saw at the barn when you drove up. Cases of shipping fever, or you probably call it BRD."

"On our ranch, we mostly call it bad. What is it you're giving them? And are your cattle getting better?"

She informed him as to what sort of antibiotic she was using before she said, "I've been treating them for the past few days. They're better now."

"I'm glad to hear it. BRD can be deadly. And this kind of weather hardly helps matters," he said then asked, "How far is it to the place we're going to spread the hay?"

"I can't tell you in mileage. Never bothered to check the odometer," she answered. "If we don't slide off the road, we should be there in about fifteen minutes."

He turned his head to look at her and, not for the first time, Pippa noticed his arresting green eyes. Did he know that only a small portion of the world's population had green eyes? And that his were especially striking?

"There's actually a road?"

She pushed in the clutch and pulled the floor shift down into first gear. The transmission made a grinding noise until she released the clutch and put the truck in forward motion. One of these days the faithful old companion was going to go kaput on her, but she didn't want to contemplate that now. She'd deal with the problem when it happened. Up to then, there was no point wasting energy on worrying.

"We've traveled the same track for years, so we call it a road. Uh—sorry. I continue to say *we* as though Debra is still here," she said ruefully. "One of these days I guess I'll finally realize it's just me. Losing family is—not easy."

Beneath the brim of his black hat, one of his dark brows lifted slightly. "I thought you said you weren't related to Debra."

She grimaced as pain squeezed the region around her heart. "I'm not biologically related. But she and Yance felt like my parents. So losing them was…well, you get the picture."

"Sure. I get it. Sorry this has happened to you—and to our family, too. My father has been planning to meet his sisters. Now I'll have to tell him one of them has passed on. He's going to be very disappointed."

She darted a glance at him but he wasn't looking her way. Without seeing the expression on his face, she could only wonder how he felt about hearing of his half aunt's death. Of course, the news hadn't cut him deeply on a personal level. He'd never met Debra. He couldn't know she'd been a kind and generous woman who'd loved everyone.

"I'm guessing that you and your family have only recently learned about having more relatives," she said as she maneuvered the truck past the last corral and straight toward a thick stand of pines.

"Technically, we learned that Scarlett had two daughters a little more than a year ago, but at that time we didn't know their names. My younger sister, Beatrice, made the trip to Coeur d'Alene to see Scarlett. Before then, none of us knew she was suffering from dementia." Shrugging, he looked over at her. "But we all figured that once Scarlett left Stone Creek Ranch back in 1970 or ʹ71, she'd likely gone on to marry someone else and could've had other children. So, I think Dad has always lived with the idea of potentially having half siblings somewhere out there."

There were dozens of questions she would like to ask him about his family, but she told herself it might not be wise to get that acquainted with the man. His presence was simply too big and masculine for a quiet country girl like her to deal with. Besides, he wouldn't be sticking around for long. What was the point in getting invested in his story?

Still, how could a few harmless questions hurt? she wondered. It would pass the time.

"Does your father have other full siblings?" she asked.

"Two younger brothers, Wade and Barton. But they're not close to my father. They occasionally exchange phone calls, but that's about it."

How sad, Pippa thought. She'd always longed to have a sibling or two. Especially when she'd been a young child and had been passed around from one foster home to the next. A sibling would have helped her face the fear over not knowing where her next home would be or if the people there would be kind to her. A sibling would've shared the trials and struggles she'd endured while in school and would've listened to the growing pains she'd experienced when she'd entered her teen years. But Pippa hadn't had a sibling, or parents. According to what she'd learned through different agencies in the state, her mother had been an unwed teenager who'd died shortly after Pippa had been born. As for her father, he'd not acknowledged he had a child, much less wanted her in his life.

"That's too bad," she said. "Do the brothers know about Debra and Taylor?"

"Yes. Dad informed them. But I don't think they have much interest in the family tree. You see, they—" He stopped abruptly and turned a rueful sort of smile on her. "Well, they have their own lives and pretty much keep to themselves."

"Nothing wrong with that. I could say the same of myself."

She thought he was going to make a reply to her remark but he didn't. Instead, he changed the subject completely, leaving her to wonder how Scarlett's absence back then had affected the Hollister family in the years since. One thing for certain, something within the family had definitely gone awry.

Think about it, Pippa. Most families are destined to tear apart. That's why you need to quit pining for one and save yourself a load of misery.

"If I'm not being too nosey, how much land does the Bell take in?" he asked.

His question interrupted the mocking voice going off in her head and she was glad. Lately, she'd begun to listen more and more to the cynical thoughts that were continually trying to encroach on her spirits. And she didn't want to be a jaded person.

"Close to seven hundred acres. Compared to your family's ranch, it's just a little patch. But it's a good piece of land. You can't tell it right now because of the snow, but there are some nice mountains meadows. I usually graze the sheep on the highest ones. The cattle forage on the lower ones. There are a couple of hay meadows, too, not far from the creek. However, the past few years, the alfalfa has been sparse because of the dry summers. Do you grow your own hay on Stone Creek Ranch?"

"Probably half of what we use. The remainder we have shipped up from Nevada. Parts of the western section of the ranch are very arid. But recently, Dad purchased a farm adjacent to our property. Since it was already equipped with an irrigating system, he's growing alfalfa and timothy on some sections of that land. So far the crop appears to save enough money to warrant the cost and labor of growing it."

She said, "The weather here in the north part of the state has been especially devastating for us these past few years. The rain and snow are either nonexistent or a deluge and the temperatures have swung just as wildly. It's difficult to know what to plan for."

They began a short climb around the side of the foothill and Pippa pressed down harder on the accelerator to prevent the truck from stalling. To their left, the ground broke away to reveal a rocky ravine. From the corner of her eye, she could see Flint's gloved hand gripping the edge of the seat. No doubt he was expecting her to slide off the side of the road any minute now.

She smiled to herself. "Don't worry," she told him. "I've driven this track hundreds of times. I've never ended up in the ravine—but I guess there's always a first time."

Frowning, he looked at her. "What if you and truck *did*

tumble over to the rock bed below? There's usually no one around to help you, is there?"

"No. You're the first person that's been here on the Bell in about three weeks. The last visitor was a guy from Bonners Ferry who drove out to see if I had any baby lambs for sale. I have some babies, but I don't want to sell. So he was around for about five minutes is all."

"Why didn't the man just give you a call to ask before driving all the way out here?" Flint asked.

"Most of the time my cell signal is very spotty. The mountains block the connecting towers. And Debra did away with the landline years ago. It was kind of worthless. The phone company never buried the line, so more often than not it was broken—and they weren't quick to come and fix it. Why bother with one customer in a hard-to-reach area? That was their motto. But as for me and the truck landing in the ravine, my dogs would go for help. They're smarter than most humans and more trustworthy, as far as that goes."

"How close is your nearest neighbor?"

"As the crow flies, maybe six or seven miles. Not too far for the dogs."

He didn't say anything to that but when the truck finally crested over onto a flat piece of ground, he said, "Ranching is hard work. What makes you want to keep doing it?"

"I've always liked working with animals. After I graduated high school, I was lucky enough to get a job helping around the vet's office in Bonners Ferry. That's how I met Debra and Yance. They needed someone to help with the chores on the ranch and they offered me room and board. I couldn't refuse. It changed my life. They taught me so much about ranching and just things about life in general that were priceless. Now, seven years later, I'm still here—but they aren't."

"But the Bell is yours," he reminded her. "That has to help dull the pain a little."

"Yes. The Bell is mine and I intend to see that it stays mine." She gestured to the area beyond the windshield. "See that group of junipers? The molasses lick is beyond them, so we're almost to our destination."

He said, "And it looks like the snow is starting up again."

"The cows will be happy to eat, no matter about the snow." She glanced over to see he was frowning at the fat flakes that were beginning to fall thickly from the dark gray sky. "Look, Flint, if you'd rather stay in the truck, I can manage this easily. Like I said, I do it—"

"Every day," he interjected. "I didn't come with you on this trip to sit in the truck."

"You didn't come to the Bell to go to work, either," she quipped.

"I volunteered. Remember?"

Yes, he'd volunteered. Now she was almost wishing she'd turned down his offer. Just being with him for this short trip was working on her senses. At the moment, they were all spinning way too fast and in a direction that was far too intimate.

She braked the truck to a halt not far from the molasses lick and pushed down on the horn. Hearing the sound, the cattle would come in a matter of two or three minutes. While they waited, she reached into the console between their seats and pulled out a raggedy set of earmuffs.

"Here." She tossed them toward his lap. "You're going to need these. The wind is even worse up here than it is down at the barn."

He plucked up the muffs then shot her a seriously comical look. "You think I need these things?"

"Well, if you want to go back to Utah with parts of your ears missing from frostbite, then have at it. At least I tried."

"Okay, okay. I admit this climate is a bit different than what I'm accustomed to."

He lifted off his hat and adjusted the muffs over his ears before cramming the black felt back onto his head. But not before Pippa got a good view of his hair. Thick and rusty-brown, it fell in loose waves all the way to the back of his neck, where it tickled the top of the collar on his coat.

He was a looker, all right, Pippa thought. But he—oh my, he could be married! Flint Hollister most likely had a wife and family somewhere. She didn't know why that idea had only come to her now. She supposed she'd been too dazzled by his presence and too rattled by his reason to be on the Bell to be thinking clearly.

Disgusted by her ridiculous thoughts, she jerked on a pair of worn leather gloves and reached for the door handle. "Here comes the cattle. They're all gentle so don't worry about being butted or trampled," she told him then climbed out of the truck before he had a chance to reply.

Outside the truck, her dogs, Chester and Rosie, were already racing toward the thicket of junipers to urge the cattle onto the haying area. Their short barks usually rang through the mountain air, but this morning the sounds were carried away with the stiff winds.

By the time Pippa had climbed onto the back of the truck to begin pushing the bales to the ground, Flint appeared at the tailgate.

"I'll bust the bales and start spreading," he told her.

"Okay," she said. "I'll leave three in this area, then pull the truck forward and leave the other four."

He nodded that he understood and the two of them went to work. The wind was howling through the evergreens and whipping across the open area where the hungry cattle gathered around the piles of alfalfa. Snow was blowing horizontally through the air and several times the fat flakes fell on Pippa's eyelashes, forcing her to pause and wipe the snow to clear her vision.

Once they had all the bales separated into piles, Pippa walked over to where Flint was standing to one side, surveying the condition of the cattle. She stepped close enough for him to hear her over the wind.

"How do they look to you?" she asked.

"They all look good," he said. "None appear to be lame or sick. And they're all carrying a nice bit of weight. You're doing a good job."

His compliment warmed her. "Thanks. I'll feed this little herd cattle cubes tomorrow along with a bit of hay. I'm keeping my fingers crossed that the weather breaks soon."

He looked at her and Pippa watched a pair of snowflakes land on his lips. Like ice landing on fire, she thought then mentally groaned at the direction her mind had taken. Since when had she ever been distracted by a man's lips? Not since her old boyfriend, Dale. And even he hadn't conjured up such fanciful notions in her head.

"You have more cattle besides these and the few at the barn?" he asked.

"Another fifty head in a sheltered area about a quarter mile west of the ranch yard. But you can breathe easy. I've already fed that herd. This is the last bunch. With this done, all I need to do is finish the chores in the barn."

She whistled for the dogs but the wind carried away the sound. "They've gone to make sure there aren't any stragglers in the woods," she said to Flint. "The dogs love this weather. It's like a tropical beach to them."

"Must be nice not to feel this frigid wind."

She chuckled before cupping her hands around her mouth and yelling loudly. "Chester! Rosie! Come on!" To Flint, she said, "Let's get in the truck to wait on the dogs. They'll show up in a minute or two."

They walked back to where she'd left the truck parked. After they'd climbed in the cab and shut the doors, Flint gestured toward the cows that were munching hungrily on the green alfalfa.

"Did you do a head count?"

"Yes. Chester and Rosie are smart, but they can't count, so they use their noses and eyes to make sure all the cattle are where they're supposed to be. All I do is double-check after them. To tell you the truth, I doubt I could do this job without them. They're like having a couple of ranch hands. Except the dogs work without pay. All they want is a bowl of food and a pat on the head."

"My brother Quint and his wife, Clementine, have four dogs to work the sheep on Stone Creek Ranch. But since they've been steadily increasing the flock, I expect them to get a couple more dogs." He looked at her. "Did you train Chester and Rosie?"

She nodded. "They were pups when Debra and I first got them from animal rescue about a year and a half ago. I'm very proud they've learned so much in just a short time. If Debra could see them now, she'd be happy."

"Perhaps she does see them," Flint suggested.

She tossed him a grateful smile. "Yes. I like to think so," she said.

Before another minute passed, the dogs emerged from the woods and raced to the truck. Once they'd safely leaped up on the tailgate of the truck, Pippa didn't waste any time turning the vehicle around and heading down the hill.

Throughout the drive back to the barn, Flint didn't say anything and Pippa was more than content to remain quiet. She'd already told this man more things about her life than she'd told anyone in years. There wasn't any need for her to spill her whole life history to him.

Inside the barn, Pippa turned on the pair of light bulbs located at the far end of the barn, where a shadowy gloom hung over three stalled horses and a cow and calf locked in a pen toward the back of the building.

Even though it wasn't much warmer in the barn than outside, the fact that they were out of the heavy snow and high wind was a relief to Flint. Yes, he was accustomed to bad winters in Beaver County, but this was extra bad. It made him wonder even more how this slip of a woman managed to deal with working in such conditions all on her own.

"Is that cow/calf pair suffering from BRD?" he asked as he followed her past the horse stalls and into a feed room.

"No. The cow gave birth only yesterday and I wanted to keep the calf inside to make sure she nursed enough to be sturdy on her feet."

"What about the horses? Do you normally keep them stalled?"

"Heck no!" she exclaimed. "They're only inside because the pastures are covered with snow and they need shelter. To the west of the house, there's a twenty-acre patch fenced away from the cows and that's where the horses normally stay. If I had to feed them grain all year round, I'd end up in the poorhouse."

"I've heard Dad make the same remark. I think we have about twenty-five head now and he says that's too many. But my oldest brother Jack—he co-manages the ranch with Dad—loves horses, so when it comes to them, they have a push-and-pull thing going on."

She lifted the lid off a barrel of sweet feed then filled three rubber buckets with the horse grain and the fourth with cattle cubes. "Do you know much about horses?" she asked.

"More than I do about cattle," he told her. "Why do you ask?"

She straightened up from her task and looked over at him. As Flint's gaze wandered over her face, he wondered if it was possible that the shadows beneath her eyes had grown darker. Or perhaps it was only the dim lighting in the barn that made her appear more haggard. Either way, he wished he could make her sit down and let him deal with the rest of the chores, but he knew it would be futile to make such a suggestion.

She said, "I have a horse that's lame on his right front and I'm not exactly sure if the problem is in his hoof or ankle. I was hoping I could deal with the problem myself and save the expense of a vet. Would you mind taking a look at him after we dump all the feed?"

"I wouldn't mind at all."

"Great. I'd appreciate your help," she told him then started out of the room with a gesture for him to follow. "Come on and I'll show you where to dump your buckets. Hopefully, the water line hasn't frozen. It's wrapped with heat tape. But I expect the ice in the troughs will have to be chopped."

And chopping ice was definitely a chore he wasn't going to allow her to do. Not while he was around.

"Okay. Let's get this done and we'll take a look at your horse," he told her.

She smiled then. It was even prettier than he'd expected and Flint found himself smiling back at her. Something about her was so endearing. He didn't exactly know what that something was, but he feared if he stayed around her for very long, he'd be in for a bit of heart trouble.

"Thanks."

They left the feed room and for the next several minutes they fed the horses and the cow and calf. In the meantime, two more dogs appeared at the back of the barn. Both were white Great Pyrenees and extremely friendly.

As Flint rubbed both dogs between the ears, he said, "Quint has two Great Pyrenees, but they aren't as friendly as these two. They always stay with the flock and rarely see humans, other than him and Clementine."

"Mine are probably more social because they come into the ranch yard every day and interact with me. It sounds like your brother's dogs are more isolated. That's probably why they're not all that sociable. As soon as these two eat, they'll go back to my little flock. The sheep are just over the rise behind the barn. I've already hayed them and made sure they could water at the stream. The only animals left to feed now are the cats and they eat later in the evenings."

Flint glanced around the area where they were standing. "I've not seen any cats around here."

"They're smart. They're up in the hayloft. The warmest spot in the barn."

"You know, I've decided you were wrong when you told me you were here on the ranch all alone. You have a menagerie here with you on the Bell."

A wan smile curved her lips. "Yes. I do have all kinds of animals to talk to. So I have plenty of conversations."

"So which one of the horses is lame?" he asked.

She motioned for him to follow her down to the horse stalls. "It's the paint. His name is Hawk and he's very gentle, so no need for you to worry about him kicking or stomping or biting."

"No worries," he told her. "I've had a few unruly horses in my day."

"Do you ride very much?" she asked. "With you working as a deputy, you probably don't have much time for ranch work."

"Not a lot," he admitted.

"Do you like it that way? I mean working more as a lawman than a rancher?"

He shrugged. "Both jobs are rewarding. But I feel—like I'm needed more as a deputy. Dad and my brothers keep things going on the ranch just fine without me."

"I see."

Did she? Flint doubted she understood his choice of career. No one really got why he'd chosen to be a lawman instead of working full-time on the family ranch. Not even his own family recognized his need to feel appreciated, or how he wanted to believe he was contributing to a cause.

She opened the gate to the stall and he followed her inside the twelve-by-twelve cubicle.

"You might have noticed all the stalls inside the barn are built of steel post. Yance did that for fire safety purposes," she told him. "He was planning to eventually replace the board siding on the outside with metal, but he passed on before he could get the job started. I think he witnessed a barn fire when he was a child and was determined to never see another one."

"No doubt. Fires are horrific. But he did a good job cutting down on the risk here inside and that's very important," Flint said then turned his attention to the horse. "You say the problem is with his right front?"

"Yes. I rode him about three days ago before the snow hit. The next day he was limping."

Flint gently rubbed the horse's neck and shoulder before he squatted on his heels to take a closer look at the foot. "Was the ankle swollen the day he started limping?"

"No. But it looks a bit puffy to me now. Does it look that way to you?"

"A little swollen, but I think that's caused by the stress coming from his hoof." Rising up, he bent over at the waist and picked up the horse's foot. After a quick examination, he said, "I see the problem. He has an abscess. Come closer and I'll show you."

She moved up behind him and peered over his left shoulder. Flint's senses were suddenly consumed with her close proximity.

He desperately needed to draw in a deep breath, but he feared she would hear him and guess that he was affected by her nearness. Instead, he cleared his throat and gave himself a hard mental shake.

"See this little hole right above the hoof line?" he asked while pointing to the spot on the horse's foot.

"Yes, I do. It looks like a tiny puncture wound. I didn't see that yesterday. What is it? It looks like something has been running from the hole and down the front of his hoof."

Flint examined the bottom of the horse's hoof before placing it back on the ground. "The little hole is from pressure of the abscess. Actually, it's much better for the horse once it burst. It relieves the pain and hopefully whatever object he stepped on will wash out as it drains."

He straightened and turned to see she was frowning at him with an expression of faint disbelief. "You mean something stuck in his foot, like a small piece of gravel, then worked its way upward?" she asked.

"Exactly. Or simply stepping on a stob of some sort or thorn could've caused it. Either way, he'll be fine. But you really need to soak his foot in an Epsom salts bath for fifteen to twenty minutes a day for the next couple of days, at least. Do you have any hoof medication?"

"Only some pine tar salve," she answered.

"No. He needs something different." He thought for a moment as she stood there looking anxious, waiting for him to speak. "Tell you what, you just concentrate on the soaking. I'll see what I can find in town, and then I'll bring the med back with me tomorrow."

Her brows arched. "Tomorrow? You're coming back tomorrow?"

He turned away from the horse to fully face her. "Uh— you said you needed time to look through Debra's papers. Or are you thinking you can do it all today?"

She pulled off her glove and swiped a hand across her forehead. "Sorry, it slipped my mind. I guess I've gotten a little distracted this morning. But yeah, coming back tomorrow would probably be for the best. I'm not really sure how many things of Debra's are packed away. I might need a bit of time to sift through all of it."

Flint suddenly felt like a heel. Yes, he'd driven a thousand miles for information, but that wasn't Pippa's fault. And resolving the mysteries of the Hollister family tree was hardly her responsibility.

"Look, Pippa, I'm causing you a lot of stress and work that you don't need. I'm very sorry about that. I intend to pay you for your troubles. Dad wouldn't want me to do anything less."

Clearly insulted, her lips flattened to a thin line. "You've already paid me by helping me with the chores. That's more than enough."

"I don't think so."

She opened the stall gate and motioned him out. "We're finished here," she said. "Let's go to the house."

As Flint followed her out of the barn, he realized that before he left Bonners Ferry, she was going to give him trouble. The sort of trouble he'd never expected.

Chapter Three

They left the barn and trudged over a snow-packed trail to the back of the house. High drifts of snow were piled around a screened-in porch that ran the width of the log structure. A set of narrow rock steps led up to a wooden screen door.

"I shoveled off the steps before I left the house this morning, but they're already getting covered again," she said then warned, "Be careful. Sometimes they're very slick."

Pippa pulled open the door and motioned for him to precede her. Flint stepped onto the porch and glanced around the shadowy space. To the left of the door a long row of firewood was stacked against the wall. To the right, a row of small-size cowboy boots snugged the wall, along with an igloo-style doghouse.

"You'll have to excuse the mess," she said as she opened a door leading into the kitchen. "During the winter season I don't have much time for house cleaning."

As the two of them moved into the room, she walked over to the cabinet counter while motioning him toward a round pine table with four chairs.

"Have a seat and I'll make us some coffee." She removed her coat and placed it over the back of one of the chairs.

He hung his hat and coat on a peg by the door then walked over and took a seat at the table. Now that she'd removed the bulky woolen coat, he was given a full view of her figure. The black turtleneck sweater she was wearing clung to the full shape of her breasts and molded to the slim line of her waist. Her hips were padded just enough to make her look all woman. But it was her hair that grabbed the bulk of his attention. Far longer than he'd expected, the copper curtain hung all the way to her butt and swished with each step she took.

"Only if you want coffee. I wouldn't want to put you out," he said then let out a short laugh. "Just like I haven't already."

"Don't worry. When you start putting me out, I'll let you know."

He didn't doubt that. She wasn't the timid or coquettish sort. She was frank and straightforward and he realized he appreciated that about her and more. So far, he could truthfully say she was unlike any woman he'd met before. If nothing else, she was making this trip to the Bell Ranch very interesting.

"Have you eaten breakfast?" she asked.

He cleared his throat and forced his gaze on a window at the back of the room. From there he could see the barn where the cattle she'd fed earlier were still milling around the feed troughs. "Yes. At the hotel. What about you?" he asked.

"Oh yes. I had mine before daylight. It's not good to go out in this cold on an empty stomach."

As she spooned coffee grounds into a filter, his gaze wandered over to the cabinet counter. Dirty dishes were stacked in the sink, while clean ones were still in a drainer, waiting to be put away. Cups and saucers sat here and there among a loaf of bread, a sack of cookies and a jar of jelly. Two iron skillets, one with a metal spatula resting over the edge, sat on a gas cook stove, while something in a big pot was simmering on the back burner. He thought it smelled like collard greens, but he couldn't imagine where she could've gotten her hands on those at this time of year. Unless she'd found frozen ones at a grocery store in town.

The white cabinets needed painting and the pattern on the linoleum flooring was worn away in the areas around the cabinets and appliances.

I'm trying to make the hay stretch, but God only knows if it will.

Now he understood better why she'd sounded a bit desperate about the hay. Financially, she had to be struggling just to keep her head above water. And while she seemed to be doing a fine job of making sure the animals were taken care of; he got the impression it was at the cost of taking care of herself.

"My mom makes breakfast for everyone at the ranch house," he said. "But it depends on my work schedule if I get to join in."

She looked over her shoulder at him. "Debra always cooked breakfast, too. Now when I walk into the kitchen in the early morning, I still expect to see her standing at the stove turning bacon or cracking eggs into the skillet. Back then I took all those little things for granted, but now those are the things I remember and miss the most."

"The little things are often the most meaningful," he reasoned.

"I think so."

He saw her swallow before she turned and walked over to the sink. After she'd filled it with soap and hot water, she washed a pair of coffee mugs and dried them with a paper towel. And all the while she performed the simple task, Flint couldn't tear his eyes off her hair and the way it flowed against her back, making his hand itch to reach out and catch a strand, see if it was as soft as it looked.

As she carried the steaming coffee over to the table, she asked, "Do you take cream or sugar?"

"A little sugar. But I can drink it black or pretty much any way."

She set the cups on the tabletop and Flint's attention was drawn to her hands. They were small with slender fingers and skin that should be pampered with creams and lotions. How had those little hands handled the heavy bales of alfalfa? he wondered. How were they strong enough to chop through several inches of ice with an axe? Strange, he thought, how much it bothered him to think of her struggling.

Once she'd placed a sugar bowl, spoons and a box of half-and-half on the table, she took a seat to his right. While she stirred cream into her cup, Flint spooned sugar into his and tried to look anywhere but at her. But he could only manage that feat for a few seconds before his gaze slipped right back to her. He'd never seen silver-gray eyes on anyone before. They reminded him of moonlight shining through a very dark night. And all that hair—it was the shade of a new copper penny and the vibrant color made her skin appear even more pale.

"I've been thinking."

Her remark broke into Flint's wandering thoughts and drew him up short as he realized how far they had drifted. It was so unlike him to get distracted by a woman like this. For the past year or more, Flint had exhibited zero interest in dating or finding someone to share his life. What would everyone think if they could see him ogling this waif of a woman with chipped nails, chapped lips and lines of fatigue beneath her eyes? They'd probably all remind him that he could have his pick of attractive women in Beaver County. But none of them had ever caught his attention like Pippa Shanahan.

"What have you been thinking about?" he asked.

"Debra and Scarlett. I don't recall Debra getting letters from her mother. And Scarlett couldn't deal with texting. But Debra did call her mother quite often, until Scarlett began to get too confused to understand who she was talking to. Then Debra would drive down to Coeur d'Alene to see her. She said her mother seemed to be able to comprehend better when she visited her in person."

Flint focused on drinking a portion of his coffee before he asked, "When you moved in with the O'Sheas, was Scarlett already living in Coeur d'Alene?"

She slanted a thoughtful look at him. "Yes," she answered then asked, "You really don't know much about her, do you?"

Flint shrugged and tried not to appear sheepish. Before Beatrice had made the trip to Idaho last year, Flint and the rest of the family had never made a search to find her. Frankly, all of the Hollisters had assumed she'd left of her own accord and never returned to see her three sons because she'd not cared about her children. Why would they be interested in contacting someone who'd deserted the family?

Yet now that Flint was away from his parents and siblings and away from Stone Creek Ranch, where Scarlett and Lionel had lived as man and wife, he found himself growing more curious. He realized that, good or bad, he wanted to know what had actually occurred to cause his grandfather to live a bitter life and his grandmother to completely disappear.

"No, not really," he answered. "My family doesn't know anything about Scarlett. She's something of a fictional person to us siblings. And to Dad...well, he can only remember a few vague images. I realize I made the trip up here to find information about Grandfather. But—I can't explain it—I suppose being here on this ranch where Scarlett's daughter used to live has pricked my curiosity about her."

She looked away from him and Flint noticed that, for the second time since they'd sat down, she was rubbing the pads of her fingers against her forehead. She was either extremely tired or something else was bothering her. A headache? Maybe stress? Over her work situation or something else? He supposed she could be having issues in her love life. She'd said she wasn't married and that she didn't have a partner who helped her run the ranch. But she could still have a special guy somewhere nearby who worked someplace else.

If so, he couldn't be much of a guy, Flint thought grimly. Whether he was a rancher or not, there were still things he could to do help, even if it was just making her coffee and cleaning the kitchen so she didn't have to.

She turned her attention back to him. "That's understandable. Especially if you have a family of your own. I'm sure you'd like to be able to tell your children something about their great-grandmother."

There was something raw about the direct way she was looking at him and Flint was shocked by a strong urge to squirm upon the hard seat. "I don't have a family—outside of my parents and siblings. I've never been married. Nor do I have a special girlfriend."

"Oh."

She licked her lips then took a long sip of coffee and Flint noticed a trace of pink color on her cheekbones.

"What about you?" he asked. "You ever been married or engaged?"

She made a noise that was something like a snort. Her lips took on a wry slant. "Something like engaged. You can see for yourself how that worked out."

"Not really. How did it work out?"

She cleared her throat. "It didn't. He's long gone."

"Sorry."

She shrugged. "Nothing to be sorry about. I'm following my dream and he's out there somewhere following his. Some people have to do their own thing, you know. Otherwise they'd be miserable."

So, she'd had different dreams from the guy, Flint mused. At least she knew her own mind and stuck to it. Still, it bothered him to think she must've believed in the man. Perhaps even loved him deeply, only to have him end up hurting her.

"Well, I'm wasting your time and mine." With the coffee mug in hand, she stood and walked over to the cabinet counter. "I'll go make a quick search in Debra's desk and see what I can find."

Flint quickly rose and carried his cup over to the cabinet. "I don't want to rush you, Pippa. I think I'll head on back to Bonners Ferry and return in the morning to see if you've been able to find anything. That way you can go through it at your own leisure."

She looked at him. "You're hardly rushing me. Although, I'm not going to promise I can get through all of her papers today."

"No matter." He walked over to the door and pulled his hat and coat down from the peg on the wall. "If you'd like, I can give you my cell number. But I remember you saying your signal is not dependable here."

She walked across the room to where a small utility table was jammed between the refrigerator and a set of open pantry shelves lined with canned goods. After a moment, she returned with a Post-it square and a pencil.

Handing the paper and pencil to him, she said, "Give me your number anyway. With this weather setting in, I doubt there will be any signal to speak of, but just in case I need to contact you later on, I'll have the number."

She was close enough for him to pick up the faint scent of evergreens clinging to her clothes and hair and some other aroma that reminded him of the outdoors. The thought made him wonder if her lips would taste just as fresh and untamed.

Releasing a heavy breath, he quickly scratched the number across the small square and handed it back to her. "Thank you, Pippa. I truly appreciate this."

"No bother. I've been needing to go through Debra's papers anyway and sort the important from the junk," she told him. "Thank you for the help with the chores this morning."

"You're welcome." Without glancing her way, he pulled the Stetson down on his head and shrugged into his coat. The heavy fabric was still damp from the snow, along with his leather gloves. "I'll—uh—see you in the morning. And if you're not around, don't worry. I'll wait."

"If you arrive and I'm gone over the mountain, just come on in the house. It won't be locked. Be better for you to wait by the fireplace than in your truck. I won't mind."

She was being gracious and that made him feel even more guilty for intruding into her time.

"Thanks. Maybe that won't be necessary," he said then asked, "Would it be easier for me to leave through the back of the house?"

"No. Your truck is out front. Follow me," she said.

They left the kitchen and passed through a short breezeway before entering a cozy living room furnished with a couch, two armchairs and a recliner. Except for the leather recliner, the furniture was wood-framed with cushions covered with a nubby fabric in dark greens and browns. At one end of the room, a low fire was burning in the fireplace. He didn't see a TV anywhere, but perhaps Pippa didn't care about such things.

As they walked toward a small foyer leading to the front entrance, Flint admired the big picture window framing the view of a jagged ridge of snow-covered mountains.

"Nice view," he commented.

"It's better in summer. Right now the creek is hidden by the snow. The meadow you see over to the left usually has wildflowers. The sheep love grazing that particular meadow, but I usually save it for the cattle. The sheep are better climbers, so I send them up the mountain."

"Hmm. You sound like Quint and Clementine."

"I don't know about how things work on your family ranch, but I have to utilize every inch of land I own."

By now they had reached the door and he couldn't think of any more reasons to dally.

Why would you want to linger here in her company, Flint? You never wanted to drive out here in the first place.

And that would have been a shame, Flint thought. Because he was glad he'd met her. Glad he'd gotten to see her pretty face and be in her company for a couple of hours.

"Goodbye, Pippa. Don't forget to soak Hawk's foot."

"I won't."

He opened the door and, after stepping onto the porch, quickly shut it behind him to avoid letting the cold air rush inside. As he walked away from the house, he resisted the urge to look back.

She wouldn't be standing at the window watching him go, Flint reasoned. No, she had better things to do besides stare after him and daydream. She was a practical woman, not a romantic. Which was a good thing, he told himself. Because he had no business daydreaming about her.

Before Pippa dug into Debra's correspondence, she carried a mixture of warm water and Epsom salts in a huge thermal jug out to the barn to soak Hawk's foot. Once she placed his hoof in the warm bath, he didn't move a muscle and Pippa figured it must have felt good to the injured foot.

While she waited for the time to pass, she used the opportunity to brush his mane and coat and, as she worked, she wondered if Flint would remember to look for the hoof medication before he returned in the morning.

If he did buy some sort of medicine to help doctor Hawk, she was certainly going to pay him back. No matter if her funds were running low and he was more than able to afford it. She didn't want to feel beholden to the man. Yes, he seemed nice enough. And yes, by the time he'd declared he was leaving, she'd already begun to feel a bit drawn to him. But she didn't want her feelings for Flint Hollister to go past friendly liking. He was here today and gone tomorrow and she'd already had too many of those brief, disappointing encounters with men in her life. She had no interest in going through another.

While Hawk finished the last few minutes of his foot

soak, Pippa checked on the cow and calf, then climbed up to the hayloft and took a rough count of what she had left. It was the middle of January. Winter would be here for, at the very least, two and half more months. That meant she needed about twenty-five ton to last her until grass started to appear.

One. Two. Three. She continued to count until she reached twenty and then reality hit her like a cold gust of north wind. From the looks of things, by the end of winter, the hay she had now would all be used up and she'd need to buy at least five more ton. Where was she going to get that much hay? And how was she going to pay for it?

A married couple who owned a ranch about ten miles east of hers, Trina and Jonas Wilkerson, might have extra hay. If Pippa could scrape up the money, they might be willing to sell her what she needed. Or if worse came to worst, she might ask the owner of the feed store in town, where she purchased all her feed, to let her buy on credit. But the man was a penny pincher and Pippa was hardly a good financial risk since everyone knew she was struggling to hold on to the ranch. Not that she didn't pay her bills. She always paid her bills on time, even if it meant selling a cow or two. But damn it, she didn't want to sell a cow or two. She'd never get her herd built up if she had to constantly peel off a couple of animals here and there. She could sell a few of the lambs, but they wouldn't bring much. Besides, she didn't want them going for meat purposes. She raised them solely for shearing.

Trying to shove the dismal thoughts out of her head, she climbed down from the loft. After finishing the task with Hawk, she went back to the house and headed to the bedroom Debra had once shared with her husband. Later, after he'd died, she'd moved his rolltop desk into the room so that she could go over the ranch's books without any distractions.

More than six months had passed since Debra had died, but Pippa hadn't bothered to tidy the desk. Most of her things were still sitting in the same spot. A can of pencils and ink pens. A coaster for her coffee cup. A stack of postcards from her sister, Taylor, along with a framed snapshot of her and Yance in their younger years.

There were times Pippa still had to remind herself that the woman was gone. Debra had suffered with viral pneumonia for more than three weeks before the consumption in her lungs had finally taken her life. During her stay in the hospital, Pippa had remained by her bedside, breaking her vigil only long enough to deal with the ranch chores.

The ordeal had left Pippa emotionally and physically drained. If she were being honest, she'd still not recovered from the trauma of losing the closest thing she'd ever had to a real mother. Now, because of Flint Hollister, she was going to have to sift through Debra's personal things and feel the pain of losing her all over again.

Later that afternoon, after a quick lunch in a fast-food restaurant, Flint returned to the hotel where he was staying. The multistoried building overlooked the Kootenai River, which flowed through the town of Bonners Ferry. Under different circumstances, Flint would be enjoying the fantastic view from his comfortable seat in the hotel's cozy lounge, but calling his father to relate the news of Debra's death was far from pleasant.

"Flint, surely you're wrong!" Hadley practically shouted

in Flint's ear. "You want me to believe my half-sister has passed away?"

Flint winced at the stunned note in his father's voice. Despite never meeting the woman, Flint had known the news would shake Hadley. He'd always been a very family-oriented man. Thus the reason he'd not been willing to give up the search for his father's birth history so he could learn how his family had wound up being related to the Hollisters in Arizona.

"I'm sorry, Dad," Flint said. "She died about six or seven months ago. From a bout of viral pneumonia."

"Pneumonia! Hell! Don't they have adequate doctors up there?"

Flint pinched the bridge of his nose and drew in a deep breath. He shouldn't be feeling exhausted. He'd gotten plenty of sleep last night and the bit of exertion he'd done this morning helping Pippa had been trivial compared to a normal day's work on Stone Creek Ranch. He supposed the emotional toll of meeting Pippa and seeing what she was going through had left him drained.

"I'm sure they do, Dad," Flint answered. "It must have been one of those resistant bugs. Or she might've had underlying health issues. I don't know. Pippa didn't go into that much detail. Frankly, I could see it upset her to talk about it, so I didn't press."

Hadley sighed then said in a gentler tone, "I understand, Flint. It's just that…well, I'm disappointed. Not just because she might've been able to give us information about my father. I feel like we'll find that later—somehow. But I had just recently learned about my half-sister and now I'll never have the opportunity to know her or for her to know me."

"Assuming she would've wanted to know you," Flint

said wryly. "Debra might not have wanted anything to do with us Hollisters. Since she never bothered to track you down, it looks like that was the case."

Hadley heaved out another long breath. "You could be right. There's no telling what Scarlett told her daughters about her first marriage," he muttered then asked, "Okay, so what about Debra's husband or children?"

"Sorry again, Dad. Debra's husband, Yance O'Shea, died a few years back and the couple never had any children."

There was a long pause before he finally said, "You know, son, there are times I wonder if I should just drop this whole matter. Every time we make a few inches of headway, another roadblock is thrown in front of us. Is God trying to tell me to leave this alone? That if I keep digging, I'm going to find out something I'd be better off not knowing?"

"I can't answer that, Dad. It does seem like one thing after another has happened. But you've gone this far and there's still a chance that Pippa or Debra's sister, can come up with some sort of helpful information. And by the way, your other half-sister's name is Taylor, not Ruthann."

"Hmm. I wonder why Bonnie's search came up with the name Ruthann?" Hadley asked thoughtfully.

"Ruthann was Scarlett's middle name. Pippa gave me that information," Flint told him.

There was a long pause and Flint figured his father was troubled over the fact that he'd not known his own mother's middle name.

"Oh. Well, tell me about Pippa," Hadley said. "You say she inherited the Bell Ranch? How did that come about? Why didn't Debra leave the property to her sister?"

"I'm only guessing, but I think Pippa inherited the place because she was like a daughter to Debra and Yance. And, too, it turns out that her sister lives in Wyoming. She might not have wanted to keep the ranch going and that's what the O'Sheas wanted. Debra must've trusted Pippa to continue on with the Bell."

"Hmm. You're probably right. But is this Pippa worthy of the ranch? I mean, does she care about keeping it going?"

It was all Flint could do to keep from groaning in his father's ear. "It's her home, Dad. From what I've seen, I think she'd probably give her life for it. And—well, I'll be honest, I can't stop thinking about her."

There was another long pause before Hadley finally said, "Why? Am I wrong to assume she's some sort of glamor girl with plenty of hands to do the ranch work? You always have turned your head toward the pretty ones."

Flint bit back a string of curse words. "Damn right, you're wrong! Pippa is so opposite of what you just described it's not even funny. In fact, everything about her and the ranch is…"

For once in his life, Flint couldn't find the words he wanted to convey to his father and he could only imagine the puzzled look on Hadley's face right now.

"Go on, Flint. Tell me about the situation."

Taking a deep breath, Flint said, "Pippa is twenty-seven and running the ranch without any hands to help her. Presently, the snow is about a foot-and-a-half deep and still falling. She's spreading hay for cattle and sheep, feeding penned livestock, taking care of horses, dogs, cats…well, you get the picture. I didn't see a tractor anywhere to load alfalfa bales. She does it by hand—out of the barn loft. The work truck she drives is at least twenty years old and low gear sounds like it's going to break a few teeth off at any given moment."

"How do you know this? You drove the truck?"

"No. But I rode in it with her—to help her spread hay. We had to go around the side of a mountain. It's as cold as hell up here, Dad. The wind chill is subzero. Just following her around a bit this morning makes me wonder how she's doing it all. The only help she has is four stock dogs. And two of those she mainly leaves on the sheep."

"What about when Debra was still living? What was the situation with the ranch then?"

"From what I can tell, Pippa and Debra were doing all the work by themselves. Frankly, Dad, I figure the place just barely makes a meager living for Pippa. A lot of it, especially the house, is run-down. The ranch consists of about seven hundred acres or so. She runs a small herd of Angus cattle and some Hampshire sheep. And she's trying to grow her herds, so she's doing her best to avoid selling any of the livestock."

Hadley said, "Sounds like she's a determined young woman."

"Mentally strong and determined," Flint told him. "Physically, though, she's a little thing."

"And you feel sorry for her," Hadley replied in a knowing voice.

"No!" Flint blurted the word with such force that a man sitting on the opposite side of the lounge looked over at him. Deliberately lowering his voice, he went on. "Pippa isn't a person to feel sorry for. She's doing what she loves. I only wish that...well, she wasn't so alone. That she had some help. We all need a helping hand from time to time. We all need someone to remind us we're not alone. Don't we?"

"Yes, son. You're exactly right. But you can't be worrying about this woman's situation. She isn't your responsibility. And you'll be leaving there soon. Uh—when do you think you'll be heading home?"

The question caused Flint to pause. When he'd climbed out of bed this morning, he'd thought how glad he would be to head back to Utah as soon as possible. But now the eagerness to leave Bonners Ferry had left him. All he could think about was going back to the Bell and Pippa.

"I can't say for certain," Flint said. "Depends on how long it takes Pippa to go through Debra's things. Why? Don't tell me you want me to head down to Wyoming to talk to the other sister!"

"Quit worrying. I have no intentions of sending you to Wyoming. I'm trying to take this whole issue one step at a time, son. You just see what Pippa comes up with and I'll take it from there. In the meantime, try to enjoy yourself. I hear it's beautiful up there. If you have your passport with you, drive on across the border into Canada and look around. Give the little ranching woman a break and take her with you," he suggested. "She'd probably enjoy getting away from things for a while."

If Flint suggested such an outing to Pippa, she'd probably laugh in his face. Take her on a leisure drive to Canada? Her first question would be *Why*? And her second would be, *Who'll take care of my animals?*

"It's a nice thought, Dad. But she doesn't have time for that kind of thing."

"Surely you could find some day hands around there somewhere who are willing to work and take care of things for a day or two."

"Probably. But she can't afford them."

"You can," Hadley retorted.

"Yes. Only, I can guarantee you that she wouldn't allow me to foot the bill for such an expense. I've already offered to pay her for searching through Debra's papers. She was offended."

"A proud woman. Well, I'm sure you'll think of some way to help her. Now, I've got to get off and head over to the ranch yard. Holt has shipped up a horse from his Three Rivers stables and Jack and Cord can't wait for me to see him."

"Okay, Dad. I'll call tomorrow to let you know what, if anything, Pippa comes up with. Tell everyone hello for me."

Hadley gave him a final goodbye. Once the signal was disconnected, Flint slipped the phone back into the pocket of his jacket and thoughtfully leaned back in the plush armchair.

Holt Hollister was a part of the Arizona Hollister family. He raised and trained horses that, more often than not, sold for six figures each. The cost of shipping a horse from Three Rivers Ranch to Stone Creek Ranch meant little to him. Flint's family in Utah wasn't nearly as wealthy as their relatives in Arizona, but they were very comfortable financially and that reality made him wonder even more about Scarlett. When she'd left Stone Creek back in the early seventies, she'd walked away from a husband and children and financial security. It didn't seem as if she'd ever found great financial wealth once she dropped the Hollister name and remarried. Apparently, getting away from Lionel had been more important to her than having money. What did that say about the woman? More importantly, what did it say about Lionel?

If only his grandmother was still in her right mind, Flint thought, they might learn the truth of the matter. As for Lionel, he'd refused to talk about his ex-wife prior to his death. And what little he had said about her had always been filled with bitterness and accusations of her being a shrew.

Flint's ponderings were suddenly interrupted by the vibration in his pocket. After swiping a hand over his eyes in an effort to clear his senses, he pulled out the phone to see a fellow deputy in Beaver had sent him a text.

Hey, buddy! Are you up there cuddled up with a ski bunny? How's it going?

Ski bunny, hell! Flint scoffed. That was the last kind of woman he'd want to be cuddled up with.

No, you want to get all wrapped up with a redhead. One with lips that had almost forgotten how to smile and gray eyes clear enough to see all the way to her heart.

Blowing out a frustrated breath, Flint quickly tapped out a reply to his friend.

No ski bunny. Cold and feeding cows.

Cows?!!

Later.

Flint sent the one-word message to him then slipped the phone back in his pocket. As he left the lounge and started toward the elevator, he noticed the hotel bar had opened.

Being a deputy, the only time he enjoyed a drink was when he was off duty. Normally, he'd never consider having a bourbon and soda in the middle of the afternoon, but this wasn't exactly a normal day, he decided. And he still had hours and hours to go before morning arrived and he drove back out to the Bell Ranch and met with Pippa again.

Even with a shot or two of whiskey, it was going to be a long, long night.

Chapter Four

Snow was still falling the next morning when Flint reached the entrance to the Bell. By the time he arrived in the ranch yard, the flakes were peppering down on the deep white blanket covering the ground, the trees, and the roofs of the barn and sheds.

Since Pippa's old truck was parked at the far end of the barn, he knew she hadn't gone around the mountain to spread hay, so he looked for her inside the building. When he didn't find her, he went to Hawk's stall and, after a quick inspection of the horse's foot, started to the back-side of the house.

She answered his knock almost instantly and as she stood there in front of him, Flint was struck with a rush of feelings pouring through him. For the past twenty-four hours, his thoughts had been consumed with her. Now that he was seeing her again, his senses were more than a bit rattled.

She stood to one side and gestured for him to enter the kitchen. "Come in, Flint. I was just cooking breakfast. Have you eaten?"

"Yes, I have. Thanks. I could use some coffee, though."

She shut the door behind him and while she walked back

over to the cabinet counter, he wiped the bottom of his rubber boots on a matt and hung up his coat. The warm room smelled like bacon and coffee and toasted bread. In spite of the shabby cabinets and worn flooring, the room had a cozy feel that drew on him. Or was it her presence that was making it all feel like home?

"Have a seat and make yourself comfortable," she told him. "I'll get your coffee."

He walked over to where she was pulling a cup from the cabinet. "You go ahead with your cooking," he told her as his eyes discreetly traveled over the green wool sweater and mud-stained jeans she was wearing. "I can wait on myself."

"All right."

Without looking at him directly, she handed him the cup then went over to where bacon was sizzling in an iron skillet. While she tended to the frying meat, Flint filled his cup from the carafe sitting on the warmer plate and, after stirring in a spoonful of sugar, carried it over to the table.

"How was the drive out here?" she asked.

From his seat at the table, his gaze slipped over her sweater and jeans. There wasn't any point in asking her if she'd already been outside, he thought. He could see for himself that she had.

"Slick, but thankfully I made it without any mishaps," he told her.

"I just returned from haying the cows around the mountain. The track up there is getting nasty. I hate putting chains on the tires, but I might have to."

"You should have waited for me to help you," he said, imagining the horror of her and the truck sliding off the mountain.

Her laugh was short and weary-sounding. "I didn't know when you might show up. Besides, I—"

"I know," he interrupted, "you deal with the livestock and the weather every day. You're used to it. Isn't that what you were going to say?"

"Yes. Only I might've used a few different words."

"I didn't notice one yesterday, but do you have a tractor?"

"Yes. It's in the shed, but the battery has gone bad. I've been trying to get by without the tractor until— Well, I've been trying to just make do with the truck," she finished awkwardly.

"I see," he said. But, frankly, Flint didn't see. Not completely. How had things gotten to this point with her and the ranch? He wanted to present her with the question, but he'd not been acquainted with her long enough to feel he had the right to pry. And even if he did know her better, she'd still probably tell him to mind his own business.

His gaze strayed back over to where she remained in front of the gas range and he couldn't help but notice the hem of her sweater was stretched out of shape and there was a hole near the neck. She'd changed her rubber boots for a pair of brown cowboy boots that had once been rough-out leather but were now worn smooth. As he watched her take a few short steps between the cook stove and the cabinet, he wondered if she'd ever worn a pair of high heels or even a pair of delicate sandals. He doubted it. He'd already concluded that she was a practical woman. She'd say a pair of high heels would be useless to her.

Pippa is practical, Flint, because she has to be. Even if she wanted them, she can't waste her money on frivolous things. She needs money for a battery, hay, horse feed and...

He was trying to mute the voice in his head when she carried her plate over to the table and sat in a chair to his right. When her gray glance traveled across the table to meet his, something in the middle of his chest made a hard jerk.

"How did your father react to the news of Debra's death?" she asked. "I thought about how that might feel, but it's impossible for me to imagine. For him to learn he had a half-sister, only to find out she'd died before he could meet her—that couldn't be easy to take."

"Dad was understandably upset. I mean he's not a man who rants or raves, or becomes overly emotional about things. But he said enough to make it clear he was troubled by the news."

She sprinkled hot sauce over a small mound of scrambled eggs then forked a bite to her lips. "Well, I realize you're anxious to hear if I found any kind of information regarding your grandfather yesterday. I'm sorry to say that, so far, I haven't."

"What do you mean 'so far'? You haven't worked your way through all of her papers?"

She shook her head and the movement lured Flint's gaze to her hair. She'd twisted the top of it into a loose bun, while the rest hung over her shoulders and down her back. He wondered what she might think if he reached over and rolled a strand of her hair between his fingers.

She said, "I went through everything I could find in her desk and I looked through the drawers of the chest and dresser in her bedroom. But there's still a chance we could find something in the boxes she put up in the attic after Yance died. At the time, she'd said it was old papers and documents that she didn't want to bother sorting through until a later date. But she didn't want to toss any of it away without first going through it. If you're willing to help, we could make a search of those."

"I'd be glad to help. When were you thinking you might have a chance to do this search?"

She took a bite of toast then placed it back on her plate. "I realize you can't hang around Bonners Ferry for days. This morning, I still need to feed the sheep and tend to Hawk's foot. After I finish with those chores, we could start—if you'd like."

Did she always look this pale? he wondered. And peck at her food? She couldn't exist on crumbs.

"I would like," he said. "But—uh, are you sure you're feeling all right, Pippa?"

"I'm fine." She frowned at him as she touched a hand to her hair. "I guess I must look rough this morning. I slept a little late and was in a hurry when I—got dressed."

He shook his head, filled with the urge to go around the table to her. He wanted to pull her into his arms and simply hold her tight. The urge didn't make sense, but it was there, and it was all he could do to keep from acting on it.

"You look fine, Pippa. I only asked because you're picking at your breakfast. Aren't you hungry?"

She sighed. "I thought I was hungry. But now that the food is in front of me, I don't really want to eat. I think I'll just finish my coffee and go tend to Hawk and the sheep. By then my appetite might fire up."

He nodded. "Okay. I'll help you. And by the way, I brought some medicine for Hawk's foot. I think it will help."

"Thank you. Just tell me how much it cost and I'll reimburse you."

Flint started to blurt out a loud no, but stopped himself.

Now wasn't the time to negotiate money with her. He figured being more subtle would work better to his advantage.

"We'll talk about the cost of the medicine later. Just enjoy the rest of your coffee. The hot drink will help keep you warm."

She picked up her cup but didn't immediately take a sip. Instead she looked directly at him and Flint was momentarily held captive by her gray eyes.

"How did your evening in Bonners Ferry go? I imagine the town is full of cross-country skiers. When there's fresh powder, hordes of ski tourists arrive."

"I didn't do much," he said. He wasn't going to admit that he'd spent part of the afternoon in the hotel bar, sipping bourbon and trying to get her out of his mind. "I drove around a part of the town and looked at the river. I did notice a few vehicles with skis strapped to the top. Have you ever skied?"

She shrugged. "When I was a teenager, I'd go with a few of my friends to do a little cross-country skiing—the kind that's mostly done in this area. It never really was my thing. I do like to ice skate, though. But it's been a few years since I've been in a pair of skates. What about you? Do you ski or skate? I imagine Utah has plenty of snow and ice for both sports."

"Utah has plenty of both. But I don't ski or skate." He gave her a guilty grin. "I never was much into sports."

"You were probably too busy becoming a deputy to think about such trivial pursuits."

"I wouldn't call sports trivial. They're important. Actually, my oldest brother makes a great living from the rodeo. He's a rodeo and stock producer."

She looked up at him, her eyes wide with interest. Her

reaction didn't surprise Flint. Most everyone was impressed with Hunter's vocation. Especially the women.

"I'm impressed," she said. "Does he have a big operation?"

"He started out small, but over the years the business has grown into a huge production. He and his wife, Willow, travel all over the western states. She handles all the paperwork involved."

"Hmm. It's nice they run the business together," she replied. "When Yance was still living, the three of us went to a rodeo in Coeur d'Alene. We all really enjoyed it."

She continued to hold her coffee cup with both hands, but he noticed she wasn't drinking.

"I guess things were very different around here while Debra's husband was alive."

"Oh yes. He was a gentle, hardworking guy. Everyone who knew him liked him. But if you're thinking his death is the reason the ranch is now operating on a shoestring, it isn't. Several problems sort of hit us all at once. Loss of calves to bovine rotavirus, bad weather, and even worse livestock markets. Once you have a couple of deep setbacks, it's a struggle to build things back. But given time, I will."

"I have no doubt you will," he said frankly while thinking he'd never met a woman with more drive and determination.

Her lips twisted to a rueful slant. "You're probably thinking I'm a fool who has no idea of what I'm up against."

"Some people probably would say you're fighting a losing battle. But I won't. You see, in spite of me working as a deputy, I'm still a rancher at heart. And I understand what a deep feeling you have for the land and how you want it to thrive. You won't cave to the hardships."

Her expression softened as she leaned back in her chair and studied him thoughtfully. "Before we go out to finish the last of the chores, I'd like for you to do something."

He'd like to do plenty, Flint thought. The first thing being to pull her into his arms and kiss her. How and why he'd developed that incessant urge, he didn't know. But it was there just the same.

"You need something done here in the house?" She probably needed an extra set of hands to deal with moving a heavy piece of furniture or something of the sort, he decided.

"Nothing like that. I'd like to hear what you and your family think about Scarlett. I realize you're searching for information about her first husband, but she's your grandmother. Or do you not recognize her as such?"

Her question surprised him somewhat. So far, he'd gotten the impression that she didn't care much, one way or the other, about his family's connection to Debra's.

"To be honest, Pippa, I never thought of Scarlett as my grandmother. I don't think my siblings do, either. But to be fair, we don't know much of anything about her. I've only seen one grainy image of her. And up until Grandfather Lionel died, Dad kept the snapshot hidden away. You see, after Scarlett left the ranch and my grandparents divorced, Lionel got rid of all the photos and mementos of his ex. Dad was just a little boy at the time—about seven, I think. His younger brother, Wade, was five and Barton was only three. Anyway, before Lionel tossed everything away, Dad managed to sneak a pic of his mother from the things and hide it from his father. That one photo is basically all Dad has of her."

"How awful. Well, I can help you out in that aspect. I

found several photos of Scarlett among Debra's things yes-terday," she told him, then with a shake of her head added, "Obviously you never knew Scarlett when you were grow-ing up. So I guess what I'm asking is your opinion of what kind of woman she must've been back when she lived on Stone Creek Ranch. Do you think she was a bad person?"

"I couldn't testify to that in a court of law," he told her. "Whatever I said about Scarlett would be hearsay. But Grandfather Lionel was very bitter about her and the di-vorce. Although, he never really explained to anyone why they split, or if he knew why she never made an effort to see or speak to her young sons." He leaned slightly toward her. "Do you know anything about Scarlett?"

She rubbed her fingertips against her forehead. "A lit-tle. Debra talked a bit about her parents and how, when she was growing up, they lived in southern Idaho, some-where around Blackfoot, I think. Her husband, Ode, was a potato farmer. Debra said her mother was in her late thir-ties when she gave birth to her and close to forty when she had Taylor."

Flint thoughtfully sipped his coffee. Of all the things he'd imagined about his grandmother, nothing had been close to her living on a potato farm. And he figured Hadley would be surprised by this bit of information, also.

"Hmm. Have any idea how she met Ode?" Flint voiced the question out loud.

"In the restaurant where she worked. Debra said Scar-lett was a waitress before she married Ode. She also told me how her mother worked very hard on the farm—even picking up potatoes in the fields when the crops were ready to harvest."

It seemed impossible that the Scarlett who picked potatoes out of the dirt could be the same one who demanded Lionel move the ranch yard further away from the house so she wouldn't have to deal with the cattle kicking up dust. The notion was too incredible for Flint to believe and yet he knew that Debra, or Pippa especially, had no reason to lie.

"So Debra and Taylor grew up on the farm?" he asked.

Pippa nodded. "The farm was their home until each of them married and moved away. But Scarlett and Ode remained there on the farm until he passed away."

"Do you know when he died? Not that it matters, but to be honest—" he shot her a sheepish look "—the more I hear about Scarlett, the more curious I am."

"I'd think you would be curious. She was your father's mother. But to answer your question, I believe Ode passed away in 2018. The reason I can recall the date is because that's when Debra moved Scarlett to Coeur d'Alene and not long afterward is when I hired on here at the Bell. Anyway, Debra always said her father's passing was the reason for Scarlett's mental spiral downward, and I'm inclined to agree. The few times I went with Debra to visit her mother—well, it was easy to see the woman was grieving for her husband. But I will say this, Scarlett always seemed to be a gentle, loving woman. And Debra never failed to describe her mother in that way."

Flint scrubbed his face with both hands. He felt like he was hearing about a woman with a split personality. "I'll tell you, Pippa, this is hard for me to absorb. Grandfather always implied that Scarlett was an adulteress and her infidelity was what sent her running away—because she didn't want to face the family with her sins. He also said she hated everything about the ranch and nagged him incessantly about living in the country around a bunch of stinking animals."

Pippa scowled at him. "Do you believe such a thing?"

Flint sighed. "You know, Grandfather Lionel was a big, authoritative man and we all respected him. How could we not? He was the patriarch of our family and built Stone Creek Ranch from scratch. He was strong and tough and he expected all of us to walk a righteous line. If you'd asked me a couple of years ago, I would have said I couldn't imagine him lying to any of us. But the more I hear about Scarlett, the more I doubt his stories about her were entirely true. Last year, when Beatrice visited the woman, she said that Scarlett was practically crying because she wanted another cat and the apartment supervisor wouldn't allow her to have two cats. Does that sound like a woman who wanted to avoid animals? Not to me."

Pippa's expression softened. "Not to me, either. And I hope— Actually, I feel like, for Debra's sake, it's my duty to clear the woman's name. And for your sake, too."

As she spoke the last words, she reached across and placed her hand over his forearm. The contact stunned him. All the time he was here yesterday, the closest she'd gotten to touching him was when she'd stood and looked over his shoulder at Hawk's foot. And even then she'd not touched him in any form or fashion.

"I...don't know what to say. Except that I... Well, it would be a heck of a lot better if I could think of my grandmother as a nice person—a loving person. But right now all I can see is a giant chasm between the woman I've heard about and the woman her other family knew."

She gently squeezed his arm before pulling her hand away and Flint was amazed at the tingling sensation left in the wake of her touch. "Maybe we'll find something among Debra's things that will help fill the chasm. But right now, I don't want to keep the sheep waiting, or Hawk's foot."

They both rose to their feet at the same time. After Flint carried his cup over to the sink, he pulled on his hat and heavy coat. Across the room, Pippa replaced her cowboy boots with a pair of fur-lined rubber boots then pulled on a red-plaid coat with a fur-edged hood.

As she joined him at the door leading onto the porch, she said, "You know, I try not to complain about the weather. Mother Nature gives us what She thinks we need. But it sure would be nice to see the sun once in a while. I'm about to forget what it looks like."

"It would be nice to see what this place looks like without a foot and a half of snow covering everything."

Her short laugh said the chances of that happening anytime soon were slim to none. "You might have to stay until spring before it all melts away."

"If that's the case, then I'll just have to imagine how it will look with grass and wildflowers."

"It's beautiful in the spring, Flint. I'll send you a pic to prove it." She tied the strings of the hood tight beneath her chin. "But for now, it's far from springtime."

Springtime on the Bell. Except for a photo, if she remembered to send him one, Flint would never see the ranch decorated with grass and leaves and flowers. For some inexplicable reason, the thought saddened him.

They left the warmth of the house and after Flint fetched a sack containing the meds for Hawk from his truck, they followed the narrow path Pippa had shoveled out to the barn. Once inside, Flint went straight to Hawk's stall and while Pippa looked on, began to treat the animal's foot.

After a moment, she said, "While you do that, I'll load the hay for the sheep."

He glanced over his shoulder and frowned at her. "No. You stay right here with me. I'm almost finished. We'll load it together."

She wanted to argue but she didn't have the energy. "If you say so. I'm just trying to save time."

"I'm not in that big of a hurry."

His comment surprised Pippa. When he'd first arrived on the ranch yesterday morning, she'd gotten the impression he was in a huge hurry to get what he wanted and head straight back to Utah. Now he didn't seem nearly so antsy to get back on the road. She didn't know what had brought about the change in him, but she was glad.

Foolish or not, she was enjoying his company and had been looking forward to his arrival this morning. And when he'd agreed to help her go through the boxes in the attic, she'd not been able to stop the little thrill of joy rushing through her.

Pippa, you don't have to wonder if you're being a fool— you are one. Flint is here on a very temporary basis. He has a life and a career back in Utah. You need to get your head out of the clouds.

Shaking away the nagging voice going off in her head, she asked, "How does Hawk's foot look to you?"

"Much better. This liquid I'm spraying on the bottom will help. And I'm going to give him a shot of antibiotics for any lingering infection."

Frowning, Pippa stepped closer to him. "You picked up a bottle of penicillin at the feed store?"

"No. This is something better I picked up at the vet's office at the south edge of town."

"How did you manage to talk Dr. Jordon into selling you the drug? Don't tell me you talked him into writing you a prescription. He's a stickler for seeing the patient before he hands out meds."

"Nothing wrong with being a stickler for that. But I had a prescription. My brother-in-law, Mack, in Beaver, is a veterinarian with his own practice. Before I left the ranch yesterday, I took a few pics of Hawk's foot. I sent them to him and called to explain the problem. Mack texted me a prescription. So Hawk is to have an injection today and the following two days."

For more than one reason, Pippa wanted to throw her arms around him and hug him tight. He'd not come to the Bell for the purpose of being her hero, but in her mind she was beginning to see him as one.

"I feel awful about this, Flint. You went to a lot of trouble for me and Hawk. And the most I can do is say thank you."

Returning the horse's hoof to the ground, he straightened to his full height and turned to her. "I don't need anything more than a thank-you. So you're all paid up," he said.

His gaze was making a slow inspection of her face and it had her feeling very self-conscious. Ever since he'd arrived this morning, he'd been looking at her with an odd look in his eyes. Like her features had morphed into someone he didn't recognize. Yes, she realized her appearance was slovenly. But she'd barely been able to drag herself out of bed this morning, much less do anything to her face and hair.

"I appreciate your help, Flint."

"I know." He picked up the plastic sack he'd used to

carry the meds and then nudged her out of the stall. "He's all finished. Let's go get the hay."

A few minutes later, after she'd parked the truck inside the barn and started the climb up to the hayloft, she recognized something wasn't quite right. Her legs felt as though someone had tied heavy weights to both ankles and it was a real struggle to find enough strength to move the heavy hay bales. She couldn't recall the last time she'd been sick. Surely, she wasn't becoming ill now, of all times. She couldn't be. Not with Flint here. Not when she had tons of work to do before the day was finished.

When she finally managed to push the third bale through the opening of the floor, she called down to him. "The sheep get three, Flint. That's the last bale."

"Right."

She climbed down slowly and found him waiting for her at the side of the truck. In spite of her lethargy, her heart fluttered at the sight of his tall, lanky body and handsome face. Never in her wildest imaginings had she pictured anyone like him coming to her remote ranch. Even now when she looked at him, she had the feeling he was a dream. Men like him didn't show up in her life for any reason—and if they did, they never stayed long. Which was why she had to remember not to get attached.

"Ready to go?" he asked.

"Ready," she said with a nod. But she wasn't exactly being truthful. Her legs were beginning to feel like two sticks of rubber. And when he turned to open the passenger door on the truck, she instinctively grabbed a hold on his arm.

Turning, he arched a questioning brow at her that ignited a fire in her cheeks.

"Was there something else?" he asked.

Her throat was suddenly tight and she tried to clear the thickness away with a little cough. "I—uh—yes, there is. Would you mind driving this time? To tell you the truth, I'm feeling a bit wonky."

A frown puckered his brows together. "I wouldn't mind at all. In fact, if you'll give me directions to the sheep, I can do this and you can go back to the house and rest in front of the fire."

Shaking her head, she said, "No. I want to see the sheep for myself. I'm okay. Really."

"All right." He opened the door and, after helping her into the passenger seat, took his place beneath the steering wheel. But as he started the engine, he slanted her a look of disapproval. "You'd make me happy if you'd go back to the house and let me handle this."

She sighed. "And you'd make me happy if you'd get us on our way."

He scowled at her but said nothing as he put the truck into forward gear and drove out of the barn and into the falling snow.

For the next ten minutes, she directed him through a couple of stands of Ponderosa pine, mountain hemlock and red cedar, all of which were tall and thick enough to blot out the gray light of day. When they emerged from the last small forest and drew near the creek, she spotted the sheep gathered at the base of a rocky cliff.

"There they are over by the mountain ledge."

Agreeing with a nod of his head, he said, "Looks like the spruce growing there shields them from the wind and snow."

"It does," she replied. "Otherwise, I'd have to herd them back to the ranch yard to one of the loafing sheds."

"Where do you want to spread the hay?" he asked.

"There's a flat space over there by those two lodge pole pines. See them?"

"Yeah."

He drove the truck over to the spot and the sheep immediately began to gather around the vehicle. Pippa tried to count the heads, but her brain was too foggy to keep the numbers straight.

"You stay put," he told her. "I'll handle this. And don't worry, I'll look them over. I know all about sheep."

"You do?"

He shot her a patient grin. "We have about a thousand head on Stone Creek Ranch. I ought to know a little about them."

Frowning, she touched her gloved hand to her forehead. "Oh. I'm not thinking clearly. You did tell me your family raised sheep."

He eyed her for a moment before he reached for the door handle. "Don't move. I'll be back in a few minutes."

As he climbed out of the truck, Pippa could have told him he needn't worry about her moving. At the moment, she doubted an explosion in the bed of the truck could make her leave the seat. If she could only close her eyes and nap for two or three minutes, the sleep might revive her.

The wishful thought was the last thing she remembered until she woke with a hand pressed against her forehead and Flint's face hovering in front of hers.

"Oh! Flint! What's wrong?" she asked drowsily. "Did I—fall asleep?"

"Either that, or you passed out," he said, sounding worried. "You're burning hot, Pippa!"

He dropped his hand from her forehead and she attempted to sit up straight. "I'm not hot. I'm freezing. Can you turn up the heater?"

He adjusted the vents on the dash so the warm air would blow directly on her. "It's already on max," he said then touched a hand to her cheek. "You told me you were feeling a little wonky back at the barn. Why didn't you tell me you were actually sick?"

She blinked her eyes and did her best to focus on his face. When her vision finally cleared, she could see his features were puckered with concern and that bothered her more than the bone-deep weariness she was experiencing. The last thing she wanted was to cause Flint any problems or worries.

"Because I—I'm not sick. Just a little tired, Flint. I'll be fine when I get home and get warmed up."

"No. You're burning up with fever. I'm taking you straight to the doctor."

She struggled with all her might to keep her eyelids from falling shut. "I don't need a doctor," she mumbled.

"Yes, you do."

He turned the truck around and as he drove them away from the feeding grounds, Pippa's head fell wearily back against the seat. Flint had already helped her so much. But maybe it wouldn't hurt anything to lean on him one more time.

The lovely thought of resting her head upon his strong shoulder drifted through her mind just before sleep overtook her.

Chapter Five

Flint had no idea if Pippa had a regular family physician for her health care or if she simply walked into a twenty-four-hour, walk-in clinic whenever she needed to see a doctor. A couple of times throughout the drive to town, he'd tried to wake her to ask where to take her, but his efforts had been futile. She'd only mumbled incoherently without ever fully waking.

Now as he wheeled his truck into the nearest parking spot he could find at the front entrance of the medical facility, he decided it didn't matter where he took her, as long as she received a doctor's care. Flint was hardly a health expert, but he could plainly see she was in a bad way. The sight of her fever-flushed face was filling him with an icy chill that had nothing to do with the brisk wind or the snow that continued to fall. What if her condition was life-threatening? What if she didn't have the strength to fight off whatever gripped her? The idea of losing her was terrifying.

She's not yours to lose, Flint. You need to remember that one important fact.

He shut off the motor, along with the mocking voice in his head, and reached over to unbuckle her seat belt. The movement of his hands next to her coat finally roused her and she looked around in a daze.

"We're in town?" she asked as she glanced around the plush cab of his truck. "How did I get in your vehicle? What are we doing here?"

"I couldn't wake you, so I carried you from the work truck over to my truck. We're now at the emergency-care clinic. Have you ever used a doctor at this facility?"

She peered at the front of the building. "Yes. But it's been a long time. I'm never sick."

He unbuckled his own seat belt and pocketed the truck keys. "Well, you are now. I just hope to heck the place isn't too busy. I don't think you're capable of sitting around and waiting for long."

Apparently, her fever-induced brain had cleared somewhat because she suddenly looked down at her dirty work clothes and let out a puny wail of dismay. "Oh, Flint! I can't go in there like this! I have mud on my jeans and boots. I— Why didn't you let me change clothes before we left the ranch?"

If he wasn't so worried about her, he would've laughed at her question. "You weren't in any shape to change clothes. You still aren't. So just sit there until I come around to help you into the building," he ordered.

Whether she'd remained in her seat because he'd told her to or if she was simply too weak to move, he couldn't say. He was just glad she'd waited until he'd opened the passenger door before she swung her feet over the side of the seat.

"I found your handbag at the end of the kitchen cabinet and brought it along," he told her, pointing to the brown-leather bag on the floorboard. "I thought you might need insurance information or something."

"Uh—yes. Thanks."

After she'd pulled the strap of the purse onto her shoulder, he reached for her hand and she wrapped hers tightly around his.

"Careful," he said. "You don't need an injury from a fall added to a fever."

She put her foot on the running board but that was as far as she got before she groaned with disbelief. "You might need to give me a moment to climb to the ground. My head is kind of swimmy."

Flint didn't wait to hear more. He reached up, clamped a hand on both sides of her waist, and lifted her to the ground. He'd already learned that she was as light as a feather when he'd transferred her over to his truck, but she seemed to feel even lighter to him as he set her down on a concrete walkway.

He shut the door behind her and pressed the key fob to lock the vehicle. "Do you think you can walk?"

"I think so," she told him then immediately clutched his arm with both hands. "If I can lean on you."

"No problem. We'll go slowly." Actually, he wanted to sweep her up into his arms and carry her into the building, but he didn't want to embarrass her. And he didn't want to scare everyone inside—no matter how scared he was himself. Seeing her go from strong and full of life one day to weak and fragile the next, had rocked him to the core of his being.

When they were finally inside the glass foyer of the building, Flint untied the strings of her hood and pushed it off her head. "There, that's better," he said as he brushed a few strands of her hair away from her face.

She looked up at him and tried to smile. "I'm so sorry,

Flint. I'm being a lot of trouble to you. I have a friend here in town who works at the library. If I call her, she might be able to come and take your place."

He urged her through the last set of doors and into a spacious lobby filled with waiting patients of all ages. Babies were crying, while most of the children and adults were either coughing or holding a tissue to their nose. From the looks of things, they were in for a long wait.

"Forget about calling your friend. I don't need anyone to take my place," he said, thinking his place was by her side for as long as she needed him.

Now where had that thought come from? He hadn't come to Idaho to pledge himself to a woman! No matter how much she seemed to be tugging on his heartstrings.

"I need to check in," she said, inclining her head toward a long counter located on the right-hand side of the room.

Behind a sliding Plexiglas window, two women were working steadily, answering the phones and taking down patient information. A sign located by the entrance had read that walk-ins were welcome, but glancing around the packed waiting room, Flint wondered if the clinic could handle any more patients.

Pippa was told a doctor could see her, but there would be a substantial wait. The woman gave her a clipboard with several papers to fill out and directed them to take a seat.

Once they'd located empty chairs where they could sit side by side, Flint removed his coat then gestured toward hers. "Would you like to take off your coat? Or do you still feel cold?"

She glanced at him and he could tell her gray eyes were growing foggy again. The same sort of fog he'd seen when they'd been driving out to feed the sheep.

"Thank you, Flint, but I'm freezing. Funny coming from me, isn't it? Compared to working outside, this room would normally feel like a hot kitchen to me. I guess I must be running a bit of fever."

A bit! She was probably going to burst the thermometer. But Flint wasn't going to tell her any such thing. She didn't need to be scared along with sick. Especially when he figured Pippa wasn't accustomed to being ill or poked and prodded by a doctor.

"Would you like for me to help you with those papers?" he asked. "I don't imagine you feel like writing down all that information."

She handed him the clipboard and pen. "Would you mind?"

"Not at all. I'm good at writing tickets for traffic violations," he said in an attempt at humor.

"You write tickets? For real?"

"Yes," he answered. "If we happen to catch someone speeding or driving recklessly."

"What if the driver is a pretty young woman?" she asked.

"You mean a pretty young woman like you? I'd probably give her a double fine," he joked, while wishing she would give him a tiny smile or some sort of sign that she wasn't growing sicker.

Shaking her head, she said, "Sorry, Flint. I can't laugh. I can't even summon a smile. I—I'm worried because I—my animals need me and I…keep remembering Debra when she first came down with the pneumonia. She had a fever, too. And I—"

He reached over and squeezed her arm. "Stop it! There's nothing for you to worry about. Everything is going be fine."

Dropping her head in her hands, she said in a muffled voice, "We'd better do those papers."

"Yeah. I'll read the questions and you can tell me the answers," he said.

Several minutes later, after the last line had been filled in on the questionnaire, Flint stood. "I'll take these over to the check-in counter," he said.

"You better take my driver's license, too. They'll probably want a copy."

She fished the plastic document from her purse and handed it to him. There was no point in asking her for an insurance card. She'd already told him to write "None" on the medical papers, a fact that hardly surprised Flint. She was self-employed and if she couldn't afford a battery for the ranch's tractor, it was a cinch her bank account couldn't stretch far enough for health insurance. The idea bothered him greatly, but he'd not said anything to her. She was doing the best she could and didn't need to be reminded of her financial status. Especially not by a man who'd always had plenty.

Forty-five minutes later, the waiting room was still crowded, even though nurses were regularly calling patients to be examined. For the first fifteen minutes of the wait, Pippa appeared to be relatively alert as she waited for her name to be called, but after a while she grew quiet. Her shoulders slumped and her chin slowly dipped toward her chest.

Normally, Flint was a patient man, but seeing Pippa in such misery made him want to stomp back to the examining room area and start yelling. But making an angry scene would hardly help her. Instead, he pillowed her head against his shoulder and urged her to sleep.

When the nurse finally called her name, Flint helped her up from the chair and made sure her handbag was fastened over her shoulder.

She clung tightly to his arm. "You will come with me?" she asked. "I don't want to go back there without you."

Placing a hand over hers, he gave her an encouraging smile. "I have no intention of leaving you. Now, come on. Let's get this over with."

The physician who finally entered the examination room introduced himself as Dr. Bartlett. Somewhere near Flint's age, the man had a head full of curly black hair and tortoise-shell glasses perched low on his nose. He stated that he recalled seeing Pippa from a visit a couple of years back and he shook her hand before turning his attention to Flint.

"Are you Ms. Shanahan's husband?" he asked.

Flint glanced at Pippa, but she was hardly paying attention.

"I'm Flint Hollister," he told the doctor. Realizing that the doctor might not allow him to be there if he wasn't a husband or relative, he quickly added, "I'm Pippa's fiancé. That's why she—uh, wanted me to be with her."

"Of course. It's perfectly fine." He shook Flint's hand. "Nice to meet you, Mr. Hollister. Now let me see what's going on with this young lady."

For the next few minutes, he examined her thoroughly then went to a small computer in the corner of the room and began to enter information. Once he was finished, he came over to Flint.

"I'm going to relay my findings to you because I don't think she's fully grasping everything I'm saying to her right now. Her fever is very high. Too high really to send her home, but I'm reluctant to admit her to the hospital. First of all, I think she'd fret herself into tailspin over what might happen to the ranch without her there, which would only exacerbate her health issues and secondly, the hospital is practically maxed out on rooms right now. Flu has been running rampant here in town," he explained. "Has Pippa been around town recently or had outside visitors?"

"Only me. Why? Does she have the flu? Is that what's wrong with her?"

"She appears to have some sort of respiratory virus. But before she leaves the clinic, I'm sending her to the lab for blood tests. Just as a way to rule out other issues. In the meantime, she might develop a cough or stomach issues. Either way, she's going to need bed rest, plenty of fluids and soft foods. Is there someone who can stay with her?"

Except for the library woman and the ranching neighbors ten miles away from the Bell, Flint hadn't heard her speak of anyone she was at all close to. But no matter, Flint would take care of her. In fact, he'd insist on it.

"I'll be taking care of her, Dr. Bartlett."

He nodded. "Good. Because for the next couple of days she shouldn't be dragging herself around trying to do everything on her own, like she usually does. But I don't think she's going to feel up to trying anyway. In the meantime, I'm calling prescriptions in for her, so make sure she takes them as soon as possible. And of course, if she worsens, bring her back here to the clinic." He started to turn away then paused and lowered his voice. "I'm remembering correctly that she's a rancher, right?"

"Very right. She takes care of over a hundred head of cows and that many sheep, along with horses, dogs, cats. She's hardworking. That's why her clothes are ragged and mud-splotched. We were out feeding the sheep when she went wonky on me."

"I see. Well, from what she's been saying, it seems she's very worried about the animals being cared for. Maybe you can ease her mind about them."

"I'll take care of everything, Doctor. Thank you for your concern."

"Of course." He shook Flint's hand then returned to Pippa who was sitting up on the end of the examination table.

After assuring her that she would be feeling better soon, the doctor exited the room. As soon as the door closed behind him, a nurse entered with a handful of papers and a dose of medicine to combat Pippa's fever.

After making sure her patient swallowed the pills, the nurse carefully explained the instructions for Pippa to follow for the next few days and made sure that Flint understood them as well. When she finally departed the room, Flint helped Pippa down from the examination table.

Swaying, she gripped his hand and he instantly wrapped his arm around her shoulders and snugged her to his side. "Don't worry, Pippa. I'm here with you. I'm going to take care of you and the ranch, so put your mind at ease."

She looked up at him and suddenly her gray eyes filled with tears. "Oh, Flint. I've messed up everything," she sobbed then hid her face against his shoulder.

His throat tight with emotions he didn't quite understand, he stroked the back of her hair and allowed her to cry.

After a long moment, she pulled her head back and attempted to wipe her eyes with the back of her hand. Flint plucked a tissue from a box on a nearby counter and gently dabbed the moisture from her cheeks.

She squared her shoulders and sniffed. "Okay. My melt-down is over. You won't see any more tears, I promise. Now let's get the trip to the lab over with so we can go home to the Bell."

As the two of them left the examining room, Pippa's re-mark lingered in his mind. *Home to the Bell.* Why did her words sound so natural to him? And why did the idea of going home with her feel so perfectly right?

Because you're falling for the girl, Flint. Because ev-erything you've ever dreamed and planned for the future has made a drastic change.

Although Flint didn't want to admit it to himself, the taunting voice was right. His plans *had* made a drastic change. Now, instead of collecting information about his grandfather, all he could think about was getting Pippa well and seeing a smile on her pretty face.

By the time Pippa and Flint returned to the Bell Ranch, darkness had fallen and she felt as if she'd traveled a thou-sand miles without stopping. Her whole body ached, her throat felt raw and, judging by the heat of her face, her tem-perature had started to rise again.

The wait at the clinic had been horrendous and they'd been put through another long wait at the lab. After leaving the clinic, they'd had to wait for the pharmacy to fill her prescriptions and then Flint had needed to go by the hotel to grab his things and check out of his room. Throughout the remainder of the afternoon, Pippa had tried her best to stay awake and alert, but several times she'd fallen asleep then jerked awake when the truck stopped and started, or Flint had opened and closed the door.

Flint.

Now, as they entered the chilled ranch house and she watched him head straight to the fireplace to stir up any remaining coals, she felt a strange ache in the middle of her chest that had nothing to do with the virus attacking her body. No, the ache was all for him and the fact that he'd stuck with her throughout the stressful day. No man she'd known before, not even Yance, would have done so much for her. And yet it wasn't only gratefulness she was feeling toward Flint. The emotions swirling around in her were coming straight from her heart. The fact scared her far worse than facing a debilitating virus.

"With the fire dying out, the house has gotten cold," he said as he piled several logs onto the bed of hot coals. "And that's the last thing you need. This will be going in a few minutes. Why don't you lie down on the couch and let me cover you with a blanket."

Just standing upright long enough to walk into the house had already taken a toll on her and she didn't argue when he helped her over to the couch.

"Does the house have a floor furnace or central heating?" he asked as he fetched a heavy afghan from the back of an armchair.

"Yes. But I have it turned down to save heating fuel."

He covered her with the crocheted blanket and carefully tucked it around her legs and shoulders. "We're not going to worry about fuel," he said. "I'll have some delivered."

"No!"

As soon as she blurted out the word, he stood back and looked at her with obvious disapproval. "Why?"

She purposely closed her eyes in hopes it would be easier to explain herself if she wasn't looking at his handsome face. But blocking out the sight of him didn't help much.

When she spoke, her voice was weak and raspy, and far from the authoritative tone she needed to make her message clear to him.

"You know why. You paid my clinic bill. You paid for all my medication. And I allowed you to because I didn't want to put up a fuss in front of everyone. But you're not going to pay for anything else I need. I'm not a freeloader, Flint. Please don't treat me like one."

"Damn it all, Pippa, now is not the time to get proud and independent on me!"

She swiped a hand over her eyes before she forced herself to look at him. He sounded angry and she didn't know what to make of his reaction. He ought to be relieved that she wasn't whining and asking him for handouts. And why would he resent her wanting to be proud and independent?

Exhausted, she pulled in a deep breath and blew it out. "Would you rather I be sniveling? Do you want me to hold out my hand and ask for money? Like hell would I ever do that. I'd rather freeze. I'd rather flatten my bank account to zero before I'd take advantage of your wealth."

His eyes narrowed. "How do you know I'm wealthy?"

If she had the strength, she'd stand and face him with her hands on her hips and fire in her eyes. As it was, she could only answer in a drained voice. "I realize I look like a hayseed, Flint. In many ways, I am. But I'm not an idiot. All I have to do is look at your clothes and your truck to know you have money. And you told me about your family ranch. You have a thousand head of sheep, herds of cattle and horses by the dozens. All of that spells money."

His taut jaw suddenly relaxed and she was more than surprised when he eased down on the edge of the couch where the indention of her waist created enough space for him to sit.

"Okay, Pippa. I'm wealthy. Should that stop me from helping someone in need? Someone I want to help?" Before she could answer, he reached up and gently stroked her hair back from her forehead. "I don't want you to feel beholden. All I want is for you to get well. You can worry about paying me back later."

The gentle touch of his hand on her hair made the fog in her brain even worse. Instead of standing her ground with him, she could only sigh.

"That might take years, Flint."

Her voice was barely above a whisper, but he'd obviously heard her, because his lips formed a wry smile.

"I'll give you a long-term loan."

She wanted to smile back at him. She wanted to grab his hand and hold it tightly. Because no matter how much she tried to protest, she'd be terrified to face the next few days without him. But she was too tired to move.

For a long moment, he sat there looking at her and then, to her utter surprise, he lowered his head and placed a kiss on the middle of her forehead. The scent of him enveloped her and the brush of his breath against her skin was like the mist of a beautiful dream.

"Go to sleep now," he murmured. "I'm going to the barn to take care of the chores. Don't try to move while I'm gone."

"I won't."

He stood and, after making sure the blanket was still tucked around her, he walked out of the living room and on toward the kitchen.

A couple of minutes later, she heard the back door shut

and then one of the dogs barked. He was going out in dark, freezing conditions to do her work. Why? And why had he promised to stay? Sure, she was ill. But she had a few friends and acquaintances around who'd come to help her if she asked. Particularly, Trina and Jonas Wilkerson. The neighboring ranchers had always been friends and had made a habit of regularly checking on her since Debra had died. She wouldn't like to impose on them, but she would if she had to. She didn't need Flint to be the one looking after her.

Maybe he was only thinking ahead to when she'd be able to help him collect information about his grandparents? Maybe he was the sort of man who'd go through hell and high water to get what he came after?

Yes, that had to be his reasons for staying, she thought. Because he couldn't be sticking around, doing her chores in single-digit weather, simply because he cared about her. No, she'd made the mistake of thinking a man cared about her before. She'd never misconstrue a man's intentions again. Nor would she ever trust another one. Not with her heart.

Tears suddenly burned the backs of her eyes, but she stubbornly blinked them away. She couldn't break down and start feeling sorry for herself. Nor could she wonder about Flint's motive to remain on the Bell. He was willing to help her through the next few days. And that was all she needed to know.

Yet as she looked over at the fireplace, she didn't see the flaming logs. She saw his face lowering toward hers and felt the touch of his lips against her skin. And as her eyelids drooped with sleep, she murmured his name.

Chapter Six

Later that night, Flint was standing in front of the cook stove, heating chicken noodle soup in a saucepan when his father called. While he waited for the soup to bubble, he quickly explained to his father that Pippa had fallen ill and he'd moved from the hotel to the Bell in order to take care of her.

"Flint, I swear, you sound just like your sister Bea. I sent her to Idaho and she ends up falling in love and getting married. Now I send you up there and you've gotten yourself involved with a woman. Is there something in the air up there?"

Flint rolled his eyes toward the ceiling. "My situation is nothing like Bea's! Before she met Kipp, she was always looking for romance. You know that that's not me. I'm here to search for information. Nothing else."

"Maybe in the beginning. Sounds like you've gotten sidetracked."

"Dad, you're only half listening to me! Pippa is very sick. She's not able to take care of herself, much less the livestock here on the Bell. Would you really expect me to just leave her and the animals to struggle through on their own? Other than me, there's no one around to help her."

There was a pause and then Hadley said, "I heard you the first time, son. And I'm wondering about her. And you. Does she not have any friends or relatives around to offer a hand?"

"Yes, but the closest neighbors she has are ten miles away and have their own ranch to take care of. She mentioned a friend who works at the library in Bonners Ferry, but I doubt the woman could handle ranching chores. Especially in this weather. The snow and winds have been brutal up here. And so far, it's not letting up. I think there's a slight chance of seeing a bit of sunshine tomorrow."

"So what you're telling me is that you intend to stay on the Bell?"

He lowered the blaze beneath the saucepan. "Until Pippa gets well enough to handle things on her own. And we go through all of Debra's things."

"Which could take days, Flint," Hadley replied. "Are you prepared to stay in Idaho for an extended period? I realize you have lots of vacation time stored up, but I doubt you wanted to be away from your job for very long."

Flint had initially planned to keep his visit in Bonners Ferry to no more than three days. He'd wanted to get the whole trip over with and get back to cruising the Beaver County roads in his patrol vehicle and working with fellow deputies. Strange, he thought, how superficial that plan felt to him now. He couldn't think about his job or anything else back in Utah. His whole focus was on Pippa and her needs. And even though he realized his preoccupation with her probably wasn't healthy or wise, he had to follow his gut feelings. And they were telling him that she needed him far more than anyone or anything back in Utah. And he needed her for reasons that weren't yet clear in his brain.

He only knew his needs had nothing to do with his finding information on his grandparents.

He said, "I hadn't planned on it. But now…well, there's no urgency for me to get back to the department. Sheriff Andrews encouraged me to take as much time as I needed. In fact, he suggested I take a long vacation—just to unwind from the job for a while."

"Hmm. Sounds as though he thinks you're getting burnt out."

Flint frowned as he left the stove and walked over to the pantry to search among the canned goods for a box of crackers. "Not exactly, Dad. He just understands that I don't do much outside of work as a deputy and a rancher."

"So he believes you need more relaxation."

"Something like that." Actually, Sheriff Andrews, who'd become his friend along with being his boss, often suggested that Flint needed to find himself a wife and start a family in order to put more meaning into his life. But Flint had always backpedaled from that idea. Why did he need a wife and kids? He had plenty of meaning in his life. Plenty of things to keep him occupied. In fact, he was so busy that he rarely took the time to go enjoy a beer with his buddies. Didn't that mean his life was full?

"Well, you sure as hell can't relax while trying to nurse a sick woman, plus see after livestock!" Hadley exclaimed then blew out a breath. "Sorry, son. I shouldn't have said any of that. To be honest, I'm proud of you for stepping up and helping a person in need. It's just that—nothing. It will all work out, Flint."

Flint held back a sigh. "Dad, you and Mom always taught us kids to treat others the way we'd want to be treated. I'm trying to follow my parents' guidelines."

Hadley chuckled. "You mean following our guidelines in this instance," he teased.

Even though his father couldn't see him, Flint grinned. "Yeah. Something like that."

"Well, at least we'll know not to be expecting any news about Scarlett and Lionel anytime soon," he said.

"Sorry, Dad. I understand you've been wanting to uncover information about your father for a few years now. This setback has to be disappointing for you."

"Listen, son. We went all these years never thinking about Dad's birth records. Your mother and I just assumed he had his birth certificate tucked away somewhere among his things. And even when I looked and couldn't find one, I believed we'd simply get the lost one replaced. Hell, little did I know that he must have lied to us."

"You mean about where he was born?"

"Of course that's what I mean. Why? What are you insinuating? You think he might've been lying about other things in his life?"

Flint thought back to all the things Pippa had told him about Scarlett. Her description of the woman had been totally opposite Lionel's. But he wasn't going to bring that up to his father tonight. Hadley had always respected his father and Flint realized it would hurt him to learn that Lionel might have been lying to the family about a host of things.

"I'm not insinuating or accusing him of anything. I'm only suggesting that if a person lies about one thing, they'll usually lie about another and another."

Hadley was quiet for a moment and then he said, "You're right, Flint. And that very idea is what's bothering me. Because it's become fairly obvious that Dad wasn't born in Parowan, Utah, like he always said. We can't even find a record of his parents—my grandparents. So we have to conclude he lied about where he came from and when."

Locating a box of crackers on a top shelf, Flint carried a sleeve of them over to the table where he'd placed a tray to hold Pippa's supper.

"Why would he do such a thing, Dad? It doesn't make sense." Unless he'd broken the law in some way, Flint thought. But for tonight, he'd keep that idea to himself.

"If we knew why, we'd probably be able to figure out everything. But who knows. People do different things for different reasons. Like you staying on to take care of Pippa."

Flint's reasons for staying with Pippa were too convoluted to fully understand. He only knew that if he left her in someone else's care, he'd never be able to rest or even face himself in the mirror. If he left the care of her livestock to a hired day hand, he'd continue to worry. No. He couldn't leave the Bell. Nor did he want to.

"Yeah. Well, I need to get off the phone, Dad, and see if I can get her to eat something."

"Okay. Just keep us informed, Flint. Meanwhile, do you need anything? If you need a doctor's advice you can always call Grace."

"The doctor who attended Pippa was thorough and left instructions for her care. I won't bother my sister, unless I have to. But I'll keep in touch," Flint promised.

After his father said goodbye and ended the call, Flint put his phone aside and finished loading the tray with her meds, a bowl of the soup, the crackers, a small glass of water and another of orange juice. He had his doubts that she'd want to eat, but he was hoping she'd try to down a few bites at least.

Since he'd helped her to the couch earlier this evening,

she'd not stirred. Even when he'd returned from the barn and gently touched a hand to her cheek, she'd not roused from her sleep. Her skin had felt overly warm and he knew it was necessary for her to take the medication Dr. Bartlett had prescribed. Otherwise her temperature would prob-ably soar again.

Minutes ago, he'd added more logs to the fire and pushed up the thermostat to the heating system. Already he could feel the warmth permeating the room. Tomorrow, in spite of her protests, he'd call and have a truck to come out and fill the propane tank. Keeping the temperature inside the house at a comfortable level would help her to get well. If he had to, he'd justify it to her by saying that *he* didn't want to be cold, and since he was staying there as well, he had a right to pay for it to be warm.

After placing the tray on the coffee table, he eased down on the edge of the couch and took a moment to drink in the sight of her sleeping image. The flames from the fireplace cast a rosy-amber glow over her face and turned her hair into a cascade of molten bronze.

Before he could stop himself, he traced a fingertip along her cheekbone. "Pippa?"

She didn't respond, so he gently squeezed her upper arm. The contact caused her eyes to flutter open and for a mo-ment she stared blankly at him.

"Flint?" she asked, her voice raspy with sleep.

"Yes. It's time for you to take your medicine and I have some soup for you. Do you think you can sit up?"

She pulled her arms from beneath the afghan and wiped a hand across her eyes. "I think so. But I'm not sure how my stomach is going to react to food."

"Queasy?" he asked.

"Yes. And my whole body aches," she told him. "But I'll try to eat."

"Good girl," he said. "Let me help you."

With a hand on her arm, he helped her scoot up to a sitting position before adjusting the blanket to her waist. When he placed the tray of food onto her lap, a long breath of air whooshed out of her.

"Are you okay or do you need to lie back down?" he asked.

"Just give me a moment," she said. "My head is a little swimmy."

She clamped a hand to her forehead then finally dropped it and glanced around her. "It's still dark. I thought I'd been asleep all night."

"No. Only for a couple of hours. I haven't been back from the barn for long."

She scrubbed her eyes with both hands then lifted her gaze to his face. "How is Hawk?"

"He's doing great. I led him out of the stall and walked him up and down the alleyway of the barn. His limp is slight. I expect it will be gone completely in a day or two."

"Thank you, Flint, for helping him to get better. I hated seeing him in pain."

He pointed to the pills he'd placed on a napkin. "Better take those or you're going to be in worse pain."

She swallowed the pills down with a short drink of water then looked at the soup as though eating was going to be a monumental task.

"I'm not much of a cook," he told her. "Mom and my sisters have always done all the cooking for the family. But I can heat things and do a few breakfast foods like bacon and eggs."

"This is fine," she said.

Her voice held a quiver that almost sounded like she was close to tears and he wondered if she was simply depressed over being sick or if she was rattled because she had never had anyone do such personal things for her.

"I found the soup in the pantry," he said. "There's not a whole lot of things in the cabinets or the refrigerator. I'm thinking I'm going to need to drive into Bonners Ferry and get some things at the market. But not until you're feeling better. Until then, we'll just make do."

"I haven't purchased groceries in a long while." She picked up the spoon and dipped it into the soup. "Did you find something for yourself?"

"Sure. I found cheese and cold cuts. I had plenty. I might even make myself some coffee before I go to bed," he told her. "And don't worry about the cats and dogs. They've all had their supper, too. The Great Pyrenees showed up to eat then left out again as soon as they'd cleaned their plates. You know, I'm going to have to tell Quint that his Pyrenees aren't as smart as yours."

She ate a spoonful of soup then nibbled on the corner of a cracker. Flint could see it was taking every ounce of strength for her to feed herself. He wanted to offer to help her, but he knew she'd insist on doing the task herself. For some reason, whether it was her pride or stubbornness, she was determined not to appear helpless in front of him.

"My dogs are smarter? I think you're just trying to make me laugh and I can't. I don't have enough energy."

"I am mostly teasing. But I'm also impressed that your dogs know to travel all the way from their flock to the barn to get their meals. Quint or some of the hands have to take feed out to his dogs."

She slipped another spoonful of soup into her mouth and though she was taking in only small amounts of food at a time, Flint was relieved that she was getting some of the simple meal down. Whether it would stay down was another question…but they'd deal with that if and when they needed to.

"I imagine your brother's dogs are working a long distance away from the ranch yard and the breed is too loyal to leave the sheep without guards for very long," she said.

"You're right. Most of the time they're miles away from the ranch house."

She took in a bit more of the soup then reached for the orange juice. "Tell me more about your family's ranch, Flint. I imagine it's very beautiful. Do you have tall mountains there?"

She sounded wistful. As though she'd never traveled very far away from home. "Yes. A mountain range to the north and the west," he told her. "The east is mostly river-bottom land. That's where the cattle mostly stay. We have lots of evergreens and some hardwood trees—like cottonwood and willows and birch."

"Is the water in the creeks clear?"

"It is until the snowmelt rushes down from the mountains and turns it muddy for a while."

"Yes. It's the same way here, too." She glanced at him. "What does the ranch house look like?"

Her eyes were glazed and he wanted to reach over and press a palm to her face to gauge her temperature. "You mean the main ranch house? Where I live?"

She nodded. "Is the outside constructed of logs, like this one?"

"No. It's two stories and has lapboard siding with native

rock work that comes up about halfway. Lots of windows, with a wide porch on the front and a covered patio in the back. When all of us children were still living at home, I shared a bedroom with my brother Quint. And my twin sisters shared a bedroom. Of course, I think they would have refused to be separated, even if there'd been plenty of bedrooms."

"And now? If I'm understanding right, your sister Beatrice lives here in Idaho and her twin is still back in Utah. How is that working out for them?"

Flint shrugged. "They miss each other terribly. But they both realize they have their own lives to live. Even if they have to talk to each other every day of the year."

"How nice that would be to have a sister to talk to." She put the orange juice back on the tray and gestured for him to move it from her lap.

"I talked with my dad a few minutes ago," he told her. "And he asked if you had friends or relatives around here. I told him you had friends, but I didn't know of any relatives. Was I right?"

Sighing, she scooted downward until she was lying prone again and her head was resting on a throw pillow. "No relatives. From the time I was born, I lived in foster homes until I turned eighteen."

He'd not expected to hear that sort of thing about her family history and he could only think how unfair life could sometimes be to people who deserved better.

"Were you orphaned?" he asked.

"Sort of. My mom was an unwed teenager. She died shortly after giving birth to me."

Flint inwardly winced. No wonder she worked so hard to put up a brave front. No wonder she'd been devastated over Yance's and Debra's deaths. For most of her life she'd had to be independent and then, when she'd finally found a home here with the O'Sheas, she'd lost them. "And what about your dad? Was he ever around?"

"Never. It seems that he didn't want any part of a baby. From what I've learned, I think the child welfare system contacted him after my mother passed, but he wasn't interested."

"That's tough."

She looked away from him and focused her eyes to a spot on the floor. "Well, the way I see it, he had to be a sorry individual. I wouldn't want to call someone like that my father. I'd rather be without one."

"I understand. I imagine I'd feel just as you do." He pulled the blanket up to her chin and allowed his hand to linger upon the thick wave of hair lying upon her shoulder. It felt just as silky as he had thought it would. "Anyway, I told Dad you don't need anyone else to take care of you. I'll be here."

She continued to look past him. "Did he tell you that you were being foolish to volunteer for such a job?"

"No." He rolled a strand of her hair between his fingers before he finally found the will to ease his hand away from her. "He understands. We Hollisters don't leave people in need."

Her gaze slipped back to his face and he could see a mist had collected in her gray eyes.

"You Hollisters must be special people," she said thickly.

He gave her a faint smile. "No more than anyone else. No more than you."

He touched his forefinger to her cheek then stood and

looked down at her. "You need to rest. Whenever you think you're able, I'll help you to bed."

"In a little while. The fire feels good."

"Okay."

She closed her eyes and he gathered up the tray and carried it to the kitchen. After washing the dishes and cleaning off the cabinet counters, he returned to the living room and found her sound asleep.

He tossed several more logs on the fire then sat down in an armchair near the couch. As soon as his long frame settled into the worn leather seat, his gaze turned to her. Except for the faint rise and fall of her chest, she was motionless. As his eyes took in her pale face and tumbled hair, it dawned on him that he'd never watched a woman sleep before. His interactions with women didn't include long hours of cuddling, pillow talk or sleeping. No, he'd always been careful to keep his dates casual without strings or ties to choke him. The only time he'd tried a serious relationship, he'd ended up looking like a fool and feeling even worse. He'd leave love and marriage to his brothers. They were good at it and he...well, he supposed he'd make a passible husband and father. But a wife and children deserved better than passible.

Pippa should've never left the couch without waking Flint. But he'd been sleeping so soundly in the armchair, she'd not wanted to disturb him. Besides, she'd not wanted to believe she was too weak to make it to the bathroom without his arm to lean on. And she had made the trip down the hall without collapsing. She'd even managed to use the facility and deal with her clothing. But when she stood at the sink to wash her hands, a wave of dizziness had struck her, followed by overwhelming weakness.

Now as she stood clinging tightly to the edge of the vanity cabinet, her body shook with violent chills. Somehow she had to find the strength to make it back to the living room to the warmth of the fire.

She was slumped over the cabinet, shivering uncontrollably, when Flint suddenly banged on the door.

"Pippa! Are you in there?"

The sound of his voice sent a wave of relief washing over her and she turned her face toward the door and answered in the loudest voice she could summon. "Flint. Help me!"

Instantly, the door flung open wide and she heard him mutter a curse as he rushed to her side.

"Damn it, Pippa! You little fool!"

He scooped her up in his arms and she clung to him as she shivered against his warm body. "I'm so cold," she said, her teeth chattering.

"Why didn't you wake me? To prove to yourself that you didn't need me?" he asked.

Without giving her an opportunity to answer, he carried her out of the bathroom and across the hallway to her bedroom. The dim light filtering through the open doorway illuminated a path to the bed. The covers were exactly as she'd left them when she'd crawled out of bed before daylight this morning. With all that had happened, it felt like that had been days ago rather than hours.

He shoved the tousled sheet and blankets aside then eased her onto the cleared space on the mattress. After he'd switched on a small lamp on the nightstand, he removed her boots and tucked a pillow beneath her head before finally covering her with two thick blankets.

"Flint, I...don't want to go to bed—like this—in dirty work clothes!" Even though she'd tried to sound emphatic, her voice had as much volume as a weak kitten's.

"I understand you don't want to sleep in those clothes. Just be still and try to warm up while I find your night-gown or whatever you wear to bed. Where do I look for something?" he asked as he glanced questioningly around the shadowy room.

"Bottom drawer of the chest. Over by the wall. There's a pair of pajamas there."

While he went to fetch the sleepwear, Pippa hugged her-self and tried to stem the tremors shaking her body. In a day or two, she was going to look back on this and be ter-ribly embarrassed. But for now, she felt too sick and help-less to care that she was having to depend on him for such private tasks.

When he returned carrying the soft flannel, he sat down on the edge of the bed and she immediately noticed the worried frown on his face. Or was it annoyance with her?

"Getting any warmer now?" he asked.

"A little. I must be having a chill. I don't ever remember shaking like this," she told him.

He reached over and cupped his palm against the side of her cheek. Even though she felt worse than terrible, his touch was both comforting and reassuring.

"If you have a thermometer, I can take your tempera-ture, but I don't need one to tell you have fever. Your face is hot." He stood and looked down at her. "I'm going to help you into your pajamas and then get your medicine. It's time you took another dose of meds and something for your fever."

She let out a weary breath. "I don't like this."

His lips pursed with disapproval. "No one likes being sick, Pippa."

"I'm not talking about me. I'm talking about you. You're—taking care of me and the animals. It's too much."

"Do I look helpless?"

He looked strong and handsome and everything a man should be, she thought. "No. But all of this is going to wear you down. And what if you catch the virus from me? Then we'll both be down!"

"If I get sick, I'll hire someone to help out. Now stop all this fretting. It's only going to make you sicker. In a couple of days, the world is going to look right to you again. But until that happens, no more getting up and trying to walk around on your own steam. Because you don't have any."

"All right. From now on, I'll stay put," she told him.

"Good." He stood and reached a hand down to her. "Now, if you can sit up on the side of the bed, I'll help you with the pajamas."

"I'm not going to undress in front of you. I'm not that weak!" she exclaimed, but she took his hand anyway and used it to lever herself up to a sitting position.

"Hell, Pippa, you think I don't know how a woman looks without her clothes?"

"I'm sure you've seen plenty of them without clothing. But that hardly means you're going to see this one!" she huffed.

He groaned with frustration. "Okay, I'll turn my back and you can cover the parts you don't want me to see—but I'm not leaving."

Pippa wasn't a prude, but she did have her pride. If Flint ever saw her intimate parts, it would be because she wanted him to and certainly not while she was sick and unsightly.

But her feverish brain wasn't working right. He'd never want to look at her in such a way.

"All right," she muttered. "I'll start with the top. You can help if you'd pull the sweater off over my head, then I can deal with the shirt underneath."

"I can do that."

He took hold of the hem of the old wool sweater and she held her arms straight up in order for him to slip the garment over her head. Once it was out of the way, she motioned for him to turn away from her.

With his back to her, she hurriedly popped the snaps on her Western shirt and pushed it off her shoulders. The cool air in the bedroom caused her shivers to start again, making her struggle to pull her arms out of the sleeves.

"Are you having trouble?" he asked.

"No!" She quickly shed her bra then slipped into the pajama top and buttoned the front. "I'm finished with the top. I can probably stand and get out of my jeans on my own," she added.

"Forget it," he told her. "Undo the button and zipper on your jeans and you can hold the cover over you while I pull the hems down over your feet."

"Oh, really, Flint. I'm not that weak," she protested.

"Don't argue. You need every ounce of energy you possess to get well."

She let out a weak sigh. "Maybe you're right. Just sitting up is making me shaky."

Thankfully, she managed to undo her jeans and while she held the blanket over her, he pulled on the hems until the garment slid onto the floor. Once they were out of the way, he put her feet into the legs of the pajama bottoms and pulled the elastic waistband as far up as her knees.

"I'll let you finish," he said and turned his back to her.

After some effort, she tugged the pajamas to her waist. The simple exertion caused her to fall sideways onto the mattress and though she needed to cover herself, she was too exhausted to bother.

Flint did the task for her and she murmured her thanks as he tucked the blanket around her and smoothed her hair against the pillow.

"I'll go get your meds," he said.

While he was gone, she closed her eyes and thought about the gentle care he'd given her since she'd come down with the fever this morning. He'd touched her with a tenderness that had taken her by surprise.

She was still thinking about his thoughtfulness when, moments later, he returned with the prescribed pills. After swallowing them with a drink of water, she said, "If you're wondering where to sleep, you can use Debra's room. The linens are clean—maybe a little dusty."

He stood looking down at her. "I'm not worried about the linens. I'm just not sure I'd feel right about staying in Debra's room. If you have an extra blanket, I can bed down on the couch."

"Don't be silly. There's a nice soft bed in there. Believe me, your aunt would be happy to know you used it."

He glanced thoughtfully over to the window where the wind was whipping the branches of a fir tree against the glass panes.

"'My aunt,'" he repeated. "That sounds odd. I do have a couple of aunts on my mother's side, along with some aunts by marriage. But I rarely ever see them. They live in California. And Dad...well, until a few months ago, I never thought of him having sisters." He turned his gaze back on her. "I could tell Dad was upset about Debra's death. I think in his mind he had hopes she and Taylor would want to get to know him and all of us. But even before I found out that Debra had passed, I didn't really hold out much hope for that to happen."

"Really? Why? Debra was a kind, open-minded woman."

Shaking his head, he said, "Well, if Scarlett told her daughters that she had children from her first marriage, neither bothered to locate them. I figure Scarlett had told her daughters to stay away from us Hollisters. But to be fair, I'm only assuming things. I have no facts."

"Why would Scarlett tell her daughters something like that? Did she have reason to be leery of your family?"

He shrugged. "I don't know. I'm only guessing," he said then shook his head. "No. I'm not even guessing. Ever since Bea visited Scarlett at the Neighbor's Place, I've had this feeling that my grandmother might have left Stone Creek Ranch in a fearful state of mind. Maybe that's just my deputy's mind at work. But none of that is important now. You need to sleep. And get well."

"I won't sleep until you promise to use Debra's bed. You'll have a hard day tomorrow and you won't sleep as well on the couch."

A wry smile touched his lips as he bent over and clicked off the night lamp. "Okay. I promise. If you need me in the night, just call out."

Need him? Yes, now that she was sick, she needed him. But she was very afraid that once she was well again, her need for the man wasn't going to end.

"I will," she murmured.

His green eyes gazed down at her for a long moment

before he lowered his head and placed a kiss in the middle of her forehead.

"Good night, Pippa."

"Good night."

Through tear-blurred eyes, she watched him leave the room. And once he was out of sight, she turned her face into the pillow.

What was wrong with her? Yes, she had a virus. And yes, she was as weak as a kitten. But she shouldn't be getting emotional over a man she'd only met yesterday.

Had it only been yesterday that she'd taken her first look at him and felt her heart take a wild leap? It felt like she'd known him for so much longer. His touch, his smell, his smile and the sound of his voice were already ingrained in her brain.

And she suddenly realized that once he left the Bell she'd be faced with a hell of a struggle to forget him.

Chapter Seven

Flint managed to sleep very little during the night and his lack of z's had nothing to do with being in a strange bed. Even a bed that had once belonged to an aunt he'd never met. No. He'd not been lying awake wondering about unknown relatives. Every thought in his brain had been focused on Pippa lying in the bed across the hallway. What if she called out and he didn't hear her? What if she became too dazed with fever to even know she needed his help?

The worrisome thoughts had him waking up every few minutes and slipping quietly into her room to make sure she was okay. Once, as he'd stood by her bed and touched a hand to her cheek, she'd stirred awake and asked him to help her to the bathroom. She'd made the trip without leaning on him too heavily and as soon as she'd crawled back into bed, she'd gone to sleep.

Now, as dawn broke over the mountains behind the ranch house, Flint climbed into the old work truck and headed to the feeding ground for the cattle. Thankfully, at some point during the night the snow had stopped and the clouds were finally beginning to break enough to show slivers of blue sky. If the sun came out, it would be the first time he'd seen it since he'd arrived in Bonners Ferry three days ago. The better weather would certainly be welcome, but what Flint wanted the most was for Pippa to be well again. Not because helping her had him tied to the Bell. No, he could deal with that problem. But seeing Pippa so helpless and weak had shaken him in ways he didn't like to admit.

Back in the ranch house, he'd left a note on Pippa's nightstand to let her know he was out handling the feeding and would return as quickly as he could. He figured she'd probably climb out of bed on her own, if for no other reason than to go to the restroom. But there was nothing he could do about leaving her alone. The livestock had to be fed and chores around the barn tended to.

Forty minutes later, he'd fed the cattle and was spreading the last of the hay for the sheep when he felt the phone in his shirt pocket vibrate with an incoming call. Thinking it could possibly be Pippa calling, he promptly dug out the phone and glanced at the identification on the face. As soon as he noted the caller was his younger brother Quint, he decided to wait until he'd climbed into the truck and had it headed in the direction of the ranch house before he returned the call.

Quint answered on the second ring. "Hey, brother, how's it going way up there in Idaho?"

The question put a frown on Flint's face. "You haven't talked to Dad? I figured he'd already told everyone that my trip is going to end up being longer than expected."

"Oh? What's the reason?" Quint asked. "You decided to drive down to Bea and Kipp's ranch and visit with them before you come home?"

As if he'd come up here for a leisurely vacation in the dead of winter, Flint thought ruefully. "No. This trip wasn't planned for fun, Quint," he said then asked, "Has Dad told you that Debra O'Shea had passed away?"

"Yes, he did give us that news. And you know, Flint, sometimes I just don't understand Dad. He actually seemed cut up over the woman's death."

The frown on Flint's face grew deeper. "Why wouldn't he be cut up? She was his half-sister."

"I realize that. But she was a stranger to him—to all of us. How could he feel grief for someone he never met or even talked to?"

Flint wiped a hand over his face. "You're not thinking, little brother. That's exactly what he's grieving—the fact that they never got that chance. Now he'll never be able to have his sister in his life, even if their time together would've probably been limited to short visits."

"Yeah. I see what you mean. Anyway, I wonder, after this, if it might be better if he'd forget this whole thing about Grandfather. I'm beginning to think the man was hiding a criminal past. There's no other reason for Lionel to have erased the facts of his birth. You're a lawman, you ought to see by now that he didn't want to be traced."

"My thoughts have run along that same line for a long while," Flint told him. "But I'm not going to talk badly about Dad's own father. Not to him, at least. And not until I have proof rather than just a suspicion that Lionel wasn't on the up-and-up."

Quint sighed. "Neither will I. So, you said something about your trip being delayed. Clementine and I worked late last night with the sheep and I didn't see Dad before we went to bed. And he's not yet come down for breakfast, so this is the first I'm hearing of it. What's wrong? Aren't you coming home soon?"

"I have no idea when I'll be heading back to Utah. The young woman who inherited Debra's ranch, the Bell, is ill. And right now I'm taking care of her and the livestock."

There was a long stretch of silence before Quint finally spoke. "How the heck did that happen? Doesn't she have a husband or ranch hands to do the work?"

Quint's assumption caused Flint's lips to flatten into a thin line. He sounded the same way Flint had reacted when he'd first arrived on the Bell and found Pippa slogging her way through a foot of snow with a feed bucket in her hand. Now the memory of his reaction made him feel foolish for making such assumptions.

"Pippa isn't married. And you know, Quint, not everyone is as privileged as us Hollisters. She can't afford ranch hands. She takes care of everything herself. Except now she's too sick with a virus to lift her head off the pillow. When you called, I was spreading the last of the alfalfa to the sheep. Now I'm headed to the ranch house and praying she hadn't tried to get out of bed while I'm not there to help her."

Quint's reaction was another stretch of silence then finally he said, "Hell, Flint, I could tell you that this woman named Pippa and this ranch called the Bell is hardly your business. But I figure I'd be wasting my breath. Sounds like you've already made them your business. So I'll just ask when did you become a nurse? It does sound like she needs help, but why does that help have to come from you? Why don't you hire someone to come out and take care of things?"

"You don't have to be a trained nurse to fetch and carry and make sure the patient drinks, eats and stays warm. As for the ranch, I don't think it would be very easy to find day help. There's probably a foot and a half of snow on the ground right now and the town appears to be full of skiers, not cowboys."

Quint grunted. "I'm fairly sure there has to be a feed and ranch supply store around there. You can always find information about day helpers at one of those places."

True, Flint thought. But he didn't want a pair of day hands out here taking care of Pippa's livestock. He wanted to do it himself. Exactly why he felt that way, he couldn't say. Except that at some point since he'd arrived on the Bell, he'd developed a possessive streak concerning Pippa.

"Probably," Flint replied. "But you know how day hands are—unreliable. Half of them wouldn't know a sick cow or lamb if it walked in front of them, much less make sure ice is busted in the water troughs. Some of these guys pour grain into a trough and pitch out a few blocks of hay and believe in their minds they're cowboys. No thanks. They're more trouble than they're worth."

"Yeah. We've had a few of them on Stone Creek before. Dad never wasted anytime running them off," he said with a chuckle then asked in a more serious tone, "So you think Pippa is going to be down for several days?"

"The doctor implied it would take a few days for her to get back to normal. I'd say three or four at least. And I'm not going to leave until I make sure she has her strength back. Plus, she hasn't yet finished going through Debra's old papers. Remember, I'm up here to find a clue to Grandfather's birth details."

"I wouldn't hold my breath on finding anything about Grandfather's life. I figure you're chasing down a dead end."

"Thanks for your confidence, Quint. Since everything is

going so well, you've managed to cheer me up even more," he said with a heavy dose of sarcasm.

"Sorry, brother. I'm just giving you my honest opinion. Hopefully, I'm wrong. Anyway, if you need help—and it sounds like you do—maybe one of us can drive up and lend a hand."

The fact that Quint was offering to send help made him feel better, even though he didn't want anyone else around. Which didn't make a whole lot of sense. Shouldn't more help be welcome? Except that the more he was here on the Bell, the more he felt like this was his home to take care of. And the more he was with Pippa, the more he wanted to think of her as his woman.

Oh man, was he ever getting off track!

"Thanks, Quint. It's good of you to offer, but I can handle things here. And tell Dad I'll keep him informed."

"I will. But, Flint—uh—do you think…you might be getting in too deep with this woman? I understand she's sick. But there has to be more to the situation for you to feel so obligated. What's going on here? Do you feel sorry for her?"

Flint slowed the truck as a small herd of elk dashed across the road in front of him. No doubt the snow was hampering their efforts to find food sources. The elk could use some alfalfa and, later this afternoon, he'd scatter some of the hay in this particular area so they'd be sure to find it. He understood Pippa couldn't afford to feed wildlife and she was trying to dole out her hay supply as sparingly as she could. But Flint was going to take care of that problem for her, too. He just wasn't going to tell her about his intentions until the hay was already delivered.

Yeah, Quint would call him crazy. As would Hunter and

Jack and Cordell. But if they were to meet Pippa and see her situation, he felt certain they'd think differently. After all, each of them had wives they'd go to hell and back for.

But Pippa isn't your wife, Flint. There's the big difference.

Shutting out the mocking voice in his head, he attempted to answer Quint's question. "Wrong, little brother. Pippa's the last person I'd ever pity. She's amazingly tough and capable. In fact, she's sort of like your Clementine. Strong, outdoorsy, knows all about livestock and how to care for them. That is, she was strong before the fever hit her yesterday."

The phone connection went quiet for a moment and Flint was thinking the mountains had broken the signal when Quint finally spoke.

"Oh. Well, that makes it all different. Is she pretty?"

Flint grimaced. "Yeah, she's pretty in her own way. What are you implying?"

"Nothing. I'm just glad you're there—to help her. It'll do you good to be around a woman for a while."

Seeing where his brother's mind was going, Flint cursed. "Damn it, Quint! I—"

"Sorry, Flint, I hear Mom yelling from the kitchen. Breakfast is ready. I'll talk to you later."

The phone went dead and Flint blew out a long breath as he slipped the device back into his pocket. It didn't matter if Quint thought he had romantic notions about Pippa. She wasn't in the market for a boyfriend or anything close to it. She'd more or less told him that she was married to the Bell and she didn't expect any man to understand her feelings. But he *did* understand her feelings. And he was beginning to think of her as a lovely woman who needed a man's arms around her. Specifically his arms.

But those sorts of thoughts weren't feasible or sensible. And the best thing he could do would be to push them out of his mind until all he could see was the highway leading him back to Utah.

When Pippa woke, the sun was sending a weak shaft of light across the foot of the bed. Stunned by the sight of it, her gaze darted over to the window. She'd slept long past daybreak! What had happened to her alarm?

She threw back the covers, but as soon as she started to swing her legs over the side of the mattress, she realized all was not well. The floor seemed to be making rolling waves and her head had a dull ache behind her eyes.

Oh Lord, she'd fallen ill yesterday, hadn't she? Memories filtered back in of how Flint had taken her to the doctor and for the rest of the day and night, she'd only been half aware of what had been going on. She recalled him giving her soup and urging her to eat. And later he'd helped her out of the bathroom and into her pajamas. After that, everything was a blur. Except...

She touched fingertips to her forehead. Just before he'd turned out the light and left the bedroom, he'd kissed her good-night. Why? Because she was sick and he'd felt sorry for her?

Groaning with misgivings, she looked over at the nightstand and spotted the note he'd left propped against the base of the lamp. He was out taking care of the livestock, it read. And would return as soon as he could.

There was no good time for a person to come down with a virus. But Pippa couldn't think of a worse one. True, she'd not invited him to make a trip to Idaho or to visit the Bell, especially during the middle of winter. He'd done that on his own. Still, she'd thrown a heap of trouble onto his shoulders and she felt horrible about it. Yet there was little she could do about the situation now.

She'd already offered to call Greer, one of the few close friends she had in Bonners Ferry, and ask her for help. But he'd nixed that idea as soon as she'd mentioned it. Admittedly, Greer didn't know the first thing about caring for livestock. And Trina and Jonas, the Wilkersons, had all they could handle taking care of their ranch. She'd wouldn't ask them for help unless it was a dire emergency. Besides, if she was being truly honest with herself, Flint was the only person she wanted near her and her livestock.

Maybe you should pretend to be sick even after you're well, Pippa. That's probably the only way you're going to keep a man like him here on the Bell.

Silently cursing at the mocking voice, she determinedly lowered her feet to the floor and pushed herself to a standing position. She wasn't going to pretend anything. She was well aware that her chances to have anything more than a short friendship with Flint were slim to none.

She managed to make the walk down the hallway to the bathroom without hanging on to the wall, but by the time she used the facility and washed her face and hands, it was a struggle to find enough strength to make it back to her bedroom.

Thankfully, she was in bed and had regained her breath by the time Flint returned to the house and entered the bedroom. Apparently he'd not taken the time to remove his coat and boots. Mud and slush from the snow had left wet splotches on the bottom legs of his jeans, while bits of alfalfa twigs and leaves clung to the front of his brown canvas coat. As he approached her bed, he swept off his hat and held it between his hands.

"Good morning," he greeted. "How are you feeling?"

Now that he was only an arm's length away, she felt like someone had given her a dose of joy. "I think I'm better. I did make it to the bathroom and back without collapsing."

"I'm sorry I wasn't here to help you."

If she wasn't so weak, she would've laughed at his remark. "You were doing something far more important. How is everything? Run into any problems?"

"No problems. The snow has stopped and the sun is out. I've let the horses out of the barn and into the south paddock. And I'm thinking maybe tomorrow, if you're well enough for me to leave for a while, I'm going to move the cattle down the hill. Yesterday I remember seeing a sheltered meadow before we got here to the house. If the snow melts a little, they might be able to paw it away and find dried grass. Feeding them in the meadow would make things easier, too. But they're your cattle and it's your ranch, so what do you think?"

"I think moving them by yourself might be tricky."

"Does that mean you want me to leave them where they are?" he asked.

"No. I'm just wondering how you can do it on your own. Jasper, the sorrel horse with the blaze face, is good with herding cattle, but with the snow so deep, I can't promise he won't slip and fall."

He suddenly grinned. "No need to worry. You're looking at an old ranch hand. The dogs will go with me and help keep the herd bunched."

If anyone else had made such a suggestion to her, she

would've told the person to butt out of her business. But it felt strangely comforting to let Flint take over and make decisions concerning the ranch for her. He wasn't a flunky or greenhorn. She trusted his judgment.

"Okay. I'm fine with you moving the herd. Especially if it will help you handle the feeding chores." She pushed her tumbled hair back from her face and wondered why he was looking at her in such a keen way. "I'm hoping I'll be back on my feet in a day or two and you'll be free of this mess you've gotten yourself into."

His eyes narrowed as he took a step closer to the bedside. "It's going to take more than a day or two for you to regain your strength. And even once your health is back to normal, there's still the matter of going through Debra's papers."

"Oh yes. Scarlett's first husband—your grandfather." She gave him a faint smile. "There for a minute, I guess I was thinking the little Irish people brought you here to the Bell just to help me."

His brows arched. "'Little Irish people'?"

She nodded. "You know. Leprechauns. My name is Shanahan, remember?"

A frown creased his brow. "Yes. But I thought—was Shanahan your mother's last name?"

"Yes. But I have no way of knowing if she knew anything about her Irish heritage. I was told, however, that she had red hair. Guess that's something." Sighing, she leaned her head back against the pillow. "Yance is the one who told me a lot about Irish folklore. His grandparents lived in the old country and he often talked about taking Debra and me over there for a visit—to see the land and the few relatives he had left there. But he…"

"Died before that could happen," he finished for her.

"Travel like that takes money. More than he had. And time passed… In the end, it was never anything more than a dream."

"Yes, but it was a nice dream," he said gently.

"Yes. A very nice dream."

He reached down and touched the back of his hand to her cheek. "You feel cooler, but I can see all this talking has tired you out. Close your eyes and rest while I go fix you some breakfast."

"Thank you, Flint. I—am a bit tired."

He left the room and, moments later, she heard the radio playing in the kitchen and the sounds of iron skillets settling against the grates of the cook stove. For whatever reason, Flint was here on the Bell with her, she thought. At least, for the next few days. And for now that was all that mattered.

The next day the sun was even brighter and as Flint rode up the foothill to where the cattle had been sheltering among the firs, his spirits lifted at the sight of the heavy snow falling from the limbs of the pines and spruce trees. Even though the ground was still covered with a deep blanket of white, he was beginning to get an idea of how the Bell would look when it wasn't winter, and he'd decided it had to be one of the prettiest pieces of land he'd ever seen. Tall mountains, rolling foothills, valley meadows and a river running through the bottomland. The scent of pine and spruce was always in the air, along with the faint smell of woodsmoke coming from the ranch house chimney.

Flint could still remember the first morning he'd arrived on the ranch and had ended up helping Pippa with the chores. Throughout the drive in the old work truck, he'd asked himself several time what she was doing living on this remote ranch alone. Why didn't she leave? Why didn't she go to town and work at an office job or as a clerk in a store where she could be with people and living conditions would be more comfortable?

But now, after the few days he'd been on the Bell, he no longer wondered about Pippa's decision to work this ranch and call it her home. There was something wild and beautiful and untouched about the place and the longer he stayed here, the more he appreciated the land.

The trip down the mountain with the cattle turned out to be easier than he'd expected. Jasper was alert to the cows and didn't require any guidance from him as they traversed the steep foothill covered with evergreens and outcroppings of rock. Plus, the dogs were like having two ranch hands to keep the cattle bunched and prevent any wayward calves from straying.

As soon as they emerged from the dense tree line, the cattle sensed the meadow was close and the herd began to trot eagerly to the open field ahead. Because the land on either side of the dirt road leading to the ranch house belonged to the Bell, it wasn't fenced, so the cattle were free to roam from one meadow to the other. And Flint didn't have to worry about opening or closing gates or making sure the cows stayed in one enclosure. His brother Cord would say the task was a snap. Even for only one cowboy and two dogs. And for Cord, moving the small herd on his own would be easy, Flint thought. Cordell had always been exceptional at riding and roping and wrangling cattle and horses. He was also a top hand at corralling men. Which was why, several years ago, their dad had appointed him foreman of Stone Creek Ranch. As for Flint, he'd always had to work harder to be as good a ranch hand as Cordell, or Jack, or Quint. Which was the main reason he'd taken up a career in law enforcement. It wasn't that he couldn't do well on the ranch—but there were plenty of others who were just as good as him or better. He wasn't really needed on Stone Creek.

However, here on the Bell, he didn't feel the need to meet his brothers' standards. He didn't feel pressured to be a top hand. And he was enjoying every minute of feeling a horse beneath him, hearing the creak of the saddle, and the cold wind slapping him in the face.

He'd reined Jasper to a halt and was sitting easy in the saddle, gazing out at the milling cattle, when he caught the sound of a vehicle far down the road.

Thinking it was probably the propane driver arriving with the fuel he'd ordered yesterday; he was somewhat surprised when a dark brown truck came into view and slowly made its way toward him and Jasper.

When the mud-splattered vehicle stopped and the passenger window lowered, Flint rode over to see who had ventured on to Bell land and why.

A woman with graying blond hair and a slightly wrinkled face eyed him with curiosity. "Good morning. We're the Wilkersons. We're on our way to Bonners Ferry and thought we'd check on Pippa. Are you helping her with the ranch?"

Recognizing the name of Pippa's ranching friends, he rode closer and climbed down from Jasper in order to introduce himself. "I'm Flint Hollister from Utah. I've been helping her out for the past few days. Pippa has spoken of you," he told the couple. "You're Trina and Jonas, right?"

The man behind the steering wheel had a gray battered cowboy hat pulled down to his ears and a thick brown muffler twisted around his neck. He looked over at Flint and grinned.

"That's us. You staying long, Mr. Hollister?"

Flint shook his head. "I'd be happy if you'd call me Flint. I'm not sure how long I'll be here. For a little while—until Pippa gets on her feet again. She's sick with a virus."

"Oh no!" Trina gasped with concern.

"Don't like hearing that news," Jonas added morosely. "Makes me think of Debra. She was healthy as a horse one day and a couple of weeks later she was gone."

"I wouldn't think in those terms, Jonas," Flint said in an effort to reassure the couple. "Pippa is following doctor's orders and her condition is already improving."

Trina looked anxiously over at her husband. "We'd better go check on her, Jonas," she said then glanced at Flint. "I imagine you've been taking care of ranching chores, but has anyone been looking after her? Poor little thing, she works so hard. And she's so independent. She should have called us for help."

"She understands you two have plenty to do on your own ranch. And I've been looking after her this whole time."

"That's good of you, Flint." Jonas spoke up. "We didn't know Pippa was acquainted with anyone from Utah."

No doubt the Wilkersons were curious about his connection to Pippa, which was understandable. From what little she'd told him about her life here on the Bell, she rarely ever had visitors. Now Flint was living temporarily on the ranch and this middle-aged couple had to be wondering why. "I'm a—relative of Debra's. I drove up here to see her. We—that is, my family and I—weren't aware she'd died."

"Oh, how terrible," Trina said then shook her head. "Losing Debra has been especially hard on Pippa. They did everything together. Now she's all alone. But you can see her situation."

"Be the same if one of us passed," Jonas told his wife. "With no kids, that means one of us will be left alone."

Trina glanced over at her husband. "God willing that won't be for a long time."

Jonas looked at Flint. "You have any kids?"

"No. I'm single." And ever since Rachel had skipped town with her ex-husband, Flint had believed being single was the best choice he could make for himself. A man didn't need a wife and kids to make him more of a man. And he sure didn't need a woman to make him look like a fool. But these past few days, the thought of a wife and babies had been pushing hard at the edges of his mind. He was handling the Bell without any problems. And he was doing a damned good job of nursing Pippa back to health. Would he be a fool to believe he was capable of being something more than a lawman?

Trina batted a dismissive hand at Flint. "You're still very young. You have plenty of time to get yourself a family."

"Yes, ma'am. I guess I do have a little time."

Jonas cleared his throat. "We'd better get on up to the ranch house, Trina, and give Pippa a quick hello. We have a lot to do in Bonners Ferry before we head back home," Jonas said to his wife then lifted a hand in farewell to Flint. "Nice to meet you, Flint. You just yell if you need us."

"Thanks. Maybe we'll see each other again before I leave for Utah," Flint said, surprising himself by really meaning it. These people cared about Pippa and he appreciated their concern for her.

"Sure thing."

Trina raised the window and the truck drove on down

the snow-packed road. Flint climbed back on Jasper and reined the horse in the direction of the ranch house.

Wrapped in a thick robe, Pippa was sitting on the couch in front of the fireplace when Flint finally returned to the house. She heard him scraping his boots on the rug by the kitchen door then his steps striding across the hallway. Just knowing he was nearby caused her heart to thump with pleasure and she couldn't help thinking that having him on the ranch had probably been better for her than the bottles of medicine the doctor had prescribed.

"There you are," he said as he entered the living room. "I thought maybe I'd find you back in bed."

"I got up to let the Wilkersons in and after they left I decided to sit up for a few minutes. I need to start getting my strength back."

"I saw their truck leaving as I was taking Jasper to the barn to unsaddle him. They didn't stay long," he told her.

He sat down on the cushion next to her and before she could stop herself, she reached over and touched a hand to his face. "Your cheek is red and freezing."

He grinned at her. "It's cold outside, but the weather is much better than it has been. I guess the Wilkersons told you I talked with them. I was in the meadow with the cattle when they spotted me and stopped on the road to introduce themselves."

She dropped her hand away from his face. "Yes. I could tell they wanted to ask questions about you, but I kept side-stepping them. The reason you're here is no one's business but yours and mine."

He shrugged. "I wouldn't have cared what you told them

about me. It's not like I have a reputation to worry about around here," he added dryly.

She sighed. "Don't get me wrong, Flint. I'm really not antisocial and they're great people. They'd do anything for me. It's just that I'm not up to chatting with visitors or explaining things that…well, would be hard to explain."

His lips twisted to a wry slant. "I'm a visitor. And I imagine I've worn out my welcome a long time ago."

Her short laugh was more like a mocking grunt. "This is going to sound crazy, but I've never thought of you as a visitor."

The twist on his lips deepened to a lopsided grin. "No. I suppose I'm what the little people sent to help you."

Smiling wanly, she rested her head against the back of the couch. "If it wasn't the little people, then it had to be Debra."

"Maybe so."

His gaze latched onto hers and Pippa wished she had the right to lean into him, to invite him to wrap his arms around her. But she didn't have that right—and maybe that was for the best. Being close to him, knowing that she could have it only for a short while, would only make it harder for her whenever he said goodbye. But she didn't want to think about his leaving now. She didn't ever want to think about it.

"Did you get the cattle moved?" she asked.

"Sure did. They're all in the meadow and already digging beneath the snow for dried grass. The dogs were better than a pair of ranch hands and Jasper was a real champ. I like him a lot."

"I like all my horses a lot." Dropping her gaze to her lap, she absently plucked at the thick fabric covering her knee.

"Since Debra is gone, two horses would be plenty to keep here on the ranch. If I sold two of them, I'd save quite a bit on the feed bill. But I can't bear to think of giving up any of them. I'll cut corners some other way."

"I wouldn't worry about cutting corners right now. Things will work out." He reached over and covered her hand with his. "You know, my dad always said that if money can fix the problem, then a person doesn't really have a problem. And he doesn't have that motto because he's wealthy. He knows that people go through trials and tribulations that money just can't fix."

She looked gratefully up at him. "I understand what your father means. If money would've made Debra well, I would've gotten my hands on it somehow, some way. But as you say, money isn't a magic wand."

He squeezed her hand then glanced at his watch. "It's getting close to lunchtime. Feel like eating?"

Smiling, she said, "Yes, I'm actually hungry. I must be getting well."

"You're definitely getting better. But I wouldn't call you well yet."

He started to rise but she caught his wrist and he looked questioningly at her.

"Is there something else you wanted to say?"

"There is something I wanted to mention. Since I'm feeling quite a bit better today, I was thinking that after lunch the two of us might start going through some of Debra's papers. You shouldn't have to go back outside for a while. Not until it's time to finish the barn chores."

He looked skeptical. "I'm not sure you're up to that much exertion, Pippa. You're just now starting to get some color back in your cheeks. I wouldn't want you to have a setback from overdoing things."

She shook her head. "The only thing I'll be doing is sitting here on the couch looking through papers. When I get tired, I'll tell you. The only hard work will be hauling the boxes down from the attic. If you can do that without my help, then we'll be all set."

His expression turned wry. "I can manage the boxes just fine. But I'm getting the feeling you're in a hurry to get rid of me."

For some ridiculous reason, a blush suddenly stung her cheeks. "On the contrary. To tell you the truth, you've piqued my curiosity about Debra's mother and her first family back in Utah. I'd like to know the truth of what occurred when Scarlett lived on your family's ranch."

"So would I," he replied then reached down and ran a hand over the top of her hair. "Thanks, Pippa."

Her heart fluttered as she looked into his green eyes. "For what?"

"For being interested. For caring."

"I only hope I can help," she told him.

"You already have."

He walked out of the room and as Pippa watched him go she wondered what he'd meant. She'd not done anything to help him so far. Quite the opposite, in fact. She'd piled a heap of troubles on his shoulders and delayed his trip home.

But, surprisingly, he'd not said a word of complaint about being stuck on a remote ranch in Idaho and burdened with chores that were far from his responsibility. No, he appeared to be taking it all in stride. Maybe that was because he'd come to the Bell for information about his grandparents and didn't resent having to work for it.

But Pippa didn't want to believe he'd hung around these past few days just on a hope he'd find a missing branch to the Hollister family tree. She wanted to believe he was staying because of her. Because, at some point during these past few days, he'd come to care about her.

You wanted to think Dale cared about you—even loved you. In the end, he only cared about himself and his wants. Do you honestly think Flint is any different? He has a career. He's wealthy. He'd never want to bury himself on the Bell.

Determined not to allow the mocking voice in her head to dampen her spirits, she rose from the couch and walked out to the kitchen to join him.

Chapter Eight

Flint must have heard her footsteps because the minute she stepped into the room, he glanced over his shoulder at her. "Pippa, what are you doing? I was going to bring your lunch to you."

"I'm feeling stronger, Flint. And walking a little will help me regain some strength."

"Or wear you out," he said as he crossed the room and placed a supportive hand beneath her elbow. "You must've been worried I was going to give you chicken noodle soup again."

The tender way he'd continued to care for her affected her deeply. She'd never had any man treat her so gently and protectively. At least, not a young, good looking bachelor like Flint. Each time he touched her, she felt her heart melting just that much more.

"Chicken noodle soup for the tenth time?" she teased. "No. I wasn't worried. You're doing the cooking. I'll eat whatever you fix."

He helped her into a chair and then crossed back over to the gas range where something that smelled like ham was sizzling in a skillet.

"I was going to surprise you with toast and scrambled

eggs," he said. "That shouldn't be too hard on your stomach. No hot sauce or jalapeños, though."

"I can do without the hot sauce this morning. And my stomach feels fine. I actually think I could handle some of that ham you're frying."

"Sorry. That's for me. You don't want to overdo things just because you're starting to feel human again," he said with a grin.

"Sure, Flint. Okay, you get the ham today. But tomorrow I'm going to eat something I can actually chew," she joked.

"You haven't bitten into my scrambled eggs yet. My little brother says they have the texture of rubber."

She watched him tending to the food in the skillet and thought how right and natural for him to be here in her kitchen, making himself at home. Which was quite a switch from the way she'd viewed him that first day he'd arrived on the Bell and she'd invited him in for coffee. He'd seemed totally out of place and she'd felt worse than awkward in his presence. Now she couldn't stop herself from thinking she was meant to be with him and he with her. Had the fever addled her? What was happening to her?

Ignoring the self-imposed questions, she asked, "And your brother would know? I thought you said your mother and sisters did all of the cooking."

"For some reason I can't recall, one day my mom and sisters were gone from the house, so I tried my hand at stirring us up a meal. I was only a teenager at the time and I didn't know the difference between a skillet and a saucepan." Chuckling, he glanced over at her. "Thankfully, Dad came in and saved us from food poisoning or worse. He dumped out the eggs and took us in to town to eat. Which was always a treat because he likes to eat at the Wagon

Spoke Café. We all still do. The old café has been in Beaver for as long as I can remember."

The smile she gave him was wistful at best. "The foster homes I lived in were okay. I had a roof over my head and a bed to sleep in and clothes on my back. But none of them had much of a family unit. I mean most all of my foster parents were nice people, but they had their hands full and couldn't give any of us much individual attention. They never bothered to try to teach me how to do things like cook. And eating out wasn't done very often. Sometimes we'd go to a fast-food place to eat. That was always a treat."

He carried a plate filled with eggs and toast and placed it in front of her, then returned to the cabinet to fetch utensils, a glass of orange juice and a cup of coffee.

"So the homes you lived in had other children?" he asked as he set the drinks and utensils next to her plate.

"Yes. All of them had kids. Some of them were the parents' own biological children and others were foster kids. I got along with most all of them, but I never thought of any of them as my brothers or sisters. I guess even as a child I was sort of a loner. Or maybe I felt like I just didn't belong. Anyway, I didn't learn to cook until I came here to live with Debra and Yance."

He fetched his own plate and cup of coffee then took a seat at the table. "I'm going to guess that's when you started feeling like you were really at home."

She nodded. "My life actually started to change when I got the job at the veterinarian's office and met Debra and Yance."

He cast her a curious glance as he shook salt and pepper over a pair of fried eggs. "Back then, were you thinking of becoming a vet?"

Her short laugh was a sound of disbelief. "Me, a vet? Oh yes, I would've loved to be a veterinarian. But that sort of college education requires lots of money. And I had none. I'm a practical woman, Flint. The very most I could hope for was to become a veterinarian's assistant. And even that was a lofty goal for me."

"Well, you must have learned a lot about animals while you were there," he said. "Or was most of your learning after you came here to the Bell and began helping the O'Sheas?"

"Both, I'd say. And once I started working here on the ranch, I knew it was my calling." She looked ruefully down at her plate. "Never in my wildest dreams did I think I'd end up owning the Bell. I didn't even know that Debra and Yance had written me into their wills until after she'd died. It was a shock. Losing her and then learning that I'd been given everything they'd ever worked for. I never felt so humbled in my life."

He reached out and curled his hand over her forearm. "Since they didn't have any children, I imagine they thought of you as their daughter, Pippa."

Her eyes misted over as she looked up at him. "Yes, I know they did. But there was Debra's sister, Taylor. Even if she hadn't wanted the property, she could've sold it for a hefty sum. The Bell isn't a vast amount of acreage, but property around here doesn't come cheap. The place would bring a hefty pile of money."

"Has Taylor ever mentioned her feelings about Debra leaving her out of her will?"

Pippa nodded. "She says Debra made the right decision concerning the ranch. Taylor and her daughters have their own lives in Wyoming and none of them would ever be interested in living here. Taylor says the Bell was too important to her sister and brother-in-law to ever sell it, but that she wouldn't have been able to maintain it herself. She's glad that I'm here to keep the place going. Except that—"

He gently squeezed her arm. "Except that you're having trouble right now making ends meet?"

She nodded again. "I lay awake at night wondering what Debra and Yance would do in this situation. And I imagine how disappointed they'd be to see the financial state of the ranch right now. I mean things were getting rough right before Debra passed away, but she believed we'd pull through it okay. And I am determined to put this place back on its feet."

"I'm betting that at one time or another, the O'Sheas faced a few rough times. Every rancher does. There are too many variables that go into the livelihood; too many unpredictable things crop up to cause little and big disasters. You push through the problems the best you can and keep telling yourself a sunny sky will show up eventually. On our family's ranch, all of us siblings try to approach life that same way."

She gave him a wan smile. "You make it sound easy."

"Nothing worthwhile is ever easy," he told her. "And, trust me, we've all had our problems."

He drew his hand away from her arm and for the next few minutes as they continued to eat the breakfast food he'd prepared for their lunch, Pippa thought about Flint's advice. She had no doubts he was an experienced rancher. But helping to work a property with thousands of acres, hundreds of cattle and sheep, and dozens of people to pitch in and share the work wasn't the same as her working the Bell. Even if the Hollisters endured losses, she was fairly certain they had plenty of financial resources to turn to, whereas she had none.

Trying to put the problems out of her mind, she finished every bite on her plate and was about to rise and carry her dirty dishes over to the sink when he gently clasped his hand around her wrist.

"Stay here for a minute," he said. "I want to ask you something."

Her eyes wide, she looked at him. "Something about searching through Debra's papers?"

"No. This is nothing to do with the Hollister family tree." His gaze met hers. "I've been wondering why you're still single. You told me you were engaged once and it didn't work out. Not all women have their heart set on having a husband and children, but I see you as the type who'd want a family. Especially since you didn't have one growing up."

Want a family. If he only knew the nights she'd gone to sleep with tears on her cheeks because she had no real parents or siblings. He couldn't guess the deep loneliness in her heart, or how she still struggled with the idea that no man would ever love her enough to make a home with her on an isolated piece of mountain land.

A lump of emotion filled her throat and she looked away as she tried hard to swallow it down. After an awkward moment passed, she forced her eyes back to his.

"You're right, Flint. From the time I was a young girl, I wanted to grow up and be a wife and mommy. I wanted my own family. One that would never leave or be taken away. Then later, after I grew to be a woman, I dreamed that one day I'd have a strong man who'd put his arms around me and call me darling. He'd promise to love and care for me and our children for the rest of my life. And for a while I thought I'd found that dream with Dale."

His green eyes swept over her face. "Dale? He was the guy you were engaged to marry?"

Frowning, she nodded. "We started dating as juniors in high school. He wasn't much of a social guy and I was somewhat of a wall flower, so I think that sort of drew us together. That and the fact that he'd also been raised in poor conditions. His family never had much and I— Well, you know my background. But Dale was a hard worker, just like me, and he had big dreams of building a better life for himself. After we graduated, he got a job in the timber industry, and was slowly working his way up the ladder to a position with better pay. That's when he asked me to marry him."

"Was this after you'd come to live with Debra and Yance?"

She sighed. "I'd been living here with the O'Sheas for about a year—a while before Yance died. Anyway, when I accepted Dale's proposal, he'd planned to continue working his job close to Bonners Ferry and we were going to build a little cabin for ourselves here on the Bell. I'd made it clear to him that I'd rooted down here on the ranch and had no intentions of ever leaving. He acted as if all of that was well and good with him...until he got a job offer in a town too far away to commute. He seemed to take it as a given that I'd give up everything that mattered so much to me and go with him." Shaking her head, she sighed. "I refused. So here I am alone and he's off somewhere. Probably married to someone else by now."

He continued to study her closely. "And you're still bitter about his decision? Or your decision?"

She stared thoughtfully at him. "I don't think I've ever questioned my decision," she admitted. "But sure, I was very disappointed when Dale decided to leave the Bonners Ferry area. But now? I can't be bitter. Dale wanted to better himself with a higher paying job and I wanted my life here on the ranch. We simply had different wants and needs. So it was best I gave him back his ring and wished him well. I would've been miserable if I'd agreed to move away with him."

He grimaced. "I don't imagine that was an easy thing for you to do, though. Ending your engagement."

She shook her head. "Actually, telling him I wouldn't leave the Bell was easy. I guess that sounds selfish of me."

"Hmm. It sounds like you knew your own mind. And that you still know it."

She looked away from him while her forefinger absently drew circles on the tabletop next to her plate. "Flint, all of my young life I'd been forced to move from one place to the next. For one reason or another, my foster parents would change. Sometimes I'd barely get settled into a place and then have to move again. Once I found my forever home here on the Bell, I swore I wouldn't leave. Dale couldn't understand my feelings. And after he left, I began to realize I didn't lose anything. He didn't love me. Not really. If he did, he'd have understood what really mattered to me and would've wanted to make sure I had it. I don't blame him for having his own dreams, but he couldn't make room for mine, and that was a deal-breaker."

"Did you love him?"

Turning her gaze back to him, she said, "Back at that time, I thought what I felt for him was love, but now I can see what I mostly felt with Dale was comfort and security. Our relationship was quiet and easy. Not hot and passionate. He wasn't that kind of guy. And I...well, like I said, I'm a practical woman."

She thought she saw a flash of disbelief in his eyes. The downturned corners of his mouth told her what he thought about her one and only serious romance.

"You know, Pippa, you might be underestimating yourself. In any case, you made the right choice when you handed him back his ring. I think you need a man with a little fire in him."

Fire? Why would he think something like that? She was far from a sexy siren.

A short laugh escaped her. "I wouldn't know about the fire, but it's taken me a long time to quit beating myself up over the breakup. To convince myself I was wise instead of selfish."

A faint grin curved his lips. "Wise. No doubt about it."

He reached for his coffee cup and as she watched him take a long sip, she told herself that since he'd had the nerve to ask her personal questions then she ought to have enough courage to ask him a few as well.

She dabbed a napkin to her lips and hoped he couldn't see how much it was shaking her to talk to him about love and marriage. "Okay, Flint, now that you know all about my failed engagement, what about you? Why aren't you married? And don't try to sidestep the question by saying you're still looking for the right woman."

Surprise flashed in his eyes, making it obvious he'd not been expecting her to turn the tables on him.

"What would be wrong in saying I'm still looking?" he asked. "I am. Well, sort of. I told myself a long time ago that if it was ever meant for me to have a wife and children, it would just happen. That I shouldn't go out looking for the right woman the same way I'd go searching for the right horse or new shirt."

"You mean you believe fate will lead you to the right woman?"

"Yeah. Something like that," he said then frowned. "I've learned that purposely trying to find a spouse...well, it just doesn't work."

Thoughtfully, she picked up her fork and absently pushed at the leftover crumbs on her plate. "So when you were younger you were searching for a wife, but later you changed your mind?"

He let out a short mocking laugh. "When I was much younger I wasn't necessarily looking for a wife. I was just— looking."

She cast him a wry smile. "I get it. You were looking for a little fun."

His expression turned sheepish. "Sort of. But most all young men want to have their fun for a while. Except your Dale, I suppose."

"He wasn't really my Dale. I never had his heart and he never had mine. Looking back, that's easy to see." Her gaze clashed with his and she was suddenly aware of the fast beat of her heart. The faint flush of heat rushing to her face. "Have you ever been engaged?"

He drained the last of his coffee then placed the mug down next to his plate. "I came close once. But she didn't know it." His chuckle was full of self-mockery. "I was getting ready to surprise her with an engagement ring, but things fell apart before that could happen."

If he was going to propose marriage to the woman, he must have really loved her, Pippa thought. The idea bothered her greatly. Which was ridiculous. She had no strings to Flint. Just because he'd kissed her on the forehead hardly meant he was interested. No, those two little kisses had merely been a way of letting her know he'd take care of her until she was back on her feet.

"She broke up with you?" Pippa asked. "Or was it the other way around?"

His lips took on a rueful twist. "Rachel was the one who ended things."

She reached for her glass. Not because she wanted the last of the orange juice but because she needed something to hold on to. "Why? She didn't like you being a deputy? Or she just wasn't that in to you?"

He let out a mocking grunt. "Now that I think about it, I couldn't tell you what she liked or disliked about me. I guess I must have been sort of blinded with infatuation. See, she wasn't a native of Beaver City. She moved up there from St. George to be closer to her parents. Her father worked for the Bureau of Land Management and had been transferred to the Beaver County area. Anyway, Rachel was divorced— had been for about two years when we started dating."

"Did she have children?"

"No, thank goodness."

She cast him a skeptical glance. "Why? Don't you like children?"

"Sure, I like children. But considering the circumstances…well, kids need stability and preferably two parents. She wasn't up to being a mother. Not at that time in her life."

Pippa couldn't stop a frown of disapproval from forming on her face. "If you knew she wasn't mother material, why would you have considered asking her to be your wife? Or did having children with her never cross your mind?"

"You don't understand, Pippa. There was so much that I didn't know about Rachel until after the fact. In the beginning, she seemed genuine and, add to that, she was easy on the eyes. She had a flashy appearance and dressed to play up her looks. Tall and long-legged with black hair, she had brown eyes that were smoking. You know?"

Pippa grimaced. "Yes. I think you're describing bedroom eyes."

"I guess so. In reality they were lying eyes."

"Where did you meet this woman?"

"She went to work as a secretary at city hall. Everyone wanted to date her. For some reason though, she singled me out. Maybe that was because she found out my family was wealthy or maybe because I wore a badge on my chest. I'll never know her reasons. But I can admit her attention fed my ego. Then later, after we'd dated awhile, she began to talk about the future, our future. Which was surprising when you think about it. She'd talked like her marriage and divorce had been stormy."

Pippa said, "She must have thought a marriage to you would be different—good."

His low laugh was full of self-ridicule. "Yeah, and I was stupid enough to believe she was serious. And I let myself think she was the one I needed in my life. I just thank God her ex-husband showed up. If not, I might have made the huge mistake of giving her an engagement ring."

Pippa frowned with confusion. "Her ex-husband? What did he have to do with anything?"

"I'll be honest, Pippa, never once while I dated the woman did I get the impression she had any feelings left for her ex. I guess that goes to show you how duped a person can be. Because she was still in love with the guy and when he showed up and asked her to give their relationship another try, she left with him so fast I should've given her a speeding ticket," he said with a heavy dose of sarcasm.

"Reunited with her ex? I never saw that coming," Pippa admitted. "How did she explain her exit to you? Or did she bother?"

His lips thinned to a straight line and Pippa wondered just how much this broken relationship had affected him and his future.

"I'm not so sure she planned to tell me goodbye. I just happened to walk into her office space at city hall and found her emptying her desk. Her explanation was blunt and to the point. She loved her ex and was going to marry him again. So I wished her well and turned on my heel and walked out. That was the last I ever heard of her."

Pippa tried to imagine him pining over a woman, but for some reason her mind refused to see him suffering over a lost love. "I suppose your heart was broken," she said.

He shook his head. "Once she was gone, everything became clear to me. I wasn't suffering a broken heart, which obviously meant I never loved her. Not the sort of love that goes with marriage and making a family. No, the only thing I felt was bitterness—mostly at myself for being such a naïve fool. And I was mortified, too, because my family and buddies had all tried to tell me she wasn't really in love with me and I was too stubborn to listen."

"Hmm. I understand. She hurt and embarrassed you." She shrugged one shoulder. "I felt the same way about Dale. It was embarrassing to have to admit to myself and my friends that he didn't care enough for me to stick around."

He reached over and covered her hand with his and she couldn't stop herself from turning her palm up and wrapping her fingers around his.

"We live and learn. Right?" he murmured.

"Yes. We live and learn."

And now they were both leery of looking for real love, she thought. Would she always be afraid to give her heart to a man? Would he always be set against falling in love with a woman? The questions caused a dark cloud to enter her mind and her thoughts must have been obvious to him because suddenly his forefinger was under her chin, lifting her face toward his.

"All of this talk about the past has made you sad," he murmured. "I'm sorry, Pippa. I never meant to make you unhappy."

She cleared her throat. "Don't be sorry. I'm not unhappy. Actually, I'm glad you told me about Rachel."

"And I'm glad you told me about Dale."

Although she tried to stop a mist from glazing her eyes, the moisture blurred her vision as she met his gaze. "Are you?" she asked softly.

Rising, he gently pulled her up from the chair and Pippa

stared at him in stunned fascination as he slowly pulled her into his arms.

"I wanted to know what kind of fool could've left you," he said in a voice gruff with emotion.

By now, they were pressed together and the contact was like an electrical jolt to her senses. Her heart started tripping over itself and her mouth had gone as dry as a desert.

"He knew what he was doing," she whispered. "You see I'm not flashy. I'm just a plain girl with manure on her boots and hay in her hair."

His hands slipped up to the back of her shoulders and as he drew her closer, she was surrounded by the scents of leather and horses and snowy wind. The smell was just as enticing as his touch and though she knew the wise thing for her to do would be to step out of his arms, she couldn't. Not when she'd been aching for him to hold her.

He said, "I know what I'm doing, too. And it isn't backing away."

"Flint, I…"

The remainder of her words trailed off as his forefinger slowly traced the outline of her lips.

"Don't talk. Just let me kiss you."

If possible, her heart kicked into an even faster rhythm. As she watched his face dip down to hers, she started to whisper his name, but he didn't give her the opportunity to finish. His hard masculine lips were suddenly on hers, gently probing and searching and sending her senses shooting off in every direction.

He tasted like coffee and blackberry jam, but most of all he tasted like a man. The man who'd slowly been making her forget all the obstacles standing between them. And now, with his lips scorching hers, all she could think about was getting closer.

Her arms unwittingly wrapped around his neck and he reacted by anchoring his hands at the back of her waist and pulling her even tighter against his hard body. When he deepened the pressure of his lips, she responded with equal fervor and for long moments she forgot about time or the fear that she might be playing with fire. Nothing mattered but him and the sweet pleasure rushing through her.

When he finally lifted his head, she had to force her eyes to open and her mind to return to reality.

"I wasn't planning on that much of a kiss," he murmured. "Are you okay?"

Even though her insides were shaking, she managed to give him a weak smile. "Of course I'm okay. I'm not *that* sick."

He smiled back at her and then, to her surprise, he pressed his cheek to hers. "You didn't feel *that* sick, either. But I—hope you don't think I was trying to take advantage of you."

Her arms were still circled around his neck and even though she knew she should release her hold on him; she couldn't bring herself to move. Not yet.

"If that was your intention, you could've easily done that three days ago when I was feverish. Come to think of it, I might be feverish now," she attempted to joke, while thinking the best thing she could do now was try to lighten the moment.

He eased his head back from hers and she was relieved to see a grin on his face.

"I think both of us might be. It could be catching." He edged her out of his arms and pointed her toward the doorway leading out of the kitchen. "You better go back to the living room and rest while I clean up here. I'll join you in a few minutes."

"All right."

As she left the kitchen, the thought struck her that she was going to need more than a few minutes to gather her senses. And not just because his kiss had jangled her nerves. From the first day she'd met him, she'd fantasized about being in his arms and having his lips on hers. As it turns out, her fantasies couldn't begin to compare to the real thing—and that scared her. She'd never felt so much hot desire swimming through her body. What would it be like if he really wanted to make love to her? Moreover, how could she ever expect to resist him?

The most you can ever expect from Flint Hollister is a brief fling before he leaves you behind. So don't let yourself dream and hope, Pippa. Your life is the Bell and your future doesn't include a rich, sexy rancher from Utah.

As she took a seat on the couch in front of the fireplace, she shoved hard at the depressing voice in her head. Yet as she stared into the flames of the burning logs, the only thing she could see was a future without anyone at her side.

Chapter Nine

A half hour later, as Flint finished the kitchen chores, he was still trying to figure out what had come over him. When he'd pulled Pippa into his arms, he'd kissed her like there wasn't going to be a tomorrow, or even a tonight. What had he been thinking? More importantly, what could she possibly be thinking about him now? Did she believe that he was a creep who'd decided to have a little fun with her while he was stuck here on the ranch?

No! First of all, he wasn't stuck. He could leave if he wanted to. But he *didn't* want to. And maybe that was the thing that was scaring him even more than the fiery kiss they'd exchanged a half hour ago.

Deciding to dwell on that worry later, Flint hung the dish towel he'd been using on a rack at the end of the cabinet and walked out to the living room.

As soon as she heard the sound of his boots on the hardwood floor, she looked up and motioned for him to join her. "I'll show you the way up to the attic in a minute," she said with a smile. "Right now I have something else to show you."

"Let me add a couple of logs to the fire first," he said. "We don't want the room to get cold."

"Speaking of getting cold," she said, "We need to turn down the thermostat on the central heat. It's been running too much."

He tossed a pair of good-sized logs onto the fire and adjusted the screen before he joined her on the couch. "Forget about the thermostat. I intentionally turned it up to keep the house warmer. The last thing you need is to get chilled while you're recovering."

"But the heating fuel will—"

"I've already had the tank filled," he interrupted as he sank down next to her. "So put it out of your mind."

Her lips parted and as Flint looked at them; the need to kiss her again stirred deep inside him. It had been a mistake to ever kiss her. Now that he knew how good it could be, he was going to have to fight like hell to keep his hands off her.

"You had it filled? I didn't hear the truck. When did it come? And how did you pay for it? The propane company won't allow you to charge the cost."

"The truck came yesterday. And don't worry about how the gas was paid for. That's my business. Not yours."

Her lips flattened to a disapproving line and he realized even when she was frustrated her lips looked oh, so kissable.

"I'll argue that point later," she said flatly. "When I get a little more strength built up."

He chuckled. "Fussing at me won't do you any good."

"I'll pay for the gas. I have enough in the bank to do that much."

Scowling at her, he said, "Now you're going to make me angry. Forget the propane. What was it you wanted to show me?"

For few seconds he thought she was going to continue to

argue with him over the fuel bill, but she must have decided it would be best to let the matter drop for now.

"Okay. We'll change the subject," she said and reached down to pick up a small box sitting on the floor beneath the coffee table. "I was going to show these to you a few days ago. But then I got sick and forgot about them."

"What do you have there? Photos of Debra and her husband?" he asked, inclining his head toward the box.

"These are photos, but not of Debra and Yance. I'll dig some of those out for you later. Your father might appreciate having a few pics of his half sister and brother-in-law." She lifted out several framed photos of different sizes and placed the stack on her lap. "These are photos of your grandmother. I thought you'd like to see them. Especially after you told me your father only owned one little photo of Scarlett."

Mixed emotions swirled through him. Growing up, all he and his siblings had ever heard about Scarlett was that she'd been a witch of a woman. Even now his father wanted to believe Lionel had been telling the truth about Scarlett being difficult and impossible to please and how she'd callously left her sons. But after hearing Pippa talk about the woman, a part of Flint wanted to believe she'd been a good and kind person.

His throat was suddenly tight. "Yes, I would like to see photos. But I—I'm not sure I have the right. Dad should be seeing these first. Not me."

Her expression was one of gentle understanding as she looked over at him. "Your father sent you here to find out whatever you could about Scarlett. And she is your grandmother. You have just as much right to see these photos as he does."

"Put like that, I suppose you're right. And all these years—especially as a kid—I tried to imagine how she looked. But now, I'm not so sure I want to have her real image in my mind."

She slanted him a pointed stare. "I think you're a man who needs to have more than an imaginary figure to hold on to. Don't you?"

Yeah, he thought. Holding Pippa in his arms would certainly be better than imagining her soft body nestled against his.

"You're right." He gave her a lopsided grin. "And I wouldn't want my fellow deputies calling me a coward."

She handed one of the larger photos to him. "I can't really say when any of these were taken. I thought there might be dates written on the back, but I couldn't find any. Judging from the style of clothing she was wearing, I'd guess this one was taken back in the 1970s."

The image was in color and Flint studied the dark-haired, blue-eyed woman with a bit of shock. "This woman is beautiful!"

"What were you expecting?" she asked ruefully. "That she'd look like a hag?"

Dazed, he slowly swiped a hand over his face. "Grandfather always described her, more or less, as a shrew. I think maybe an idea had already formed in my mind she'd have a hard look on her face. But nothing about this woman looks hard. Her eyes are soft and her expression gentle."

Pippa nodded. "Debra always described her mother as gentle and kind. Don't you think it's odd that your grandfather said the exact opposite of his ex-wife? Or maybe it isn't so odd, after all, Flint. The man you describe sounds as though he was very bitter about their divorce."

Flint continued to study the young smiling woman in the photo. "Bitter wouldn't begin to describe Grandfather. And it wasn't just about Scarlett. He was a hard man in many ways. He expected us all to walk a very straight line. If we veered off and disappointed him, there was hell to pay."

She began to hand him the other photos and as Flint sifted through them, he could only imagine how different Stone Creek might have been if this lady had been around to buffer Lionel's abrasiveness. To love and nurture her sons and grandchildren.

He pointed to one of the smaller snapshots. "Are these two little girls with Scarlett her daughters?"

Nodding, she said, "Debra is the taller one. She had dark hair like their mother. Taylor's is lighter, like her father's. I'm sure there are some pics of Ode around here somewhere, but I haven't run across any yet. He was a tall, raw-boned man with big hands and an equally big smile. From what Debra said of her parents, they adored each other."

Smiling wanly, he looked over at her. "I'm not sure what my dad would think to hear that his mother ran off from her three young sons and found happiness with another man. I don't know—to me it would feel like an ice pick to the heart."

Her head swung from side to side. "It would be an ice pick to the heart for me, too—if it were true. Somehow I don't believe Scarlett just ran off. And I certainly don't believe she deliberately left her sons behind. That doesn't sound like her. But to be fair, I only know one side of the story."

He breathed deeply. "I only know one side of the story, too. That's why I'm hoping you can help me find the other side."

She reached over and clasped her hand on his forearm and he realized her touch was more than a warm reassurance to him. It was a bond. A connection that he never wanted to break. Was this the way a man felt when he lost his head over a woman? If so, then he was headed toward deep trouble.

"I'm hoping we'll find some answers together." She gave his arm a gentle squeeze. "Come on. I'll show you how to get up in the attic."

He followed her out of the living room and down the hallway past the bedrooms. When they reached the end, she pointed to a small square opening with a latched door in the ceiling.

"If you can reach the chain dangling from the handle, you should be able to pull down the door. A built-in ladder will come down with it," she explained.

Flint reached up and grabbed hold of the chain and pulled. With the door opening, the ladder extended all the way to the floor and stretched up into the dark entrance of the attic.

"Maybe I'd better have a flashlight. It looks dark up there," he said as he stepped onto the bottom rung.

"No worries." She reached over and flipped a switch on the wall of the hallway. "Two lights should be on up there now."

"So what do these boxes I'm bringing down look like? Do you know where they're located?"

"If I remember right, Debra had some of the things packed in a plastic storage container and others were in plain cardboard boxes. There are a few boxes with Christmas decorations and old clothes up there, but they're all in the back of the attic and marked. The ones you need should all be stacked close to the entrance of the attic. If you can't find them, I'll climb up and help you."

He leveled a look of warning at her. "You're not to step one foot on this ladder," he ordered. "In your weakened condition, you might get dizzy and fall."

She gave him a hopeless grin. "Has anyone ever accused you of being a mother hen?"

He chuckled. "Okay, I admit I might be overdoing it. But I've never played nurse before."

"Might be? You're above and beyond overdoing it. But I'm not going to complain. I'll be back to pitching hay soon enough."

Like when he'd gone back to Utah, Flint thought. He hated to admit it, but each time the thought of leaving the Bell struck him, his mind revolted. What would his family think if they knew he was going through some sort of emotional upheaval? What would Sheriff Andrews and Flint's fellow deputies think if he told them he wasn't certain he wanted to continue to be a lawman?

Damn it, Flint, don't let a woman make a fool of you again. Just because Pippa fills you with these soft feelings, it doesn't mean you really want this sort of life with her. It doesn't mean you'd be content to root down here with her on this isolated ranch.

Root down. Hell, he was even beginning to think in her words. Shaking away the unnerving thoughts, he said, "You won't be pitching hay until I see that you're strong enough."

He started up the ladder while down on the floor he could hear her chuckling.

"Bossy man," she called up to him.

Thankfully, Flint managed to find the boxes of documents and papers quickly and after hauling them down the ladder, Pippa helped him carry the containers out to the living room.

For a large remainder of the afternoon, they slowly sifted through the cards and letters, old receipts and other documents, which mostly held no value. Flint was on the verge of calling it quits for the day when Pippa opened a handwritten letter and quickly scanned the front page.

"Oh, here's something that might give you some clues. It's from your grandmother to Debra, shortly after Ode passed away," Pippa told him. "At first she's discussing the weather and some of her friends and then she moves on to this. 'Darling daughter, I hope you never have to go through the pain of losing a husband. I've done it twice and both times were equally painful. The first was not by his death. No, it was the death of a love I thought was true. Now the death of your father was different. Ode's love for me was always true. The only reason he's gone from my side is because God called him home. Even so, my grief is heavy and I pray that you'll never have to be without Yance—that the two of you will go together.'"

Pippa glanced over at him then back to the letter. "She goes on to say she's seriously thinking about selling the farm and how sad it makes her to see the fields empty. And how she should probably move closer to Debra."

Frowning thoughtfully, Flint shook his head as he tried to decipher what Scarlett could've possibly meant. "'No, it was the death of a love I thought was true,'" he repeated her words. "What do you think she meant?"

"I'm afraid to say," Pippa answered glumly. "It's just all so sad. And I...well, from this letter, it sounds like your grandfather might've betrayed her in some way. Maybe she thought he fell out of love with her because they'd been fighting. Or maybe she found out he'd been unfaithful."

"Yes, that was the same idea I was getting. Do you think Scarlett might have been suffering from the beginnings of dementia when she wrote this letter? That maybe she wasn't thinking clearly?"

"It sounds to me like she was thinking clearly. I first met her after she moved to Coeur d'Alene and while she'd started getting confused by then, it used to come and go. Most of the time, she seemed to have her mental faculties intact. And this letter was written even before that time."

"I see." He let out a heavy breath. "I'm not sure I want to let Dad know about this just yet. Not until we find something more concrete about Scarlett's marriage to Grandfather. I don't want to upset him unnecessarily."

She put down the letter and squared her knees around to his. "Do you think it would upset him? From the little you've told me about your father, he's not one to sugarcoat things. And I can't imagine that a man with eight children and a spread the size of Stone Creek Ranch would be too fragile to handle the truth about his father."

"You're right. Dad is a bear of a man. Both emotionally and physically. He can take the truth. I just want to make sure it *is* the truth before he hears it."

She nodded then gave him a hopeful look. "Well, there's not much left for us to go through. Maybe something else will turn up before we finish."

"We've been at this a long time," he told her. "You need to rest and I need some fresh air. We'll look through the last of this tonight. If we don't find anything, then what? I suppose I'll have to go home and tell Dad he needs to forget the whole thing."

"No!" she quickly blurted. "Don't start giving up now. I'm not certain these containers you carried down from the attic are all that's left of Debra's papers. Besides, we might think of some other route—some other person privy to Scarlett's past."

He reached for her hand and when she wrapped her fingers around his, the feeling was so utterly strong and sweet, he knew with certainty that it was like nothing he'd felt before. Nor had a woman ever made him feel so much with just a simple touch. Had a part of him been asleep before he'd met Pippa? Why was she making him look at himself and the world as if it were all brand new? He was afraid to answer himself.

"Pippa, I don't want you to feel like you have to do any of this," he said gently. "I'm causing you trouble. Trouble that you don't need."

A wry smile slanted her lips. "I'm causing you trouble, too. The kind you never asked for or wanted. So, we're even, I suppose. And as far as I'm concerned, it's nice to think we can help each other."

"I'm glad you think so," he said then swallowed as he felt his throat begin to thicken. "Pippa, about that kiss... I—"

Frowning, she quickly cut him off. "I was just about to say I hope you didn't take me too seriously. I guess you can tell I'm not all that experienced with men. And I... well, just want you to know that I understand it was a casual thing for you."

Casual? Was she kidding? He'd thought his whole head was going to spin off and hit the ceiling. "You think our kiss didn't mean anything to me?" he asked quietly.

Her gray eyes narrowed skeptically. "Of course. It couldn't. You're you and I'm me. And we're from different worlds. I'll admit we had a very nice moment. And I enjoyed kissing you—obviously. But we both know…" She paused and shook her head. "You'll be heading out soon."

What could he say? He did have to leave Idaho sooner or later. And yet he didn't want her to think their kiss meant nothing to him. Not when it had been everything and more. How the hell had this happened to him?

"Maybe so. But you're wrong about our kiss. It did mean something to me."

Shadows darkened her gray eyes before she looked away to a spot across the room. "What kind of talk is this, Flint? It's futile and we both know it. We need to be smart and just regard each other as friends."

Frustration clamped his jaw. "I can't think of you as just a friend. Not anymore."

His voice was gruff with emotion and the sound must've caught her attention because her gaze suddenly turned back to him. "Then it's probably a good thing you'll be leaving soon. I'm not in the market for a broken heart."

He grimaced. "You think I'm looking for one?"

Not bothering to answer, she rose from the couch and walked over to the fireplace. With her back to him, she extended her hands toward the warmth of the flames.

Rising to his feet, he walked over and joined her on the hearth. When she glanced his way, he placed his hands over the tops of her shoulders and turned her toward him.

"Look, Pippa, I don't understand what's happening between us any more than you do. But whatever it is—I don't think we should ignore it. Do you?"

Her eyes were sad as her head moved back and forth. "Flint, I just explained to you what happened with Dale. I don't need or want to go through that sort of thing again.

And don't start telling me a bunch of lies—we both know your life is in Utah. I can accept that. And I think you can accept that my life is here on the Bell."

Could he? he asked himself. He didn't know. But one thing he knew for certain, she'd never budge from this ranch for any reason. Not even for love and marriage.

"Yeah, I guess I'll have to accept it," he said sourly. "I only wish that we—could've met under different circumstances."

Her expression turned mocking. "Under different circumstances you would've never noticed me. I'm—"

He interrupted her words by wrapping his hand around her chin and tilting her face up to his. "You're a beautiful woman, Pippa. You'd be noticed anywhere."

Her gaze clung to his and he could see heavy doubts clouding her eyes.

"Don't make this hard for me, Flint. Don't try to convince me we could have a relationship. It's impossible. And—"

"I'm not convinced it's impossible," he interjected.

Surprise parted her lips and Flint couldn't pass up the opportunity to kiss her again. Only this time, he forced himself to keep the contact soft and brief.

When he eased his head back from hers, her eyes were closed and he could see the pulse in her neck throbbing with each beat of her heart. The rhythm matched the hammering in his chest and he had to believe the strong reaction they had to each other was more than chemistry.

"I'm going to the barn," he told her. "I'll see you later."

She opened her eyes and immediately looked away. "Okay. I'll finish going through Debra's things. If I find anything of interest, I'll lay it aside."

He wanted to keep talking about him and her. He wanted to keep touching her, kissing her. But for now he could see the more he pushed, the more she was going to back away.

And perhaps she was right, he considered as he walked out of the living room. Life was taking them in different directions. It would be impossible for the two of them to have a relationship. But, foolish or not, he desperately wanted to prove her wrong.

The next morning Pippa woke early and feeling better than she had in days. After sluicing her face with cold water and wrapping a robe over her pajamas, she hurried out to the kitchen to find Flint stirring something in a big mixing bowl.

He was wearing a red-plaid shirt with his jeans and the color made his tanned skin and rusty-brown hair appear that much richer. By now she'd had enough time to memorize the shape of his face, the angles and lines of his features, the deep green of his eyes and the way his lips often expressed his feelings. He was not pretty-boy handsome. His looks came from maturity and toughness and that made them all the more appealing to Pippa. Yet most of her waking hours were spent warning herself not to be swayed by his looks or his kisses.

"You're stirring whatever that is as if you know what you're doing. What are you making?" she asked as she sidled up to him.

He looked at her and grinned. "Can't you tell it's pancake batter? I found a mix and the directions said all you have to do is add water. I thought that should be simple enough for me to do."

"It is. Except they'll be sort of bland without adding a

little sugar and oil. And then you have to cook them. Do you know how to cook pancakes?"

"Never tried it. But I've watched Mom flip a few. Looks easy."

She chuckled. "I imagine it is easy for her after doing it a million times. There's a knack to it. Maybe you'd better watch me. Then you can try."

He gave her a playful scowl. "Worried about eating a burnt breakfast?" he teased then stepped back and looked her up and down. "What are you doing up this early anyway? Are you feeling better?"

She smiled at him. "A hundred times better. I feel like getting dressed and going to the barn this morning. And please don't argue. I'm going stir crazy in this house."

"I won't argue. In fact, I was going to ask if you'd like to ride into town with me later this morning. I have a few things I need to pick up and I thought we might have lunch. Is there anywhere special you like to eat?"

She didn't have to ponder more than a moment. "Debra and I always loved to eat at the Blue Moose. It's a diner in the old part of town. They have grilled food and daily specials. Nothing fancy, but everything tastes good."

"Then the Blue Moose it shall be. As long as you feel up to it."

"I'm feeling great. I'd love to go. I've not been to town since I went to the medical clinic. And that doesn't count as a real visit. It might be good for me to see civilization again," she joked.

"Okay. After I finish the feeding this morning, we'll head for town."

She reached over and took the mixing spoon from his

hand. "Better let me do this. You can fry the sausage and make the coffee."

He chuckled. "You mean stick to what I know?"

"Something like that."

She laughed along with him and it felt so good that she decided then and there to quit worrying about tomorrow. Today, Flint was here with her. She needed to enjoy his company for as long as she could.

Pippa couldn't remember the last time she'd taken any kind of pains with her appearance. These past months since Debra had passed, her trips to town had only consisted of the grocery store and places to buy ranching supplies. The most she'd done for those occasions had been to change into clean clothes and make sure her hair was pulled into a neat ponytail.

But today was different. She was going to be in Flint's company and for once she wanted him to see she was capable of putting in an effort to be attractive. At least he could go home to Utah with one nicer image of her, she thought as she fastened the sides of her hair back with a green barrette to match her button-down shirt.

With her hair in place, she leaned closer to the dresser mirror and peered closely at the light makeup she'd applied to her face. A little mascara, a dab of color on her cheeks, and a swipe of pink lipstick was hopefully enough to brighten her appearance without looking overdone.

Once she was ready, she tossed her coat and purse over her arm then left the bedroom to find Flint sitting at the kitchen table. He was talking to someone on his cell phone, but the moment he spotted her, he quickly wound up the call and rose to his feet.

"I didn't mean to interrupt your call. If it was important, call the person back. I'll go wait in the living room," she offered.

"I'll finish the call later." His eyes grew wide as he took a step toward her. "Pippa, is that you?"

Her smile was totally self-conscious. "I can clean up a little—when necessary," she added with a little laugh.

He walked over and touched a forefinger to the turquoise stone dangling from her earlobe. "You're wearing earrings!" he exclaimed then, bending his head, sniffed her neck. "And you smell like violets. Mmm, nice. Did you do all this for me?"

She was grateful for the impish grin on his face. Right now, she was far better equipped to handle his teasing. She would have been far more rattled by a serious glint in his eyes.

"Maybe," she said coyly. "By the way, how does a lawman and rancher like you know how violets smell?"

He chuckled. "Mom keeps several pots of violets growing in the kitchen window. I sometimes sneak a sniff."

"Oh, so your ability to identify the smell of violets didn't come from sniffing the neck of a past flame?"

Laughing again, he said, "You know, the sheriff's department could probably use you as a detective. But just for the record, none of my past flames wore violet-scented perfume."

"I believe you," she said then asked, "Are you ready to go?"

"I'm ready." He glanced at his watch. "If we leave now, we should get there at lunchtime."

"I've parked the truck out near the front gate and shoveled off the walkway. You should be able to reach it without getting your feet soppy with melting snow."

By now his thoughtfulness shouldn't surprise her. Over these past days, he'd done all sorts of little things to make her life easier and more pleasant. Yet she continued to be touched by the kindness he showed her.

"Thank you, Flint. But you shouldn't have gone to so much trouble."

He clasped a hand around the back of her arm and urged her out of the kitchen. "No trouble. I needed the exercise."

"About like you need a hole in the head," she said dryly.

"Samuel, the guy I was just talking to on the phone, thinks I must've fallen and knocked myself goofy. He can't believe I've stayed away from work for this long."

"Is he a fellow deputy?" she asked as they made their way to the front door of the house.

"No. One of our dispatchers. He's worked the job for years and I've been friends with him forever."

She glanced at him. "I imagine all of your coworkers are wondering why you've been up here for so long. Did you tell them you had a sick girl on your hands?"

"No. I just explained that I've not finished my business here. Which is true."

Sometimes Pippa had to stop and remind herself why he'd come to the Bell in the first place. In her mind, she wanted to think fate had brought him here.

Fate could just as easily make him leave, Pippa. So get your head out of the clouds.

Shaking away the mocking voice in her head, she said, "I'm sure you're missing your family and friends."

He arched a brow at her. "I'm not missing anyone—yet."

Forty-five minutes later, Flint and Pippa were sitting in a booth at the Blue Moose, a fair-sized diner on the west edge of town. Similar to the Wagon Spoke back in Beaver, the eating establishment had a long bar equipped with several swiveling stools on one side of the room, while a row of wooden booths ran the length of the opposite wall. In between, at least a dozen round tables with wooden chairs were covered with blue-checked vinyl tablecloths. A loop of old pop and country tunes playing in the background competed with the noise of conversations and laughter.

As the two of them sipped coffee and waited for their meals to arrive, Flint inclined his head toward a Christmas tree with twinkling lights in the far corner of the room. "I guess the folks running the Blue Moose are still celebrating the holidays."

Smiling, Pippa nodded. "Either the celebration is still going or they haven't found the time to take down the decorations. I like seeing the tree, though. With Debra gone, I wasn't in the spirit to decorate the house. Next year I'll do better," she said with a sigh.

He thought about the big family Christmases that always took place on Stone Creek Ranch. His mother always made sure the house was full of food and drinks and everything was decorated beautifully. However, it was the love and laughter with all the family members that made the holiday truly special. But Pippa wouldn't know how it felt to be in the middle of a big family celebration, he realized.

"You spent Christmas alone?" he asked.

She nodded. "A couple of friends invited me to join them, but like I said, I wasn't in the mood. Did you have a nice holiday?"

"Very nice. And this year it was unusually eventful," he said. "My oldest brother, Hunter, brought his ex-wife home with him for the holidays. Only, she didn't know she was his ex-wife."

Pippa frowned with confusion and then laughed. "This has to be some sort of joke. Isn't it?"

He sipped his coffee. "Not at all. You see, Willow disappeared four years ago and even though she sent Hunter divorce papers in the mail, he never quit loving her. But after four years of never seeing or hearing from her, he'd given up on ever finding her. And then, while he was putting on a rodeo out at Red Bluff, California, he unexpectedly ran into her. She didn't recognize Hunter. She'd been suffering amnesia for four years and was going by the name of Anna Jones."

"Oh! That's unbelievable! So what happened? Did you all tell her who she really was? Dear Lord, I can't imagine how that went over."

He placed his coffee cup back on the tabletop. "We didn't tell her anything. We just acted as though we'd never seen her before. See, our sister Grace, the doctor, advised Hunter it might send Willow into shock if we broke the news to her before she was mentally ready to deal with it. But, thankfully, it all turned out great. Being back on Stone Creek or perhaps seeing all of us, caused something to click in her. Anyway, her memory all came flooding back on its own."

"So what happened with her and Hunter? Are they still divorced? Was she angry at him and the rest of you for keeping the truth from her?"

He smiled at the memory of Hunter and Willow wrapped in a loving embrace. Yes, they'd had their troubles, but now those were all in the past. "She wasn't angry. She was thrilled to finally be home again. And her and Hunter have already remarried."

"Oh, a happy ending. How nice," she said. "Apparently she must have still been in love with Hunter even when she'd gotten the divorce."

"She was," Flint replied. "It's a long story. I'll tell you about it later. Right now, let's concentrate on today. Do you need to do any shopping or see a friend while you're here in town? I have some things to do—personal things—so I thought I'd drop you off while I tend to them. That is, if you don't mind."

She drummed her fingers against the tabletop. "No shopping. I mean I should go to the grocery store, I suppose."

"I'll go there with you. Before we head home," he said quickly. "Anything else you'd like to do?"

She let out a sly chuckle. "Flint, I actually think you're wanting to get rid of me."

"I am," he admitted. "But only for a few minutes. I promise."

"I'm teasing. Take all the time you need. My word, after all you've been through with me this past week, you deserve lots of minutes for yourself."

He started to say how much he'd enjoyed being with her since he'd come to the Bell, but the arrival of their meals interrupted him.

The waitress, who was different from the one who'd served their coffee, was carrying a tray loaded with their plates. She took one look at Pippa and let out a squeal.

"Pip! Where have you been? It's been ages since you've been in here! I was beginning to get worried about you," the tall blonde said as she placed the loaded plates of food onto the table. "Did you have a good Christmas? I mean as good as you could without Debra."

Pippa said, "To be honest, Haley, I've been sick for a few days, but I'm all good now."

"Glad to hear it. The flu has been nasty here in town. Four of our waitresses had it. Thankfully, not all at the same time." She placed wrapped silverware next to both plates before she cast a second curious look at Flint. "Aren't you going to introduce me to your friend?"

"I'm sorry, Haley. This is Flint Hollister. He's been staying out at the Bell. He's—uh, a relative of Debra's. And, Flint, this is Haley Lancaster. We've known each other since high school."

Haley turned a bright smile on him. "Nice to meet you, Flint. You must not live around Bonners Ferry. Pip hasn't mentioned you before."

"I'm from Utah," he said, purposely leaving off an explanation for his visit.

"Well, I hope you enjoy your stay," she told him. "And, Pip, don't be so much of a stranger around here. You know I enjoy hearing what's been happening on that ranch of yours."

"I'll try to make it back sooner," Pippa promised.

"Hey, Haley! Can we have some coffee over here?" a man called from a table across the room.

With a good-natured roll of her eyes, she refilled Flint and Pippa's cups. "I'll check on you two later," she said then hurried over to the table with the noisy coffee drinker.

Once she was out of earshot, Pippa said, "I hope you didn't mind me telling her you were a relative of Debra's."

He shook his head as he dipped his fork into a mound of mashed potatoes covered with brown gravy. "I didn't mind at all. I am related to her."

"Yes. But you've not known Debra was your aunt for very long and something like that takes time to digest."

"Trust me, Pippa, it's all fine. Now, back to my errands. I'll—"

"I have someone I'd like to see," she cut in. "If you could drop me by the library, that will suit me fine."

"Great," he said then pointed his fork toward her plate. "Eat up. This is delicious."

"I told you it would be."

As Flint watched an impish smile curve her pink lips, he decided she was right about the food. It was very good. But it was her company that was charming him and making him think things about himself that he'd never felt before. Like maybe being a deputy wasn't his true calling in life. And maybe being here in the Idaho mountains with her on a full-time basis wasn't such a farfetched notion.

Flint, you need to forget these foolish ideas about you and Pippa. You wouldn't be happy stuck on the Bell. And she wouldn't be happy anywhere else. So eat your lunch and think about your family back on Stone Creek. They need you.

But his family didn't really need him, Flint reflected as he fought off the mocking voice. Not like Pippa needed him. Or did she? Physically, she was getting stronger every day. But he wanted to think she might need his company, his kisses, as much as he was beginning to need hers.

Chapter Ten

The two of them took their time over the meal and once they departed the Blue Moose, Pippa suggested he drive a mile on down the highway to the animal clinic where she'd once worked.

"So this is where you met Debra and Yance." Flint peered out the windshield at a large cinder-block building painted white and trimmed with green. Several vehicles were parked in front of the building, while on the side, a few trucks pulling stock trailers were parked at odd angles. "Is this the vet you use for your livestock on the ranch?"

"Yes. But only when the problem is something I can't handle myself."

"What about vaccinating your cattle and sheep? Surely you get help for those jobs."

"The last time I vaccinated the cattle, a young guy who helps the Wilkersons from time to time came over to give me a hand. But in the middle of the job, he got an emergency call—something to do with his parents—and had to leave abruptly. I finished the job alone."

Yes, Flint could believe she completed the arduous task alone. She appeared to be unafraid to tackle jobs that would send most people running for help. Yet he was beginning to see there was something she feared and that was to give her heart to someone. Or was it only Flint she feared? He wasn't yet ready to ask her that question.

As they drove to the library, Flint commented on the beauty of the town with its snowcapped-mountain views and the Kootenai River running through it.

"How did you end up here in Bonner's Ferry anyway?" he asked. "Were the foster homes you lived in always in this area?"

"Most of my childhood was spent around Coeur d'Alene. And then the last family I was with, the Morrisons, decided to move up here in order to follow my foster dad's job. I was just entering high school. Luckily they remained here until a couple of years ago."

"Do you keep in touch with them or any of your other temporary families?" he asked while trying to imagine how it would feel to uproot and change homes at the drop of a hat. Flint and his siblings had always enjoyed a loving, stable home. Without the solid foundation his parents had given him, he figured his life would be far different than what it was now.

"I keep in touch with the Morrisons. They live down by Pocatello now. And another family, the Parkers. They moved to Boise some years ago and operate a tire shop there. I lived with them and their two biological children during my junior high school years." She pointed to a one-story, red-brick building surrounded by tall fir trees. "There's The Book Shelf. The parking area is to the left."

"You been coming here for a long time?" he asked as he wheeled the truck into a small graveled parking lot.

"Since I was a teenager," she answered. "Because the business is privately funded, the person in charge has made the place like a combination library/bookstore. So you can either buy a book or just check one out."

He parked the truck in a spot where most of the snow had been pushed to one side. So far today, the sun had continued to shine, but the temperature was still too cold to allow the mounds of ice and snow to melt. As for the green fir trees, the wind had blown most of the heavy white weight from their limbs.

"If you wouldn't mind too much, I'd love for you to come in and meet Greer," she said as she unbuckled her seat belt and shouldered the strap of her purse.

"Sure. I'd like to meet your friend," he said then asked, "How did you two become friends?"

She chuckled. "I read a lot. At least, I used to. Now that I'm working the ranch alone, I don't have as much time for reading. And when I do have time, I usually fall asleep. Anyway, over time, Greer and I began chatting about books and our friendship eventually grew. Now she's one of the closest friends I have."

He switched off the motor and unfastened his seat belt. "In that case, I'd like to meet her."

Once inside the building, they passed through a short foyer and into a large open room. The walls were lined with shelves of books, while several rows of tall shelves filled with more books took up the center of the room. To one side, a long couch was joined by three round tables and folding padded chairs. Presently, an older man and woman were seated at one of the tables. Neither looked up from the books they were reading as Flint and Pippa made their way toward a wide desk situated on the opposite side of the room.

A blond woman, somewhere in her mid-thirties and

wearing a heavy white sweater, was seated behind the desk. Her focus was on a monitor until she spotted their approach and quickly stood. When she recognized Pippa, she skirted the piece of furniture and gathered her into a tight hug.

"Pip! It's so great to see you! Where have you been? Have you been snowbound on the ranch?" Before Pippa had time to answer, she stepped back and took a long survey of her friend.

"We've not been snowbound," Pippa told her then gestured toward Flint. "Greer, I'd like for you to meet Flint Hollister. He's currently staying on the Bell with me."

Greer quickly introduced herself. "Hello, I'm Greer Reynolds."

Flint extended a hand to her. "Nice to meet you, Greer."

"Flint drove up from Utah." Pippa quickly spoke up. "He's Debra's nephew—through her mother's side of the family. He—uh—hadn't heard about her passing."

The woman's expression suddenly took on a mixture of dismay and suspicion. "How terrible! You traveled all the way up here, not knowing she'd died?"

Flint realized the situation sounded dubious, but he wasn't going to try to explain the convoluted family dynamics or the reason for his trip to Idaho.

"Unfortunately, yes," he said. "But my journey hasn't been in vain. Pippa fell ill not long after I arrived. So I'm glad I've been around to help her through the worst of it."

Frowning with concern, she looked at Pippa. "You've been sick? Why didn't you call and let me know? I would've gone out to the ranch and taken care of you."

"The morning Flint took me to the clinic, I was going to call you, but he insisted he could see after me. And, frankly, I didn't want to put you out," Pippa explained to her friend.

"You would've had to find someone to take your place here at the library. Besides, the road out to the Bell is still barely passable. Even in Flint's truck."

The librarian cast a calculating glance at Flint before she turned her attention back to Pippa. "I understand. And I would've been useless at looking after your livestock. Whereas, Mr. Hollister probably knows about cows and sheep and all those ranching things."

Pippa leveled a pointed smile at him. "Flint does know all about ranching. He lives on a big family-owned cattle and sheep spread down in Beaver County, Utah. He's also a deputy sheriff. So he wears dual hats."

Flint self-consciously tugged at the brim of his black Stetson. "I have a little experience in both fields," he said then, touching a hand to Pippa's shoulder, added, "I'd better go get my errands taken care of. I'll pick you up in a little while."

"Fine," she told him. "Take as much time as you need."

With raised eyebrows, Greer watched Flint exit the room before she turned on Pippa. "What is going on, Pippa? Who is that man, really?"

Pippa kept her chuckle quietly under her breath so as not to disturb the couple sitting at the table. "He's exactly who I told you. He really is Debra's nephew. Actually, you might say he's her half nephew. His father and Debra are half siblings."

Greer glanced over at the man and woman, who appeared to be oblivious to anything but the books in front of them. "Let's go back to the break room where we can talk. I can keep an eye on the front from there."

Behind Greer's desk was an open doorway leading into

a small room furnished with a portable card table, two folding chairs and a cabinet equipped with a coffee machine, a microwave and a minifridge.

"Want some coffee or a snack?" Greer asked.

"No thanks. Flint took me to the Blue Moose for lunch and I'm stuffed."

Pippa eased into one of the chairs, while Greer took a seat then adjusted her chair in order for her to have a view of the outer room.

"Okay, now that we can talk, tell me everything," she said. "You say Flint Hollister is related to Debra. Are you certain about that? He could be a phony."

Holding her laughter down to a quiet chuckle, she said, "Does Flint look like a phony?"

Greer rolled her eyes. "We're in a building full of books. And you know the old saying—the cover doesn't exactly tell you what's inside."

Her smile indulgent, Pippa said, "I can assure you Flint is genuine. Debra's mother is his grandmother—who was married twice. First to Flint's grandfather then later to Debra's father. The Hollisters have been working on their family tree and only recently learned that Debra and Taylor existed. It's a long story and not yet completed. So I've been helping him search for information regarding his relatives."

"Hmm. I'll take your word for it, but what is he doing staying out at the Bell? You've been out there all alone? With him?"

Pippa could hardly hold back a laugh. "Well, yes. Why? Do you think he's dangerous?"

Greer's mouth dropped to comical proportions. "Dangerous? Are you kidding? That's hardly the word for the man! He's drop-dead sexy!"

"My oh my, Greer. I've never heard you talk this way about a man before."

Greer's demeanor suddenly turned sheepish. "I've never seen a man like him before. And certainly not with you. Honestly, it's been years since I've encountered a man anywhere close to his caliber. Is he married or engaged?"

"No. He's not even seriously involved with a woman," Pippa told her. "He got burned pretty badly a while back and I think he's kind of given up on relationships since then."

Her eyes narrowed as she carefully studied Pippa. "And what do you think?"

"About Flint being single?"

Her friend nodded and Pippa tried not to frown or appear hopeless. She didn't want Greer to guess that she was falling for her sexy visitor. She didn't want the woman to know she was naïve enough to hope and wish Flint could actually begin to care for her in a serious way.

Pippa answered, "Oh, I think he'll eventually find the right woman to settle down with. Someone who fits in his world."

"Hmm. You think so? I didn't get that sort of impression from him. But five minutes is hardly enough time to judge a person's character," Greer commented then added, "So what's so different about his world?"

"Well, it's in Utah, for one thing. And, also, he comes from money. To be honest, when he first arrived, I was a little embarrassed for him to see how things had become run-down on the Bell. And it's been ages since I've purchased myself any new clothes. But he hasn't said anything derogatory about me or the ranch. In fact, he's been working very hard taking care of me and the livestock without any help. I honestly don't know what I would have done without him. It's like he was an angel who showed up at just the right time."

Greer leaned back in her chair and gave Pippa a long, calculating look. "You're definitely pale and you're some-what thinner than when I last saw you, but those things aren't concerning me now. You're falling for this guy. I can hear it in your voice—see it in your eyes."

"You're not seeing anything. Except for gratitude and, well—appreciation, I guess. It's been so nice to have his company." Frowning, she leaned across the table toward Greer. "And before you start preaching to me, I understand perfectly well that Flint will be leaving soon. So don't start worrying that I'm getting permanently attached to him. It's impossible."

"Really? Can a woman actually stop herself from get-ting permanently attached to a man? I wished I'd known that trick before I'd ever met Chad. It would've saved me from making the mistake of marrying a freeloader, among other things," she added with a hefty amount of sarcasm.

Pippa sighed. "I'm not the type of woman to be bedaz-zled over a man's charms," she said flatly. "Dale walking out on me taught me to follow my head not my heart."

"Is it really so easy, Pip?" Greer asked then, rising from her chair, she moved to the cabinet and poured coffee into a foam cup. "After I divorced Chad, I thought it would be a cinch to avoid men. To shut myself off and play things safe. But it hasn't been so simple or painless. I look at my-self and keep thinking my life is swiftly ticking by—and I always thought I'd have children by now and a husband who actually loved me. I don't know about you, Pip, but it hurts me to be alone."

There had been times since Debra died that Pippa had been intensely lonely, but she'd focused on her work and talked to the animals just to reassure herself she hadn't lost the ability to carry on a conversation.

"It's not always pleasant," Pippa admitted. "You know how it is with me. Sometimes I go for a couple of weeks without seeing another human being. But I can deal with that sort of isolation much better than I can deal with having my dreams crushed. Of a man brushing me aside as though I mean nothing."

Greer nodded solemnly. "Well, foolish or not, I still want to think that one of these days I'll run across a good man who'll take a second look at me."

Even though the room was warm, Pippa felt a cool draft pass over her. Flint had kissed her with an urgency that made her want to dream and hope of a future with him. But a man couldn't be measured by his kisses, she thought.

"I hope you find him, Greer. You deserve to be happy."

"And you don't?" Shaking her head, she carried her cup over to the table and returned to her seat. "Look, Pip, I'd like to tell you to grab on to Flint Hollister and don't let go. But, like I said, he's dangerous. He's the kind of man you'd have a hell of a time forgetting."

Pippa had already reached that conclusion. Now she could only wonder how much longer it would be before he said goodbye and the forgetting process started.

River Valley Ranch Supply was located on the far edge of town, within view of the meandering Kootenai. From all appearances, the business had been open for far more years than Flint had been alive. The front of the large rambling structure was built of corrugated iron and painted a rusty-red color. Huge storage barns of the same color were connected to each side of the building. Both had double doors opened far enough for Flint to get a glimpse of stacked hay and feed sacks.

Presently, the wide, graveled parking lot was filled with trucks and trailers, some of which were being loaded down with feed and bales of hay. Pippa had told him this was where she purchased supplies for the Bell whenever they were needed and Flint had decided two days ago that it was past time her barn was stocked with needed items. He just hadn't told her his plans. Undoubtedly, she'd have a fit about him taking matters into his own hands—and paying for them out of his own wallet—but once the supplies were delivered to the Bell, there wouldn't be much she could do about it, except yell at him. And he could deal with her yelling. It was those kisses of hers that turned his insides to helpless mush.

A cowbell jangled over the door as he entered the supply store, causing several heads to glance in his direction. A few customers were waiting their turn at the counter, while the clerk taking orders was busy entering information into a computer.

Seeing it would be a few minutes before his turn would arrive, Flint ambled through the aisles of riding tack, horse blankets, liniment and endless bottles of equine hair care products. At the far end, he picked up an iron horseshoe and recalled how as a boy he'd go with his father to buy things they needed on the ranch. Along with being a great dad, Hadley had been a stickler when it came to teaching his sons and daughters about each little thing that was needed and used on the ranch. Whether that be a horseshoe nail or the type of oil to use in a chain saw. Odd, how those lessons had stuck with Flint. Even now, when most of his days back in Utah were spent patrolling the county.

Glancing up he saw the last customer leave the counter and he quickly walked over to give the man his order.

"Sorry you had to wait so long," the clerk said to him. "Can I help you find something?"

Somewhere in his late fifties, the man was tall, with wire-framed glasses and an extremely lean face. Although the interior of the store was heated, he was wearing a heavy denim jacket and a sock cap pulled over his ears.

"I need feed and hay delivered out to the Bell Ranch."

The man hesitated as he gave Flint a closer inspection. "Uh—yes. We can deliver. But—Ms. Shanahan usually hauls whatever she buys with her own truck. Saves the delivery cost."

Flint couldn't imagine Pippa's rickety old truck making such an arduous trip from the Bell to town, especially loaded down with tons of supplies. But apparently Pippa risked the vehicle holding together just to save a few bucks.

"This order will be more than Ms. Shanahan's truck can manage," Flint explained. "So I want it delivered. And don't worry about the delivery cost. I'll be paying."

The salesclerk was doing his best not to look surprised as he positioned a small notepad on the counter in front of him and pulled a pen from his shirt pocket. "Okay, what do you need?" he asked.

"For starters, five ton of alfalfa hay. Do you have enough on hand to sell five ton to one customer?" Flint asked, thinking he'd better cover all the bases with this man.

"Yeah, I think so. It's just that..." Frowning, he looked up. "I don't think— Ms. Shanahan only purchases a half a ton at a time."

"She's not making this purchase. I am. I just told you I'd be paying," Flint said bluntly.

Flustered now, the man tapped the pen against the note-pad. "Uh—yeah, you told me. I just thought you meant paying for the delivery cost."

"I meant paying for everything."

The man must've decided Flint meant business because he quickly wrote down the order then looked up at Flint. "Okay. Was there anything else you wanted?"

"Yes. I need a ton of your best cattle pellets. A half ton of lamb grower, a half ton of your best horse feed and ten mineral blocks. Also, I want two hundred pounds of dry dog food and a hundred pounds of dry cat food. Make those the best you have," Flint told him then asked, "Do you sell molasses licks?"

The salesclerk continued to write the huge order, his eyes growing wider with each new addition. "We do," he said. "But we're out of stock. There should be some arriving in the next few days if you'd like to check back. We do have the molasses on hand, though."

"Okay, give me a tub of it. And I'll check back later for the lick. Thanks." Flint asked, "How soon can you have these things delivered to the ranch?"

"Early in the morning. Both of our delivery trucks are tied up for the remainder of the day. Some folks are still having trouble getting into town after the latest snow-storms." He moved over to the computer keyboard and began typing in Flint's order. "You from around here?"

"No. I'm from Utah. Beaver County."

"Oh. That's a fair distance from Bonners Ferry." He darted a curious glance at Flint as he continued to punch buttons on the keyboard. "It's none of my business, but did you buy out the Bell?"

It wasn't any of the man's business, but Flint understood his curiosity. Especially since Pippa was a regular customer. "No. What makes you ask?"

The man grimaced as he waited for the bill to emerge from the printer. "Well, I shouldn't talk, but most folks have heard that Ms. Shanahan is having trouble trying to run the Bell by herself."

Flint silently counted to ten and told himself he shouldn't take offense. People talked. Most of the time, they didn't mean any harm by it. And it wasn't like they were wrong—he'd been able to see for himself that Pippa was struggling to make ends meet. The only surprise was that anyone would think she'd sell out. Clearly, this clerk didn't really know her at all.

Releasing a heavy breath, Flint said, "It isn't running the ranch that's giving Pippa trouble. It's the high cost of feed and hay."

The man's face turned beet red before he let out an awkward cough. "We do the best we can to keep our prices manageable."

Flint said, "I'm sure you do. Just like Pippa is doing the best she can."

The salesclerk pushed the bill over the countertop to Flint. He glanced at the total amount before pulling a debit card from his wallet.

As Flint dealt with the electronic payment, the clerk asked, "Will there be someone at the Bell to help the driver unload? I'm not sure we'll have an extra hand to send on deliveries tomorrow."

"I'll be there," Flint assured him. "Thanks."

After folding the receipt and stuffing the paper in his pocket, he turned to go and nearly barreled into a stocky gray-haired man wearing a black cowboy hat and heavy brown coat.

"Oh, sorry. I wasn't looking," Flint apologized. "Did I step on your feet?"

The man chuckled. "Don't worry, you missed me," he said then asked, "Did I hear you mention Pippa?"

Flint's gaze remained on the stranger while he stepped to one side in order to clear the way to the customer counter. "You did. Do you know her?"

Smiling broadly, he said, "I was friends with Yance and Debra for years. And then I got to know Pippa when she went to work for them. My name is Clive Brayman. My place buts up to the north side of the Bell."

He extended his hand to Flint and he gave it a firm shake. "Glad to meet you, Clive. I'm Flint Hollister. I came up here from Utah expecting to see Debra, only to learn she'd died."

Clive's expression turned sad. "Yeah, her dying was a real shocker. She was as healthy as a horse and then suddenly she was gone. That kind of thing makes you want to stop everything and just appreciate breathing."

"It knocked me for a loop," Flint admitted. "Even though I'd never met her. My family just recently learned we were related to Debra and her sister. So that made her death even more shocking."

Clive nodded solemnly. "After she died, I offered several times to give Pippa a hand at the ranch. But she always refused. I finally quit offering. She's an independent little thing. And determined. I only hope she doesn't end up having to sell the place."

The man's comment caused Flint's eyes to narrow on the man's left hand. There was no wedding ring on his finger, but that hardly came as a surprise. He didn't have that husband vibe like Flint's brothers and married friends back in Utah.

"Why would you think she'd sell?" Flint asked.

He shrugged. "That's what a person normally ends up doing when they're backed in a corner. I'd offer her a loan, but I know she wouldn't accept it."

And Flint wouldn't want her to, he thought as jealousy streaked through him. Clive Brayman was a few years older than him and several older than Pippa. But when a woman fell in love, she often times seemed oblivious to a man's age. If Clive decided to make himself conveniently available to Pippa every time she turned around, feelings of gratitude could grow into something deeper and she might get interested in the man.

"That's generous of you, Mr. Brayman. But you're right. She wouldn't accept it. And I wouldn't be concerned, if I were you. Pippa is getting the ranch set up nicely for the remainder of the winter and, come this spring, she should have a productive calf crop."

Surprise flickered across the man's face. "Well, that's great to hear," he said then glanced around to see the customer counter was open. "I'd better get my business taken care of. Nice to meet you, Mr. Hollister. Tell Pippa if she needs me all she has to do is call."

Flint kept his response to a simple nod and quickly strode out of the feed store.

When Flint finally arrived back at the library, Pippa was curious as to why he'd been gone for so long but she didn't question him. And then when he helped her into the truck, she saw the reason. Several plastic sacks filled with groceries were piled on the back floorboard. She could smell bananas and freshly baked bread from the deli.

"You've been to the grocery store! Why did you go without me?" she asked.

He gave her a lopsided grin. "Because you would've tried to limit my buying. And you definitely would've steered me away from all the junk food."

She laughed softly. "I might have done that. Do you like junk food?"

"Of course. Doesn't everyone?"

"Well, I can't deny I love barbecue potato chips," she admitted with a guilty chuckle.

He laughed knowingly and as her gaze slipped over his sexy image she thought about her conversation with Greer. Her friend had been right. There was nothing easy about following her head instead of her heart when it came to how she felt about Flint. Even so, she was strong enough to be sensible. She had to be.

"Flint, I've been thinking about your grandmother and the information you need regarding your grandfather. I was going to mention this to you before, but then I got sick and everything was hazy for a while. But I believe I should call Taylor and ask if she has any idea about her mother's first husband. She hasn't lived near Scarlett in a long time, but she might remember something from years ago. Or have an idea to help us."

He glanced at her. "Do you think she'd mind? Or resent the idea of helping me?"

Pippa frowned thoughtfully. "I don't think she'd resent you at all. Debra wouldn't have, either. But don't worry, since you've never met her in person, I'm not going to put you in the awkward position of talking to her."

"Thanks, Pippa. For being so thoughtful."

The grateful smile he gave her was enough to melt her heart to a helpless puddle. "After all you've done for me? I can't possibly thank you enough."

He reached over and clasped her hand in his. "We're helping each other. Right?"

She smiled back at him. "Right."

Later that evening, after Flint had gone out to the barn to do the evening chores, Pippa sat down with her phone at the kitchen table and punched Taylor's number. Unless her schedule had recently changed, Taylor's office job at an insurance company normally ended at five in the evening and then she worked several more hours for a local animal rescue agency in Sheridan. Pippa hoped the woman had a few free minutes.

Thankfully, Taylor answered after the third ring and Pippa quickly asked if she could spare a few moments to talk.

"For you, Pip? Of course. I'm doing basic chores this evening. Cleaning cages and laundering cat and dog bedding. Having you to chat with me and keep me company sounds great actually."

"I'm glad I'm not interrupting something important," Pippa told her. "I should've waited until later tonight to call, but I have something important on my mind."

"Good thing you didn't wait. By the time I get home, I usually fall right into bed. And I'm so glad to hear from you. How is everything in Idaho?"

The sound of her cheerful voice put a smile on Pippa's

face. "Cold and snowy. I've been under the weather a bit, but I'm feeling much better now. What about you?"

She chuckled. "Don't think you have a corner on the cold and snow. The weather has been brutal here. But everything is fine with me and the twins. I've been meaning to call to check on you, but something is always taking up my time. Are you sure you're okay?"

The concern in her voice was obvious. "I'm perfectly okay, Taylor. Don't worry."

She sighed. "Sorry, Pip. I just can't help it. Even though I know I'm driving the twins crazy, I'm constantly checking on them to make sure they're safe and well. But after Deb died so unexpectedly, every little thing puts me on edge. She was so vibrant and full of life and then suddenly she was gone. And Mom—well, we lost the mother we knew years ago. It's like my family is dwindling away. That's why I want you to take care of yourself, Pip. You're family to me. You realize that, don't you?"

Pippa swallowed at the sudden lump in her throat. She'd met Taylor and her daughters, Lilly and Rose, shortly after she'd come to live and work for the O'Sheas. Pippa had felt an immediate kinship to Taylor and the twins and throughout the following years, she'd looked forward to their limited visits to the Bell.

"Sure, I do. And speaking of family, I—uh, have something to tell you. And it's going to be a surprise."

There was a pause and then Taylor let out a squeal of delight. "Let me guess! You're getting married?"

Pippa glanced around the kitchen where, less than an hour ago, she and Flint had worked together to put away the groceries he'd purchased in town. For a moment, the shared task had almost made it feel like the two of them were a married couple. But just as quickly she'd reminded herself it was all temporary. Soon the two of them wouldn't be sharing anything other than an occasional phone call, perhaps.

"You're way off base, Taye. I'm married to the Bell. You should know that."

Taylor sighed. "Yes, I do. But I also know that livestock and a piece of land can't keep you warm at night."

Oh yes, she'd be more than warm in Flint's arms. But for how long? Two or three nights? A week at the most? No, that would only make things harder when he did drive away from the ranch.

"That's what electric blankets are for," she told her.

Taylor let out a good-natured groan. "Okay. So your surprise isn't a man. Then what is it? Something to do with the ranch?"

"Actually the surprise is a man. But not in the way you're thinking. I've had a visitor for the past few days. He initially drove up here from Utah to meet with Debra."

"Meet with Deb? I wasn't aware my sister was acquainted with anyone from Utah. Who is this man?"

There wasn't any way to say it gently, Pippa decided. And maybe gentleness wasn't what Taylor needed when it came to hearing she had more family. A family that Pippa believed would enrich Taylor and her daughters' lives.

She breathed deeply then blurted, "His name is Flint Hollister. His father, Hadley, is your half-brother."

"What?"

The one word was a blast in Pippa's ear. "Yes, you heard me say 'half-brother.' Your mother had three boys during her first marriage. Judging by the shock in your voice, you didn't know about them. And since Debra never mentioned anything of the sort to me, I'm assuming she was in the dark about this, also."

"Three boys! No! Mom never mentioned other children! This can't be right, Pip. She wouldn't have kept her own children a secret."

"When you hear the whole story, I think you'll believe it, Taye. Can you recall Scarlett saying anything about her life before she married Ode?"

Pippa's question was met with a long stretch of silence and she understood the woman was trying to collect herself.

After a moment, she said, "Only that she was working as a waitress when she met Dad. As for her first marriage, she simply didn't talk about that time of her life. I only recall her saying they lived in a rural area and that she often felt alone."

"Was the rural area in Utah?" Pippa asked.

"She mentioned living there as a child. But Deb and I just assumed she and her first husband had resided in southern Idaho. We didn't press her with questions about the past. Even as kids we could see it upset her."

"You and Debra must have been curious about your mother's young life," Pippa replied.

"Well yes, we were curious. Debra and I talked among ourselves and we wondered about her childhood. She sometimes talked about being a little girl and some of the pets she'd had. But she always seemed reluctant to tell us about her life after she grew up and met her first husband. She never discussed her marriage or what might have happened. She'd clam up if we asked, so we quit asking. But we sometimes wondered if she might've had kids. But we both decided that was just our imaginations running wild. After all, if she had other kids, they'd be with her—with us—right?"

Pippa could hear the disbelief in Taylor's voice and she regretted the fact that she was causing the woman such angst. But from what Flint had told her, Hadley had already made plans to make himself known to Debra and Taylor. So maybe it was best that she got over the initial shock now. Taylor would likely take it better coming from someone she knew rather than from a man who—despite their blood connection—was a total stranger.

"Taylor, I'm sorry I've caused you such a shock. There just didn't seem to be any other way of telling you."

"But who are these Hollisters? Why are they just now surfacing in our lives?"

Pippa took a deep breath and quickly explained how the situation had come about. "So you see, Flint came up here believing Debra might help him find information about his grandfather—your mom's first husband. Yesterday we went through most of Debra's old papers she had stored in the attic. We were hoping there might accidently be something written on an old document that belonged to your mother. But so far we've not found anything helpful."

There was a long stretch of silence and Pippa wondered if Taylor resented the idea of her helping Flint dig into Scarlett's past. But surely she'd want the truth of the matter to be revealed. Especially if it would help put her mother's image in a better light for her other family.

"This is so incredible, Pippa." She finally spoke. "Are you sure about this man who's staying on the ranch with you? Maybe all of this is just a sham."

"For what purpose, Taye? Scarlett doesn't have any assets or money to speak of. And trust me, the Hollisters don't need it. They're very wealthy."

"How do you know that? Just because Flint Hollister told you so?"

"Flint didn't tell me he was wealthy. He didn't have to. This morning I was at the library and while I was there, just out of curiosity, I used one of the computers to look up the Stone Creek Ranch website. There are photos and a bit of information about the family. The ranch is a beautiful, massive spread that's been in existence for over sixty years. Besides, Flint works as a deputy sheriff for Beaver County, Utah. He's hardly in a position to lie."

"Oh. Well, I'm sorry I'm being so suspicious and skeptical. It's just that—"

"I understand. It's a shock. But really, Taye, you should be happy. You have more family now and I'm betting they'll be happy to meet you."

"I'm not so sure. But we'll see," she said. "And as far as knowing anything about Mom's first husband, that's a blank for me. Other than I heard her mention the name Lionel. I didn't know who she was talking about and she said that was her ex's name. I remember because I thought it was an unusual name."

Pippa rose from her chair at the kitchen table and walked over to the window above the sink. The sun was beginning to slant long shadows across the trail to the barn. It would most likely be dark before Flint returned to the house. He was a stickler for making sure each and every animal was healthy and fed and the barn itself was in order. He might spend the majority of his time working as a deputy sheriff, she thought, but he was clearly a rancher at heart.

"Flint is going to be disappointed," Pippa told her. "But I'm not ready to give up yet. We still might find something among Debra's old papers."

There was a pause and then Taylor said, "Actually, Pippa, an idea just came to me. Mom has a safety-deposit box in the bank at Coeur d'Alene. I have no idea what's in it, but Deb told me that Mom insisted she put some of her important papers and things in there for safekeeping. Poor thing, I doubt they would mean anything to Mom now."

Taylor's suggestion gave Pippa a glimmer of hope. "Oh, that's an idea, Taylor. But I'd have to have a key. And even if Debra had one, wouldn't you or Scarlett be the only ones who could get access to the box?"

"When Mom moved to Coeur d'Alene, Debra became her conservator. When Debra died, her will and testament requested that you to be appointed her executor, right?"

"Yes. I think she more or less did that because you lived so far away and she knew I'd be here on the ranch."

"Oh, come on, Pippa, she willed you the place and appointed you executor of her estate because you were like a daughter to her. And, frankly, I'm very glad she did. So are the twins. You deserve everything and more that Debra left you. But anyway, if you can find the key, then as her executor you should have the right to collect the contents of the box."

"You could be right. At least, it would be worth a try. After all, there could be things in the box that you and the twins might eventually need or want. If I can find the key. You have any suggestions as to where it might be?"

"No. Knowing Deb, it was probably thrown in with the extra tractor or truck keys. I'm sure you'll find it somewhere," she said.

"I'll start looking right now. Thanks, Taye. You've been a big help. And I'm sorry if I've upset you with all of this."

"You haven't upset me. I'm a little dazed and you've

given me a lot to think about. Which is probably something I needed right now. These past few years Debra and I didn't get to spend much time together. Not as much as we both wanted. Her death has really affected me in ways I never expected. I'm wondering...well, I don't want to get into my troubles. However, before you hang up, I'd like to hear a bit more about Flint Hollister."

Pippa frowned. "You're still worried he might be a scam artist?"

"No. You've convinced me, he's the real deal. But I'll be honest, I'm a bit surprised you're going to all this trouble to help the man. When he first showed up at the ranch, you obviously didn't know him."

"No. But it didn't take long to get to know him," Pippa told her while thinking back to that first morning when Flint had walked up and introduced himself. Just looking at him had addled her senses and she wasn't sure she'd ever gotten them back completely. "To give you a quick rundown, he's thirty-one. Nice-looking. Rugged and masculine. When he's not working as a deputy, he works on the ranch helping his dad and brothers. Actually, since I've been sick, he's taken care of my livestock and—other things here on the Bell."

"Well, that's a mark in his favor," she said thoughtfully. "Does he have a wife and kids of his own?"

Pippa momentarily closed her eyes. She didn't want to discuss Flint's marital status. It only reminded her of the huge chasm between them. "No. He's never been married."

"Oh."

Taylor's insinuation with that one-word reply was enough to burn Pippa's cheeks. "He doesn't want one, either. So don't start speculating."

"Well, I can hope, can't I? You need a man in your life, Pip. You were made to be a wife and mother."

"So were you," Pippa countered.

Taylor groaned. "I had my try at love and marriage. It didn't work. It's your turn."

"My turn will come," Pippa told her. "When someone suited to me happens by."

But who could possibly be better suited, she asked herself, when everything about Flint felt so right for her? Except that he was totally out of her league. Not to mention out of her state.

"Okay, Pippa, I won't dig into your private life. We'll talk later," Taylor replied. "Let me know if you find anything interesting in the safety-deposit box."

Pippa promised she would then ended the call and headed to Debra's old bedroom to look for the key that could possibly unlock some of the mystery to Scarlett's first marriage. And perhaps send Flint home to Utah sooner than she wanted. But she couldn't dwell on that dismal thought. More than anything, she wanted to help him and make him happy. If that meant she was falling for him, then she'd deal with that problem later.

Chapter Eleven

Flint was late coming back from the barn and he half expected to find Pippa in the kitchen putting something together for their evening meal. When he didn't find her there, he walked out to the living room. A fire was burning in the fireplace, but she was nowhere around.

Worried that she'd physically overdone things to the point where she'd had to lie down, he started toward her bedroom, only to have her call out to him.

"Flint, I'm in here. In your room."

Turning on his heel, he crossed the hallway and peered into the open doorway to see her going through the small drawers of a rolltop desk.

"What are you doing?" he asked. "I thought you'd probably laid down to rest."

Rising from the wooden chair, she quickly walked over to him and reached for his hands. "Come help me. I'm hunting for a key. To Scarlett's safety-deposit box."

He stared at her in wonder. "Scarlett's? Where is the box? And how did you find out about it?"

"I called Taylor and told her all about you and your family trying to finish your Hollister family tree."

"And what did she think about learning she had 'other' relatives?"

"She was stunned, naturally. But before we ended the call, she was coming around to the idea. I think it's too soon for her to know exactly how she feels about learning she has three half-brothers."

"Did you ask her if she knew anything about Lionel?"

"I did. She recalled hearing her mother say his name, but that's about all. She said Scarlett was always closed-mouthed about her early life. But she did bring up the safety-deposit box. It's in a bank in Coeur d'Alene. She said her mother wanted Debra to put her important things in safekeeping. Who knows what might be in it, Flint! Maybe the information you need!"

She squeezed his hands and suddenly he forgot all about his grandparents and even the reason why he'd come to Idaho in the first place. All he could think was that her hands were warm and her eyes were trusting and her lips looked so soft and delicious. What would she think if he told her he wanted to make love to her? Would she tell him to leave the ranch? Tell him she wasn't into casual affairs?

Hell, Flint, you already know that much about Pippa. With her, it's all about love and family. Not hot sex and then a quick goodbye.

"Flint, what's wrong? Why are you looking at me that way?"

Clearing his throat, he asked, "How am I looking at you?"

She frowned faintly. "I don't know. Like you're upset, I guess. Is anything wrong?"

"No. Nothing is wrong," he answered quickly then gave her hands a reassuring squeeze. "I was only wondering how you'd get access to the deposit box. Now that Debra is dead and Scarlett is suffering from dementia, who's in charge of it?"

"Technically, I believe I am. Once Scarlett was diagnosed, Debra was made her executor. Then in Debra's will she made me conservator. I have a document proving everything has been turned over to me, so I shouldn't have any trouble accessing the box."

Thankfully, the sudden fierce urge to sweep her into his arms and make love to her had cooled somewhat. At least enough for his brain to digest what she'd been saying about the deposit box.

"Okay. Then we definitely need to find the key," he said.

With her hands still on his, she pulled him over to the desk. "Come on and help me. I've gone through several drawers, but not all of them."

He shot her a wry glance. "Aren't we going to eat first?"

His question caused her to laugh with disbelief. "Are you kidding? The key is more important. We'll eat later."

Flint didn't argue with her. He figured the best thing to do was find the key as fast as possible.

For the next half hour, they searched through the many small drawers located on the antique rolltop desk, but so far the only keys that were found belonged to the truck and a generator that had gone on the blink more than a year ago.

"This is not looking promising," Flint suggested as he closed a drawer on the desk and straightened to his full height. "Maybe Debra didn't put the key in this desk. Could be she placed it in a jewelry box or something of that sort."

His comment caused Pippa to suddenly snap her fingers. "Good thinking, Flint. Deb kept a little cedar chest full of odds and ends. I'll get it from the closet."

Flint watched as she pulled a small box from a shelf in

the closet and carried it over to the bed. "She never was one to wear much jewelry. And I think the only real piece of jewelry she owned was her gold wedding band and she was buried wearing it. But she had a few costume things that she wore on special occasions like Christmas and her and Yance's wedding anniversary."

After placing the small cedar chest on the edge of the mattress, she lifted the lid and began to sift through the costume jewelry. Flint stood next to her and tried to ignore the scent of her skin and hair, the warmth emanating from her body.

"A string of faux pearls. Glass beads. Gold hoop earrings. Oh, this little reindeer Christmas pin is adorable!" she exclaimed then looked at him and grinned. "Sorry, Flint, I'm getting sidetracked, aren't I?"

"Only a little," he said with a grin. "Actually, I'm surprised you're interested in these things. Today is the first day I've seen you wear any jewelry."

She looked over at him as she absently touched a finger to one of her earrings. "Even though I'm a ranch woman, I like girly things. But I usually wait to wear them when the occasion warrants. I'm like Deb. I only have a few pieces of costume things. Except for the earrings I'm wearing. These were a gift from Greer on my birthday. I scolded her for splurging on real silver and turquoise."

As Flint watched her return to digging through the items in the chest, he thought about how much pleasure he'd get out of showering her with clothing and jewelry, or anything else her heart desired. Strange that he'd never felt such a need to gift things to a woman until he'd met Pippa. Not that he was a stingy man. He was always giving to charities and buying gifts for friends and relatives. But with Pippa the idea of giving took on an even deeper meaning.

Her sudden gasp broke into his thoughts and he looked over to see her holding up a small cloth pouch with a drawstring at the top.

"Oh, oh! Flint, I think this might be it! I feel a key inside!"

She hurriedly fumbled with the ends of the drawstring until she managed to open the pouch. A wide grin spread across her face as she pulled out a key with a small square of paper taped to it.

"Is that a note?" Flint asked.

She carefully peeled the paper away and read, "'Big Lodge Bank and Trust. Mom's box.'" Looking up, she gave him a joyous smile. "This is it, Flint! And you know what I'm thinking? I have the feeling this is going to give you what you're looking for."

He might've come up here looking for his grandfather's birthdate, but along the way he'd found much more. A woman who'd opened his eyes and enabled him to see life in ways he'd never seen it before. A woman he wanted more than he thought he could ever want anything.

Stepping forward, he slipped his hands around her waist and pulled her to him. "I think we need to celebrate—with a kiss," he murmured.

Her hands flattened against the middle of his chest as her head tilted back in order to peer up at him. "There are other ways of celebrating."

"Probably. But they couldn't be nicer than this."

He lowered his head and relief rushed through him when she didn't turn her face aside. Instead, she angled her lips to meet his. The soft sweetness of her mouth was exactly as he remembered and it was all he could do to keep from pressing her body to his and deepening the kiss. Yet even with her lips warm and giving on his, something told him she wasn't ready to make love to him.

The thought was enough to give him the strength of will to lift his head. Her eyelids fluttered open and the tip of her tongue came out to moisten the center of her bottom lip.

"That was—uh—an especially nice celebration," she said.

Her voice was barely above a whisper and the raspy tone sent delicious shivers down his spine. For one second, he considered lowering his head and kissing her again. But one more kiss would lead to another and another. And for now, Flint decided there were too many unanswered questions between them to carry their relationship to a deeper level.

He gently brushed his fingertips against her cheekbone. "I'd like very much to repeat it," he said huskily. "But I think we both need to take a deep breath."

Her brows arched in question. "You do?"

His grin was wry. "Okay. I admit a moment ago I wasn't being very cautious. But for both our sakes, I'm trying to be levelheaded now. Besides, I have another sort of celebration in mind that I want to discuss with you."

She smiled faintly. "More celebration? Flint, we only found a key."

"Yes. But you have a good feeling about what it might expose. Besides, you deserve a little festivity for getting your health back." He curved a hand around the back of her arm and urged her out of the bedroom. "Come on, I'm starving. Let's go to the kitchen and I'll tell you my plan over sandwiches."

A few minutes later, they were sitting at the table eating salami-and-cheese sandwiches with potato chips on the side. Outside the window, the wind was whistling and

Pippa could just make out the branches of a red cedar being tossed about.

"The wind is getting stronger," she said. "I hope it's not bringing more snow with it. Not with us needing to travel to Coeur d'Alene tomorrow."

He looked over at her. "I haven't checked the weather. But no matter about the snow. I wasn't planning on heading down to Coeur d'Alene tomorrow."

Surprised, Pippa stared at him. "You're not? But I thought you were in a hurry to look at Scarlett's documents? Aren't you excited to think you might get the information your family needs?"

Glancing away from her, he shrugged one shoulder. "Sure, I'm excited about the safety-deposit box. There's a possibility we might find my grandparents' divorce papers. Or, wonder of wonder, their marriage license. On the other hand, we might uncover nothing more than a few documents pertaining to her and Ode. Either way, I'm content to wait another day to make the trip. That will be Friday, so the bank should be open. Tomorrow I have—some other things I want to tend to."

He continued to avoid looking in her direction and she wondered what could possibly be going on with him. Had he started to regret that kiss he'd given her in the bedroom? Was he worried about being cooped up in the truck with her for the two-hour trip to Coeur d'Alene? Did he fear she might make an embarrassing pass at him?

Pippa, you're being silly. You're alone with Flint here on the ranch around the clock. You don't need to take a trip to make a pass at him.

Frowning, she shut out the mocking going on in her head and asked, "Other things? What could be more important?"

"There're some things at the barn that I've been working on. I'd like to get them done before we take off."

He was being evasive and she couldn't begin to guess why. "What kind of things? I realize there are boards and tin that need to be nailed down better and the water float in Ruby's stall doesn't always work right, and the gate in the sheep paddock is sagging, but those aren't urgent."

He looked at her and smiled. "Don't worry about fixing those things or anything else at the barn. And don't worry about our trip to Coeur d'Alene. We'll go Friday."

Why should she argue the point? she thought. Putting off the trip would give her one more day with the man. And in the end, that's what she wanted most. More time with him. More time to soak in the pleasure she received from his company.

Shrugging, she reached for her water glass. "Okay. That's fine with me."

"Good. Now that we have that settled, I wanted to discuss tomorrow night with you," he said.

Her gaze darted back to him. "Tomorrow night? What are you talking about?"

"Remember? I said I wanted for us to celebrate. Well, I wasn't just saying that. I want to take you to Bonners Ferry for a nice dinner with wine and scrumptious food where you won't have to lift anything more than a glass and utensils."

Ever since that kiss he'd given her in the bedroom, he'd continued to confuse and mystify her. But this invitation to dinner was downright shocking.

"Flint, you're being very nice to offer, but such a dinner is—totally unnecessary. Just because I came up with a safety-deposit box key doesn't mean I deserve to be wined and dined."

His eyelids lowered as his gaze slowly perused her face. "Well, first of all, you absolutely do deserve to be wined and dined. As a thank-you or a celebration—or just because you're wonderful and deserve to have nice things. But anyway, this invitation isn't just about the key. You know, you've been a very gracious hostess and encouraged me to make myself at home here on the Bell. That in itself means a lot to me, Pippa."

A spot between her breasts winced with longing and a sense of loss. She could feel their time together winding down. She knew that he'd head back to Utah soon after they searched his grandmother's deposit box. The knowledge burned her throat with tears and yet she fiercely told herself it would be wrong for her to cry. Just having the chance to be near him for this length of time had been an unexpected gift. And she had to be grateful for that much.

"Well, it's meant a lot to me that you've been here to help me through a bad stretch. I won't forget it, Flint. Ever."

He gave her a quick grin. "Then we both have a right to enjoy an evening out, don't you think?"

She couldn't look at his handsome smiling face without feeling her spirits soar and she instinctively smiled back at him. "Yes. I do. So I'll try to find something in my closet to wear. Other than jeans and a flannel shirt," she joked.

"I'm not a bit worried. I'm confident you'll look beautiful."

Beautiful. There would come a time when she would remember back to this night and hearing Flint call her beautiful. And she'd cherish the memory.

Because Pippa seemed to be completely over her virus, the next morning Flint couldn't think of one excuse to keep her in the house while he went to feed the livestock. Especially when he knew how eager she'd been to get back outside and see for herself how the cattle and sheep were faring. But how was she going to react when the semitruck and trailer from River Valley Ranch Supply drove up to the barn? Surely, she wouldn't tell the driver to take it all back. Not after he'd driven forty minutes over rough roads to get here to the ranch. But without a doubt, she was going to be shocked and angry. However, Flint was hoping that once she got past the resentment of him taking matters into his own hands, she'd look at all the hay and feed and be happy and grateful for his help.

"I really think I need to catch Ruby and trim her front feet," Pippa said as she peered through the corral fence at the four horses gathered around the hay manager in the middle of the large paddock. "Her hooves are looking like skis. I don't want her to start stumbling. Did I tell you she's going to have a foal this summer? Or maybe you could already tell by looking at her."

"I thought she looked in foal. What's the sire?"

"He's a paint quarter horse. Debra had made a deal with his owner some time back. She traded him a couple of calves for the stud fee."

"A baby," Flint said fondly as he gazed out at the sorrel mare. "You're going to enjoy watching it grow. That is if everything goes well with the birth."

She darted him a look of concern. "What do you mean?"

He hadn't meant to alarm her, but seeing he had, he quickly tried to smooth over his comment. "I only meant some mares have problems when it comes to foaling, that's all."

She regarded him thoughtfully. "I suppose you've helped bring a foal or two into the world?"

Nodding, he said, "I have. It's a task that Dad insisted all of us be experienced with."

Shrugging, she gazed across the paddock to the sorrel mare. "Well, it's a cinch you won't be around when Ruby foals. So I'll try to get prepared before her time arrives."

You won't be around. Strange just how hard he'd been struck by her remark. Yes, in the back of his mind, he realized he'd soon have to return to Utah. But that rapidly approaching day was something he didn't want to dwell on. For the first time he could ever remember, he felt truly needed and he wanted to hang on to the precious feeling.

"Well, don't worry. Ruby appears to be in great shape. You'll probably wake up one warm sunny morning and see a baby at her side."

She smiled. "I hope that will be the case. But right now I'm going to the barn and gather my farrier tools. It's turning out to be a beautiful morning and I don't want to waste it."

Flint inwardly groaned. It would make the situation far easier if she wasn't around when the delivery truck arrived. "Pippa, why don't you forget Ruby's feet for now? Don't you think you should go to the house and rest for a while?"

Turning, she leveled a look of disbelief on him. "Rest? Don't start that again, Flint! I'm so sick of being cooped up in the house, I was on the verge of cracking! I feel wonderful. So quit being a mother hen!"

She took off in a long stride toward the barn. Stifling a resigned sigh, he followed at her side. Halfway there, she heard the sound of the truck at the same time Flint heard it and she instantly lifted her head and peered curiously out toward the road leading up to the ranch.

"I hear a vehicle coming," she said with faint surprise. "Someone must be lost."

Flint realized he couldn't keep his secret any longer and he shook his head. "I don't think anyone is lost. I'm expecting a delivery."

She stopped in her tracks and slanted him a suspicious glance. "A delivery? What have you done, Flint?"

By now the truck was in view and he gestured to the vehicle steadily making its way toward the ranch yard. "I only purchased a few things from the feed store," he told her. "Don't worry. It's all usable."

"Why didn't you haul it in your truck yesterday?" she asked warily.

He grinned at her. "Because I wanted to surprise you."

Not bothering to say more, she took off in a long stride and Flint hurried after her. By the time they reached the semitruck and trailer, the young, huskily-built driver and another tall young man wearing a furry cap had already climbed down and were waiting for further directions.

With a polite nod to Pippa, the driver turned his attention to Flint. "Are you Mr. Hollister? And is this the Bell Ranch?"

"Right on both counts."

The driver said, "That's a relief. It's a rough trip out here." He motioned to his helper. "I'm Grady and this is Lyle. I wanted to make sure we were at the correct place before we unloaded all this stuff."

From the corner of his eye, Flint could see Pippa's mouth had fallen open, but so far she'd not uttered one word.

"What comes off first?" Flint asked. "The hay will go in the barn loft. Behind the building, there's a winch lift to help with that job. The rest will go into a feed room. It's located on the north end of the barn."

"The hay will come off first," Grady told him. "If you'll show me the best way to get this rig to the backside of the barn, we'll get started."

"Just follow me," Flint told him. "We'll go around the north end of the barn."

The men climbed back into the truck and Flint looked over at Pippa. "Coming with me?"

She blew out a heavy breath. "Darn right, I'm coming with you! And maybe you'll be kind enough to explain all of this! You were talking about hay. Just how much hay did you order?" she asked as she joined him in a quick stride.

"Five ton of alfalfa. But I don't want to hear you complain," he told her.

She let out a short, mocking laugh. "Like I'm not going to complain about five ton! Flint, have you slipped a cog? I can't pay for five ton of alfalfa right now!"

She practically yelled the last sentence at him and Flint was glad the men were inside the truck with the windows up. He didn't want them to hear her chewing on him.

"You're not going to have to pay for it," he gently explained. "I already have. Just calm down. Everything on the truck is paid for. Along with the hay, I ordered a ton of cattle pellets, a half ton of lamb grower, a half ton of horse feed and ten mineral blocks. Along with a hundred pounds of dry dog food and the same amount for the cats. I didn't get as much for the dogs and cats because they won't eat it up as quickly."

Her expression took on a bewildered look and, for a couple of seconds, he thought she might burst into tears, but then she groaned and covered her face with both hands.

"Oh God, what am I going to do?" she murmured.

"We'll talk about that later," he said then, wrapping a hand beneath her elbow, he hurried her forward. "Come on, let's go help the men set up the hay lift."

More than an hour later, Pippa stood just inside the doorway of the feed room and stared with wonder at the neat stacks of sacks. Even when Yance had been alive, she'd never seen the ranch this well stocked. He always drove in to Bonners Ferry on a weekly basis to pick up whatever feed was needed. Small amounts at a time were always easier to pay for, he'd say.

She didn't know why Flint had done such a thing, or what he'd stand to gain by spending so much on her and the Bell. But no matter his motive, she was totally shaken.

"How does the feed room look to you now?"

At the sound of his voice, she turned to see him entering the doorway.

"There's barely enough room in here to turn around!" she exclaimed.

He walked over and joined her in the small open area where she was standing.

"Don't worry. You'll have plenty of space soon enough," he told her.

"Have the men left?" she asked.

He nodded. "About two minutes ago. I signed the delivery slip and they're headed back to town. I'll say one thing. Both men were great help."

"Yes, especially considering how much they had to unload." She drew in a bracing breath and turned to face him. "Okay, now that they're gone, Flint, we need to discuss this."

"There's nothing to discuss. I bought supplies for the Bell. No big deal."

Maybe a few thousand dollars was no big deal to him. But to her it was like climbing an impossibly steep mountain. "We obviously don't think in the same terms," she pointed out. "This past month as the weather has worsened I've lain awake at nights, wondering what I was going to do about stretching the hay and feed. I thought about asking the bank for a loan. I considered selling a cow or two. Or one of the horses. None of those would be a permanent solution. And none appealed to me. But I—now you've done this and I—"

"You don't have to worry anymore," he interrupted. "And I can feel good about helping you."

To her horror, tears began to gather at the backs of her eyes and she quickly turned aside so he couldn't see her face. "I will pay you back for this, Flint. Somehow," she said, her voice low and strained. "Even if I have to pay you a hundred dollars a year for the next thirty years!"

"Well now, Pippa, there's no use in you being in such a hurry to pay it back," he gently teased. "I can extend the note to fifty years if that would help."

She turned an anguished look on him. "You're impossible, Flint! I don't understand this. Why did you do it? To make me feel beholden? Or small?"

Quickly stepping forward, he wrapped his hands around her upper arms. "Don't ever say that again, Pippa. Don't ever think it! Why would I want to hurt you in such a mean way? I thought by now you'd know I'm not that kind of guy."

Suddenly she couldn't hold back the emotion that had been stirring in her for the past two hours. Tears spilled onto her cheeks and with a little cry, she flung herself at him and buried her face against his chest.

Her voice was muffled by the front of his coat when she finally managed to speak. "I'm sorry, Flint. I know you're not that kind of guy. It's just that I can't believe you'd want to do so much for me."

His hands moved to the back of her shoulders and gently kneaded her flesh through her heavy woolen coat.

"Pippa, one of these days you're going to realize you're worthy of receiving help—and that it doesn't have to have strings attached," he said gently. "Besides, I've grown very fond of the Bell. I want to see it prosper."

She tilted her head back to look up at him. "If that's the way you feel, then thank you."

His lips twisted into a faint smile. "There. You can mark the feed bill paid. A thank-you is all I needed."

Her mouth opened to utter a protest but he quickly went on before she could speak. "Pippa, listen. I'm not one to go around bragging or talking about my money or assets. That's not me. But in this case, I think you need to understand that what I spent at the feed store is not going to cause me any hardship. Not in the least. Okay?"

She nodded and he wiped the tears from her cheeks with the pads of his fingers.

"Okay," she murmured.

"Good. So let's go to the house and take a break with a cup of coffee. What do you say?"

She did her best to give him a smile. "After the surprise you've given me this morning, I could definitely use something warm to drink."

Grinning, he slipped his arm around the back of her waist and urged her out of the feed room. As they walked away from the barn, Pippa realized she was slowly but surely handing the reins of the ranch and herself over to him—temporarily. But giving him control, even for a short while, might end up affecting the rest of her life, she thought helplessly. And no matter how charming or how merrily her heart danced whenever he was near, she had to keep her resistance up and her common sense in place so that she could figure out how to move on once he was gone.

Later that evening, Pippa didn't argue when Flint told her to remain at the house and let him deal with the last of the barn chores. She needed the extra time to get ready for their dinner date. Or perhaps she'd be overstating it to call the outing a date. He was simply treating her to a nice dinner. She'd be foolish to tack anything more to his motive.

But no matter his reason for inviting her to dinner, Pippa wanted to look her best and that meant she needed to find something to wear that looked better than worn jeans and muddy boots. Problem was, her closet was far from stuffed with fancy garments. She owned only a few dresses and those were worn mainly when she went to church. As for shoes, that was another drawback. With snow still on the ground, it was far too cold to wear the only pair of heels she owned, which were open-toed. Other than galoshes and old penny loafers, that only left a pair of knee-high fashion boots. She'd had them for nearly four years, but because she'd splurged and invested in real leather, they were still in good shape. So that meant she had to find something to go with the boots.

Eventually, after rifling through her closet for more than a half hour, she decided on a mid-length prairie-style dress with long sleeves that ruffled at the cuffs while a row of small buttons fastened the front of the close-fitting bodice. The fabric was a tiny gold-and-brown-flowered print that brought out the copper in her hair. Not that Flint would notice such a thing. But at least, the dress was nice enough that he shouldn't be embarrassed to be seen with her.

They'd planned to leave the Bell by six o'clock in order to give them plenty of time to make their seven o'clock reservation, and Pippa was ready fifteen minutes early. After gathering her coat and purse, she went out to the living room to wait, only to find Flint already there securing the safety screen in front of the fireplace.

Hearing her footsteps, he looked around to see her entering the room. As she walked toward him, he slowly straightened to his full height and stared at her.

"Pippa! Wow! You look—incredible!"

Her face flush with warmth, she stopped a few steps away from him. "Thank you, Flint. But you don't need to overdo the compliment."

"Can I not speak the truth?" he asked as he stepped off the hearth and came to stand in front of her. "Incredible—gorgeous. Neither one of those adjectives is overdoing it."

His compliment caused pleasure to ripple through her. "Okay, if we're speaking the truth, then you look very handsome, Flint. I like your gray hat."

"Thank you. The black one is my work hat. This is my going-out hat," he explained then added on a teasing note, "And I did take time to shower off the hay and dirt."

His green eyes held a subtle glow as they traveled over her face and the sight caused her breathing to go shallow.

With a nervous little smile, she murmured, "Me, too. And I think I managed to get all the hay out of my hair before I pinned up the top of it."

"Let me check," he said with a playful wink.

She stood stock-still as he made a complete circle around her. "No hay. Just beautiful hair and pretty sparkly pins holding it all in place." He reached for her hand. "I hope you're looking forward to tonight."

"I'm very much looking forward to it," she told him.

As soon as she'd entered the room and he'd walked over to her, the rhythm of her heart had jumped into overdrive. And now that he was holding her hand, she felt practically giddy. There was something particularly sensual about the sound of his voice and the way he was looking at her that had her all aflutter.

"So am I."

He lifted the back of her hand to his lips and Pippa practically swooned as heat rushed from her feet all the way to the top of her head. If they didn't leave the house right now, she feared she might do something totally reckless. Like take him by the hand and lead him straight to her bedroom.

Clearing her throat, she said, "Maybe we should get started. We don't want to be late."

He kissed her hand one more time before he released his hold on her. "Right. If we lost our reservation, it might not be easy securing more tonight. And you know what that means?"

She walked over to the couch to collect her coat and handbag. "No. What does it mean?"

"We would either have to go to a fast-food joint or come home and eat corn dogs."

Home. He'd called the Bell home, she thought. Maybe he'd used the term in an offhand way, but even so, just hearing him say the word had touched her.

She breathed deeply and willed her senses to hold together. "I like eating corn dogs and there's nothing wrong with fast food. Especially when you're hungry."

Chuckling, he said, "I'm only joking. No corn dogs tonight."

He walked over and, taking the coat from her, held it open so she could slip her arms into the garment. Once she had the coat on, he stepped around and began to button up the front. The touch of his fingers, even against the thick fabric, left an imaginary trail of fire leading from her belly button all the way up to her throat.

"There," he said softly when the last button was securely fastened. "That ought to keep out the cold wind."

"Thank you, Flint," she murmured. "I'm not used to getting this kind of attention. You're—spoiling me."

His gaze met hers and, after going ninety miles an hour, her heart very nearly stopped. Was she wrong to think she saw tenderness in his eyes? Was he really looking at her with genuine affection?

"I happen to think you deserve special attention."

She didn't say anything. She couldn't. If she spoke, it might break the mystic spell that seemed to be swirling around them. And she didn't want the magic between them to end. At least, not tonight.

"Flint, I—"

Whatever else she was about to say no longer mattered as he lowered his head and placed his lips upon hers.

The kiss was soft and tender, causing sweet emotions to pour through her. It wasn't until he lifted his head that she realized her hands had curved over the ridges of his shoulders and she was clinging to him as though she never wanted to let go.

"As nice as that was, I think we'd better be on our way," he said huskily. "Ready?"

Everything inside her was trembling and she wasn't sure her legs would remain steady, but she gave him an agreeable nod anyway. "Yes. I'm ready."

Chapter Twelve

The Deer Crossing restaurant was a rambling structure built on the bank of the Kootenai River. The outside consisted of cedar siding accented with native river rock. Endless plate-glass windows wrapped around one end and extended across the front.

"I hope the food is as good as the outside of the place looks," Flint said as he ushered Pippa to the glass door entrance. "I searched the web on my phone and read the reviews, and they all seemed pretty positive. Do you know anything about it?"

She said, "Not much. It's beyond my pocketbook. But Greer's parents brought her here for a birthday celebration and she loved it. So that's a good recommendation. Besides, Flint, anytime I can sit down and be served, it's nice for me."

One of the things that amazed him about Pippa was how easy she was to please. Most of the women he'd dated in the past, including Rachel, would insist he take her to the very best dining establishment. Pippa truly wouldn't complain if they ate corn dogs on paper plates. But then, the problem he'd had with demanding women had been his own fault. He was the one who'd chosen to date that kind of woman instead of seeking out someone who was truly compatible with him. He'd been too caught up in surface charms. Especially with Rachel. Yeah, she'd been glamorous, but like the old saying went, glitter didn't mean there was gold underneath. Strange that it had taken meeting Pippa to teach him that much.

"Okay, I won't worry if the service is poor and the food is tasteless," he teased.

Inside the building, they emerged from a long foyer to be met by a hostess with wavy black hair and a long red skirt and white blouse.

After giving her his name, the young woman checked the reservation list then gave them a welcoming smile. She plucked two large menus from a nearby stack and motioned for them to follow. "Right this way," she told them. "I have a table for two next to a window."

The hostess led them through a large dining area filled with round tables and covered with white-linen tablecloths. The accompanying chairs were made of ornately carved wood with padded leather seats. Flint noticed many of the tables were already occupied, making him glad he'd called yesterday for reservations.

Once they reached their designated table and were comfortably seated, the hostess handed each a menu and assured them a waiter would soon be with them.

After she'd walked away, Flint looked over to see Pippa studying the interior of the ritzy restaurant rather than the menu.

"Greer had described this place as fancy. And she was right. It is fancy, but not too much." She chuckled under her breath. "I mean it doesn't make me feel like I want to crawl under the table and hide."

He chuckled with her. "I'm grateful. I'd hate to have to throw scraps to you under the tablecloth."

She started to reply just as a young waiter with curly blond hair walked up to their table and peered at them through thick-lensed glasses.

"Welcome to the Deer Crossing." His cheerful grin was directed mostly at Pippa. "What would you two like to drink? Cocktails? Wine? We have a wide assortment of both. Or, of course, we have coffee, soda and tea."

"Bring us a bottle of your best red wine and a plate of your most popular hors d'oeuvres," Flint told him.

"I'll be right back," the waiter assured him.

Once he stepped away from the table, Flint said, "Sorry, Pippa. I should have asked if you like wine. If not, you can order something else when the waiter returns."

She shook her head and he couldn't help but notice how the golden hooped earrings dangled against her neck. While he'd told her she looked incredible, that had been an understatement. With a faint touch of makeup adding color to her face and the top part of her hair done up in an elaborate knot, she was like a lovely rosebud on the verge of bursting into full bloom.

"I'm fine with red wine. But I'm not accustomed to drinking spirits, so don't let me overdo it or you'll be carrying me out of here."

He smiled at her. "I'll limit your refills."

She turned slightly and gazed out at the view beyond the window. Presently, a nearly full moon was making the river appear as a shiny ribbon curling its way southward.

"I feel like we're far, far away from the Bell," she said thoughtfully. "I imagine it really feels like you're a world away from your home in Utah."

"It does," he agreed. "In more ways than one."

Her gaze settled on his face and Flint couldn't help but notice the silver moonlight beyond the window matched the color of her eyes.

"You've not mentioned getting homesick yet," she said. "But have you felt that way?"

"Have I been homesick?" His lips twisted to a wry slant. "Don't tell my family, but I've been doing just fine without seeing their smiling faces. And my coworkers, oh man. The first few days after I got here, they bombarded me with text messages. Thankfully, those have stopped. I think they've given up on me coming back to work."

Her brows arched with speculation. "Did you explain to them exactly why you were making this trip?"

"Not completely. I only told them I had to deal with a family matter. Which was true enough."

"Oh. Well, the situation with your grandparents is hard to explain. And I don't know your coworkers, but I'm not sure they'd understand why your family is so dead set on digging up the past. Most people prefer to leave the past behind them."

Nodding in agreement, he said, "Before this is all over, Dad might be wishing he'd left the past alone. But then, he wouldn't have learned about his half-sisters. And I would've never met you. And that is something I can't imagine. Not now."

She pushed her hand across the tabletop until her fingers were resting over his. The contact caused a wave of warm emotions to pour through him. Little by little, day by day, she was becoming the most important thing in his life. And he didn't know what he could do about his swiftly growing feelings. Or even if he could do anything. She'd more or less told him she'd closed her heart after Dale had walked away. Did he dare believe she'd open it for him? Moreover, would she be willing to welcome him inside?

"When you showed up on the Bell that first day, I wanted to scream with frustration," she said with a wry smile. "Now I can't imagine the Bell without you. Funny, isn't it, how quickly the two of us have…well—grown close."

"Grown close. Yes." He turned his hand over and wrapped it around hers. "We have done that."

Her lips parted to make a reply just as the waiter arrived with the wine and hors d'oeuvres. By the time the young man had served them and departed their table, the intimate moment between them had passed. But as far as Flint was concerned, it was far from forgotten.

For the next few minutes as they sipped the fruity wine and nibbled at the assortment of cheeseballs, Pippa asked him to talk about his work as a deputy sheriff. He related some of the more colorful situations he'd encountered over the years. He'd always been proud of being a lawman. He liked the idea of helping people and, hopefully, making them feel safe as they went about their lives. And, too, he liked that it set him apart from his brothers. And yet the more he'd grown to know Pippa, the more he'd begun to recognize that he didn't need to make himself different from Hunter and Jack, or Cordell and Quint. All he needed was to be himself. And find the place where he truly belonged.

More than two hours later, after Pippa finished the last of her grilled fish and vegetables, she leaned back in her chair and pressed a hand to her midsection.

"Flint, I'm going to pop if I try to eat another bite," she

insisted when he suggested she try a dessert. "You go ahead and enjoy something sinful. I won't mind watching you eat all those rich calories."

He chuckled. "Actually, I don't think I can manage any more food tonight. I'm on the verge of popping myself. But I'll be the first to say my steak was cooked to perfection, as was everything that went with it."

"Oh yes. Everything has been wonderful, Flint."

"So what would you like to do now? Do they have a movie theater around here with a late show? Or a nightclub where we can go dancing? Whatever you'd like to do, just tell me. We're celebrating, remember?"

"Oh yes, the key," she said impishly. "Well, I realize this is going to sound like I'm throwing cold water on the party, but I think I'd enjoy just going home and the two of us sitting in front of the fireplace. But after being cooped up on the ranch these past days, that idea probably sounds boring to you."

Shaking his head, he reached across the table and squeezed her hand. "Pippa, you can't know how perfect it sounds to me. Truly."

"Then, if you're ready to go, I am."

He motioned for the waiter to bring their check and after he'd taken care of the bill, they donned their coats and left the restaurant.

The night air was frigid and as they walked to Flint's truck, Pippa shivered against the wind. He immediately wrapped his arm around her waist and snugged her close to his side.

"You're freezing. Let's hurry and get in the truck." He helped her into the cab and, after joining her, quickly started the engine. "If you have a relapse over this, I'll never forgive myself."

She let out a good-natured groan. "Flint, are you always such a worrywart?"

"No."

"Then why are you doing it with me?" she asked.

He looked over at her. "I'm not sure. Except that when you were sick, Pippa, you looked so fragile—you scared me. Especially that first day you came down with the fever. You were half delirious most of the time. I doubt you even realized what you were saying. The only time I'd ever seen anyone that sick was Grandfather Lionel when he had a stroke. It wasn't pretty."

She thought about those days he'd nursed her so tenderly. She'd not expected anything like that from him. "Oh, Flint. I'm so sorry I put you through such an ordeal. I could never thank you enough. Never repay you for all that time you spent caring for me."

A pained look crossed his face and then suddenly he was leaning across the console and reaching for her. When his hands came around her shoulders, she scooted closer and curled her arms around his neck.

"You little fool, don't you understand that you've already given me far more than I deserve? Taking care of you was an honor. And one kiss from you is more than enough payment."

"Only one kiss?" she breathed against his ear.

He chuckled and then, with a forefinger beneath her chin, he drew her face around to his. "Well, I'd take more if you'd like to give them."

"I would like," she whispered before she leaned in and pressed her lips to his.

They kissed for long, long moments and when he finally pulled away and straightened himself behind the steering wheel, Pippa realized that something had drastically changed between them. All this time, it was like a magnet had pulled them together, and now it felt as if it had locked tight. The reality of where they were headed should probably frighten her, but it didn't. For years now, she'd shut herself away from the affection and pleasure a man could bring to her life. And she'd thought she was doing fine without those things. Until Flint had come along and given her the vision of a whole new world.

"The heater will be warm in just a minute," he promised as he put the truck into gear and maneuvered the vehicle out of the parking area.

She reached over and touched his forearm. "No worries. I'm as warm as toast now."

The glance he gave her could only be described as scorchingly sensual.

"All the more reason to get you home."

During the drive back to the Bell, neither Flint nor Pippa had much to say. The only thing they discussed was the possibility of another snowstorm hitting the area in the next couple of days. Flint had no idea what might be going through Pippa's mind. But he definitely knew what was rolling around in his. He had to get her into his arms. He had to feel her body pressed tightly to his or he was going to crack right in two.

When they finally reached the ranch house, Flint parked at the back and they entered through the kitchen, which was lit by a small light over the stove.

"I'm going to go check on the fireplace before I make coffee," she told him.

Flint followed her out of the kitchen and on to the living room. The logs in the fireplace had burned down to a mound of glowing embers that cast a rosy hue over part of the dark room.

Not bothering to switch on a light, she slipped out of her coat and placed it and her handbag on the arm of the couch. A few steps away, Flint quickly shed his own coat and hat and dropped them both in the seat of an armchair.

She walked over to the hearth and pulled back the safety screen. "The fire is nearly burned out. We need to add more logs."

Joining her on the hearth, he tugged her into his arms. "We don't need more logs, Pippa. The fire is just now starting."

With his arms circling her waist, she tilted her head back and gazed up at him. Flint could see a mixture of wonder and wariness in her eyes.

"Flint, are you sure about this—about me?"

A burning sensation filled the middle of his chest and he realized nothing would take it away except the touch of her lips against his, the softness of her body giving to him.

"I'm very sure I want you more than anything I've ever wanted in my life," he said, his voice hoarse with emotion. "And I'm hoping you feel the same way about me. Do you?"

She reached up and touched his cheek. "Oh, Flint, I think I've wanted you from the moment we met," she whispered. "I was just too afraid to tell you. And I didn't want us to make a mistake."

Groaning with need, he buried his face against the side

of her neck. "This couldn't be a mistake, Pippa. It feels too right, too good."

Her arms slid trustingly around him and Flint was suddenly filled with the need to protect her. To cherish everything she was offering him.

"Yes," she murmured. "It's felt right from the very beginning."

Lifting his head, he found her lips with his and, for the next few moments, he carefully reined in his hunger as he kissed her softly, adoringly. It wasn't until he felt her hands clench the back of his shirt that he bent down and scooped her up and into his arms.

With her head snuggled against his shoulder, he carried her down the hall and into her bedroom where a tiny night-light illuminated a portion of the bed and the night-stand next to it.

When he eased her onto the side of the mattress, she looked around her and then at him. "We're in my room. I thought you'd want us to be in yours."

"That room was Debra's. I don't think I'd feel right taking you to bed in my aunt's room."

Smiling softly, she stood and slipped her arms around his waist. "She wouldn't haunt you. I think she'd be proud to call you her nephew."

He smiled back at her. "I'll never know about that. But I do know your sheets probably smell nicer than mine."

Her arms tightened their hold on him. "Who cares about sheets?"

The sultry tone of her voice was like a burning match tossed into a bed of straw. The flames inside him were instant and all-consuming. With a helpless groan, he lowered his head and covered her soft lips with his.

This time he couldn't tamp down the desire burning inside him. With his arms wrapping her tightly against him, he kissed her deeply and hungrily until they were both starving for oxygen.

When he finally lifted his head, she spoke through ragged breaths. "I think—we should get undressed. Don't you?"

"The quicker, the better," he agreed.

While she pulled off her boots and slipped out of her dress, he hurriedly removed his boots and shirt and finally his jeans and left them all in a pile on the floor. When he turned back to see her standing beside the bed wearing only her bra and panties, his throat suddenly grew tight with emotions that had nothing to do with sexual desire and everything to do with the strange burning sensation that persisted in his chest.

Stepping over to her, he touched his hands to the tops of her shoulders then slid them downward until they were cupping each breast. "I didn't have to see you without clothes to know that you'd be beautiful. I just didn't expect you to be *this* beautiful," he murmured.

She said, "The wine we had at dinner has obviously clouded your vision."

Reaching to her back, he unclasped the pale pink bra and lifted her arms so the garment would slide away from her body and onto the floor. When her breasts were finally exposed to him, he dipped his head and touched his lips to one pale pink nipple.

"My vision is crystal-clear. And all I'm seeing is you." He spoke against the soft flesh of her breast.

She groaned and arched her upper body toward his mouth as, for long, delicious moments, Flint tasted her sweet skin. Finally, after he'd lathed both nipples into hard buds, he pulled back and lifted her onto the bed.

As soon as he'd stretched out next to her, they reached for each other at the same time. And once the fronts of their bodies were aligned, Flint's hands began a slow search of her warm curves. At the same time, her hands were doing their own exploring as her fingers trailed down his back then around to the hard muscles surrounding his belly-button.

Her touch was like a lighted torch, burning a path across his skin. In the back of his mind, he knew her touch would never leave him but remain seared forever in his memory.

"I don't want to think," she whispered. "I only want to feel. I want to feel your hands touching me—in all the places I've never been touched before. I want your lips to keep kissing mine until neither of us can think of anything except this—and us."

Easing his head back just enough to gaze into her eyes, he murmured, "My darling Pippa, let me make love to you now. This very second."

"Yes," she said thickly.

He shifted his body until he was poised over her and then it struck him that in the heat of desire he'd forgotten one important thing.

When he paused, she frowned with confusion. "What's wrong?"

Blowing out a heavy breath, he eased himself back to the mattress. "I wasn't thinking, Pippa. We need birth control. I might have a condom in my wallet, but it's probably so old the rubber has turned to dust."

Turning slightly toward him, she skimmed the palm of her hand across his chest and down his abdomen. "You don't need a condom," she said gently. "I take oral contraceptives—to keep my periods regular."

Relief poured through him and caused a grin to twist his lips. "I didn't figure you'd be taking them just in case you ran into a man you wanted to have sex with."

"A man like you?" she teased.

Chuckles rumbled from deep in his chest and he could only think how perfect Pippa was for him; how special she made him feel.

Resting his forehead against hers, he said, "Definitely like me."

Her lips found his and, after a deep kiss that shot his senses straight up to the ceiling, he positioned himself over her. With one knee, he parted her legs to allow himself entry.

A quick glance at her face told him her eyes were closed and the corners of her mouth were tilted faintly upward. Her red hair had come loose from its pins and now tumbled onto the pillow and down over her shoulders.

The beautiful sight of her was the last thing he saw before he closed his eyes and lowered his hips down to hers. He felt her thighs part even wider and then his manhood was slipping into her moist heat, drawing him into a dark velvety vortex.

A mix of wild sensations shot through his entire body and, for a moment, the shock very nearly took his breath.

He wasn't supposed to feel this lost!

The frantic thought was swirling around in his mind when her hips lifted toward his and her hands slipped to his buttocks. For a split second, he was paralyzed with the depth of his feelings and he could only imagine what she was thinking. But just as quickly a burst of feeling shot through him and he began to move his hips and savor the incredible pleasure of having her surround him.

These past few days, Pippa had fantasized about making love to Flint more times than she could count. In her mind, it had always been an incredible experience. Yet now that it was truly happening and their bodies were locked together with searing heat, she realized how ridiculous her fantasies had been. Making love to Flint was so much more than just incredible; it was mind-bending. It was shocking her senses and sending them shooting off to the sky like July fireworks.

His hands were touching her anywhere and everywhere while his lips were plundering hers with a hunger that fed her desire like accelerant on an already-raging fire. She never wanted so much, needed so much, and she realized she wasn't just losing control of her body, her heart was going with it. And yet in the heat of the moment, that reality didn't scare her. She wanted to love. Really love.

From somewhere outside, she heard one of the dogs bark and then farther away a calf bawled. Inside her bedroom, she could hear the wind howling beyond the window, Flint's sharp intakes of breath and the faint ticking of the alarm clock on the nightstand. But none of those sounds could match the loud thud of her heart thrumming in her ears. And with each and every beat, she clung to him desperately. Her body needed relief, but she didn't want their special connection to end.

Sooner rather than later, though, she felt her grip tightening. As his thrust grew harder and faster, it became impossible to hold back. Crying out, she clutched his arms and arched her body in search of relief and as his arms slipped around her waist, she felt herself flying off into the starry darkness.

"Oh! Oh, Flint! Hold me! Don't let me go!" she pleaded.

Burying his face in the curve of her neck, he whispered, "I have you, darling. I won't let you go. Ever…"

His voice trailed away on a guttural groan and then he was clutching her tightly, spilling his warm climax inside her.

Flint decided he must have traveled to another planet when he opened his eyes and stared in confusion at the foot of the four-poster bed. Where was he? And what had just happened? The room was spinning and, no matter how hard he tried, he couldn't suck in enough oxygen.

"Are you all right?"

The question came with the palm of her hand resting gently against his cheek and he turned just enough to see her head resting next to his on the pillow.

"Yes. Just don't ask me to stand right now," he mumbled. "I'm not sure my legs would work."

Smiling impishly, she reached down and tugged the comforter over them. "As far as I'm concerned, you don't have to move a muscle."

He pulled her head down against his shoulder and pressed a kiss to the middle of her forehead. "I don't plan on letting you out of this bed. Not until daylight."

"And then I can get up and cook breakfast. Right?" she asked with a pointed smile.

"Exactly," he said with a chuckle. "Your eggs taste a lot better than mine."

Strands of her hair were tangled against her cheek and he used his fingers to tuck it behind her ear.

"My hairpins must have fallen into the bedcovers," she said. "I'll search for them later."

Stroking a hand over her bare shoulder, he marveled at the soft glow of her skin and how it felt like satin beneath his fingers. If he touched her for the next hundred years, it wouldn't be enough to satisfy him.

"You asked me if I was all right, but you didn't mention how you are," he said. "I hope I didn't disappoint you."

His remark drew a chuckle from her. "Do I look disappointed?"

Her lips were pink and puffy from his kisses and her silver-gray eyes held a soft, contented look. "No," he answered.

"Good," she said, "because I feel totally wonderful. And I'm excited about our trip tomorrow. We are still planning on leaving after we feed the animals in the morning, aren't we?"

After what had just occurred between them, he'd very nearly forgotten the trip to Coeur d'Alene tomorrow. And a part of him wanted to forget it entirely—to put off the trip and further delay his return to Utah. But to do that he'd need excuses to give Pippa and his family. And he wasn't quite ready to open himself up to her that much. Not until he knew for certain how she felt about him.

Yes, she'd just made love to him as though she truly cared and wanted a future with him. She'd given herself to him as though he was the only man she'd ever want touching her in such an intimate way. But she'd never said or even hinted that she loved him. He'd been fooled before by a woman, and this time he wasn't going to assume anything.

"Yes," he told her as he tried to focus his thoughts on tomorrow. "The sooner we leave, the sooner we can get back."

Lifting her head from his shoulder, she studied his face. "You don't sound very excited. Are you dreading the drive? Or are you concerned about what you might, or might not, find among Scarlett's things?"

Strange, Flint thought, how a grandmother he'd never known seemed to be steering the direction of his life. "I've decided not to get my hopes up too much about this, Pippa. Why would my grandmother keep something pertaining to her first husband? A man she apparently hated? It's a long shot."

His negative remarks had her sitting straight up in the bed and staring at him concern. "I don't know what's come over you, Flint. But I think you're wrong."

Reaching over, he took a strand of her hair and rolled it between his fingers. "About what? Thinking the chance of finding anything to answer my questions in the deposit box is a long shot? I don't think that's wrong. It's using common sense."

"I'm not talking about the box. I'm talking about Scarlett. I just don't believe she hated her first husband. She gave him three sons. I don't believe any woman could do that with hate in her heart. Unless she viewed giving him children as her wifely duty."

Would Pippa be willing to give him three sons? he wondered. Would she stick by his side through thick and thin? Or would she leave him and their children high and dry as Scarlett had left Lionel and their sons?

The questions rolling through his mind must've put a crease between his brows because she leaned over and gently smoothed the spot with her forefinger.

"Why are you frowning? I thought this was a night for

celebrating," she said softly. "Are you…having regrets about us?"

Her question jerked him out of his wandering thoughts and he groaned with self-recrimination as he recognized a shadow of uncertainty on her face.

"Oh, Pippa, no! Don't ever think such a thing." With a hand on her arm, he pulled her upper body down until she was draped against his chest. "I could never regret making love to you. Not this moment. Not ever. Do *you* wish it hadn't happened?"

Sighing, she cupped her hand against his jaw. "My only regret is that this didn't happen sooner—to give us more time together."

Yes, more time. The more Flint thought about it, the more he realized that was the real reason for his reluctance to open his grandmother's deposit box. He didn't want this time with Pippa to end.

His fingers slid up the ridges of her spine until his hand was at the back of her neck, drawing her lips down to his. "That's why we shouldn't be wasting the rest of this night with talk."

With a groan of agreement, she slipped her arms around his neck and, as her lips responded to his, Flint closed his mind to tomorrow.

Chapter Thirteen

Thankfully, the sky was clear and sunny as the two of them made the drive to Coeur d'Alene. It had been a long time since Pippa had traveled any distance from Bonners Ferry, and she enjoyed the scenery. As for Flint, he was somewhat quiet and preoccupied, but she didn't press him to talk. She realized he had a lot on his mind.

This morning, after they'd returned to the house from feeding the livestock and she'd started cooking breakfast, Flint had called his father and explained the situation with Scarlett's deposit box. Although she'd not heard the whole conversation, she'd heard enough to pick up the strained thread in Flint's voice. It drove home to her that, more than anything, he didn't want to disappoint his family.

"Flint, you've never told me exactly why you were the one your father sent up here to Idaho to delve into Scarlett's history. Was it because you're a deputy sheriff and more experienced at gathering information?"

His features took on a wry twist as he shook his head. "No. I think it was more of a process of elimination. Jack and Bonnie had already done their part in the family tree search. Hunter and Willow just had their miraculous re- union and Quint and Clementine are tied up with their expansion of the sheep division. Plus, they just announced she's expecting a baby. Cordell is foreman of the ranch. Dad can't do without him. And Grace has a doctor's office she can't possibly leave. So, that left me. Since I had vacation time stacked up, I couldn't refuse."

She cast him a penetrating glance. "Somehow I don't think you would've refused your dad even without the extra vacation time."

He shrugged and the movement drew her gaze to his broad shoulders. Before they'd left the ranch, he'd changed into clean jeans and a denim shirt with pearl snaps. The close-fitting garment emphasized his perfectly fit body and it was all too easy for Pippa to recall the strong muscles of his arm and shoulders, the narrowness of his lean waist, the washboard abdomen and the line of brown hair growing from his navel and disappearing into his jeans. Last night, when she'd turned and seen him standing next to the bed without his clothes, her breathing had gone totally haywire. And now as she looked at his long-legged body sitting behind the steering wheel, it amazed her to think she'd made love to him.

"You're right. I don't think any of us kids could ever refuse Dad. Especially when he doesn't ask us for favors very often. Actually, he and Mom aren't the type to butt into their children's private lives very often at all. Not unless we seek their advice."

"Must be nice to have parents like yours," she said wistfully.

He looked over at her. "Trust me, Pippa, they're not perfect and they'd be the first to tell you so. But they're loving and supportive and those are the most important things."

She wanted to say how much she'd like to meet his parents and siblings, but she didn't want to sound as though she was hinting or pushing at him to make some sort of commitment to her. As much as she wanted him to give her some sign that he was thinking of a long-term future with her, she didn't expect to receive one. No, he'd come into her life like a dream and she figured he'd leave her with only that, a beautiful dream.

It was close to noon when they entered Coeur d'Alene. Because they wanted to make sure they visited the bank before it closed for the day, they decided to head there first and worry about lunch later on that afternoon.

"Do you know where the Big Lodge Bank and Trust is located?" he asked as they traveled deeper into the city.

"I have directions pulled up on my phone," she told him. "The bank appears to be about five more blocks down this main drag, on the left side of the street."

"That sounds easy enough." He braked at a red light and as they waited for it to change to green, he glanced over at her. "My sister, Beatrice, talked about how pretty this town was. I need to tell her to visit Bonners Ferry, she'd love it."

"Has she been back here to visit your grandmother since that first time she saw her?" Pippa asked.

"Once, I think. Her husband is pretty busy with the ranch where they live—the Rising Starr. And besides running a boutique in Burley, Beatrice designs Western clothing. So they don't have much time for traveling."

"I see. Well, I'm sure she and the rest of your family will be anxious to hear about what you find today," Pippa remarked.

"If we find anything," he said.

She reached over and clasped her hand around his arm. "I feel hopeful, Flint."

With his gaze focused on the traffic in front of them, he lifted her hand to his lips. "Thank you, Pippa."

Flint half expected Pippa to run into trouble when she requested access to Scarlett's safety-deposit box, but to his relief, her identification and other documents were enough to satisfy the bank clerk.

Once Pippa had gone to the security area to retrieve the box, Flint took a seat next to the window in the lobby. Working as a deputy for all these years, he'd learned not to get nervous or uneasy over an uncertain situation. It fogged a man's senses and ruined his ability to think clearly. But today, as they'd grown closer to Coeur d'Alene, an anxious feeling had settled over him that he'd been unable to shake. Pippa had said she felt hopeful. But what should he hope for? To find his grandfather's birthdate? To find something that would explain or justify his grandmother's absence from the family? Yes, those things would give him a sense of gratification. But they wouldn't fix anything about his situation with Pippa. And that was Flint's major worry.

A few minutes later, Flint was standing, staring mindlessly out the plate-glass window at the passing traffic, when Pippa appeared at his side.

She patted the tote bag hanging from her shoulder. "I took everything and returned the key to the bank. There's no reason to keep them here. I figure Taylor should have her mother's things. Scarlett can't deal with them now."

"Guess this means we're ready to leave," he said.

After glancing around the busy lobby, she nodded. "I think we should go somewhere more private to look everything over."

"I agree."

With his hand under her elbow, he ushered her from the building and into his waiting truck in the parking area. Once they were settled in the warm cab, he asked, "Do you want to look at everything here? Or go to a coffee shop or somewhere that's not too busy."

She looked down at the tote bag on her lap and thought for a moment. "I think we should leave this parking lot and get out of the way of the other bank customers. There's a little park not far from the apartment building where Scarlett lives. Why don't we go there? We can sit in the truck where it's warm and have our privacy while we look over everything. Then, depending on how you feel about what we find, you can decide whether you want to see your grandmother or not."

"Fine with me," he said then cast her a wry glance. "To tell you the truth, Pippa, I haven't considered the idea of seeing Scarlett. I guess I've been too busy thinking about—other things."

"A lot has happened since you first arrived in Idaho," she said gently. "You've had plenty to think about and I've hardly made things easy for you."

He started the truck and quickly backed out of the parking slot. "Without you, Pippa, I wouldn't be here. Besides, nothing worthwhile is easy."

Once they were headed down the street, Pippa navigated him to the park and, five minutes later, he parked the truck in a sunny area next to a row of blue spruce trees.

Pippa opened the tote and began to place the papers and letters on the console between them. "I didn't take the time to scan anything," she told him. "I just wanted to empty the box and get out of there."

He chuckled. "You make it sound like you were pulling a heist."

"I sort of feel like I have. These things aren't mine. I mean legally they are, but otherwise…well, I'm just glad you're Scarlett's grandson. Somehow that makes this snooping seem okay."

"Snooping? Yeah, I suppose in a way that's what we're doing." He picked up a folded piece of paper and unfolded it. "But the way I look at it, if Grandfather Lionel had been more forthcoming with his family, none of this would be necessary."

"True," she agreed. "So let's see if we can find anything of importance."

There were several documents pertaining to property that Scarlett and Ode had owned in southern Idaho, along with their marriage license and his death certificate. They also discovered Scarlett's birth certificate, which stated she'd been born in Nevada in 1943.

"Looks like Scarlett was good about keeping her important papers together," Pippa said as she picked up a manila envelope. "This feels heavy. Could be a bunch of photos."

"I'm thinking this might be something," Flint said as he opened a heavy tri-folded paper. It was stained brown in spots and the edges were ragged. When he spotted his grandfather's typewritten name, he studied the document closer. But the more he examined the paper, the more confused he grew. "Pippa—this looks as though it could be Grandfather's birth certificate. But I don't understand. This says he was born in Bedford, England! How could that be…?"

Her cheek very nearly touched his shoulder as she leaned in to inspect the paper in his hand. "Lionel G. Hollister," she read. "'Father, Peter Hollister.' Is there a Peter in your family?"

"He was supposedly my great-grandfather. But we could never find a Peter Hollister listed on any of the genealogical sites. Not one anywhere close to the right age."

"Hmm. Here's the listed name of his mother—Audrey Gibbons. Are you familiar with that name?"

Flint nodded. "I recall Grandfather saying his mother's name was Audrey. If he ever said her last name, I never heard it. Like I told you before, he didn't talk much about his childhood. But he did speak of his mother from time to time."

Pippa pointed to the date of birth. "Nineteen forty-three. Would that fit Lionel's age, you think?"

"Yes, that would make him around eighty-two now, if he'd lived. He was in his mid-seventies when he passed away."

She turned her head to look at him. "Flint, this has to be Lionel's birth certificate. Why else would Scarlett have kept the document?"

Bewildered, he shook his head. "Yes, but England? Why did he tell us he was born in Parowan, Utah? That's a hell of a long distance from Bedford, England. And how did he end up in Utah? It's crazy."

She blew out a long breath. "I agree it's odd, but not unreasonable. Think about it, Flint. 1943. England. World War II would have been raging at that time. Peter Hollister, whoever the man was, could've been in the military and stationed there."

He nodded thoughtfully. "True. But none of Dad's family had anyone in the military! I think Dad mentioned that one of the Arizona Hollisters was in the army, but he was never seriously considered a part of the equation of the family tree because he was killed in the war."

"Did your grandfather mention having any siblings?"

"No. That was one thing he made clear. He was an only child. Unless he was lying about that, too," Flint added grimly.

"Well, you now have the mother's last name. Your sister, Bonnie, could make a search for Audrey Gibbons and it might reveal something."

"I hope. And we could find more information here among Scarlett's things," he suggested. "Let's keep digging."

"I'll start with this," she said of the large manila envelope. "It's full of something."

She dumped the contents in her lap and they both stared in wonder at the pile of white envelopes with handwritten addresses.

"Letters!" Pippa exclaimed under her breath. "And look, Flint, the return address is Bedford, England!"

Flint picked up one of the envelopes and studied the faded cursive handwriting on the front. The letter was addressed to Lionel Hollister at General Delivery, Beaver City Post Office. "This is unbelievable, Pippa. I never thought…"

"We'd find anything like this?" she finished for him. "Neither did I. Are you going to open them? Or wait for your father to look at them?"

"We're not going to wait," he said with a shake of his head. "Dad trusted me to do this job. If I called him right now, he'd tell me to start reading. And I want to see just what's in these letters before I call Dad with the news of what we've found."

She glanced down at the pile of letters. "Maybe we should read them in order of the post-stamped date. They'd probably make more sense of them that way," she suggested.

"Right. Let me help." He reached for a handful of letters and together they placed them one by one on the dashboard according to their date. "Looks like 1961 is the earliest I have. What about you?"

"Mine are all later," she told him. "Mostly in the mid to later sixties."

"Okay. I'll start with this one," he said. After retrieving two small, carefully folded papers from inside the envelope, he began to read aloud.

"My Dearest Grandson,
It was a relief to hear you made the trip to the United States safely. Our hearts were torn to watch you go. With Audrey gone and buried now, you're all the family we have left. But you're young, Lionel, and we understand your need for adventure. You inherited that from your lively father. He had big dreams for Audrey and himself and you. We've often told you how your mother never was the same after Peter was killed on the beaches of Normandy. Your grandfather believes her heart never recovered from losing the love of her life. But having you, Lionel, made her happy. If you remember anything about your mother, remember that.

Now that you're in the States, we're anxious to hear how you're getting along. We know you want a big ranch someday, but you must realize these things don't happen overnight. Anyway, we pray you'll stay

*far away from your father's family. They've already
proved they're not to be trusted. It's a shame Peter
died without their love and support or a dime of all
that money, but that's in the past. What's important
now is for you to forge ahead and follow your own
dream."*

Dazed by what he'd just read, Flint looked away from
the letter and over to Pippa. She was staring at him in
stunned fascination.

"Can you make any sense of that?" she asked.

Slowly, Flint nodded. "It's beginning to make a whole
lot of sense. This Peter must have been the member of the
Arizona Hollisters who was killed during the Normandy
invasion. From the way Dad explained it, this particular
son was estranged from his father. And if I remember correctly, his legal name was Parnell. But he must've been
going by Peter."

Pippa said, "Now we know why your sister wasn't getting a genealogical hit with her searches. She was looking for the wrong name. But why was he estranged? The
mother mentions the Hollister family wasn't to be trusted.
You think that could be why Lionel never mentioned the
Hollisters in Arizona? Why he kept his birthplace a secret?"

Flint's mind was racing with everything he'd just read
and the reality of what he knew about his grandfather. It
seemed surreal that the man had left England at the incredibly young age of eighteen or nineteen and come to
the States, in particular, Utah.

"Your guess is as good as mine. But obviously, Grandfather must have been frightened of the Hollisters in Arizona.
I suppose their vast wealth and land holdings must have

intimidated him in a way. See, they started Three Rivers Ranch in 1847. It's a part of Arizona history." He tapped the letter he'd just read with his forefinger. "According to what his maternal grandmother is saying here, Parnell must have been shut out of their wealth. Must have been some bad blood there."

Pippa glanced thoughtfully across the park to where a group of swings and monkey bars sat empty in deep drifts of snow. "I can understand Lionel being too distrusting to approach his relatives in Arizona. But to hide his birth identity in order to avoid being linked to them seems…well, a little farfetched. Lionel's mother and grandparents must have driven fear and resentment into him."

Flint grimaced. "The cause of the initial break between Parnell and his parents might take a lot of deep unraveling to figure out. Right now, the questions in my mind are about Scarlett. Why did she have Grandfather's birth certificate and all these letters? I can't imagine it being common for a woman to hold on to her ex-husband's letters—written to him by his grandparents."

"Maybe Scarlett is mentioned in these later letters," Pippa suggested. "Let's scan through them and see."

For the next several minutes, each of them read through the letters written by Elizabeth and Cedric Gibbons to their grandson Lionel. In one, they mentioned visiting Audrey's grave and decorating it with roses. Another revealed that the couple lived on a small farm and raised sheep along with a few dairy cows. In another letter, Elizabeth remarked about keeping Audrey's rose garden blooming and how hard it was becoming for her and Cedric to carry out their chores as they aged.

"Here's something," Flint said as he scanned through

one of the few remaining letters. "Cedric is telling Lionel how glad he is to hear that his grandson has a loving and dedicated wife. He writes '*Scarlett sounds very much like your mother—making a fuss over her young sons and the livestock you have on the ranch. It's a blessing that she takes such good care of your boys and it's a bonus that she also wants to help you care for the animals. The two of you working together will make your ranch grow that much quicker.*'"

Flint swiped a hand over his face. "A good mother? Helping with the livestock? This all feels like some sort of fantasy. It's so different from everything my grandfather ever said about Scarlett. Except that it's real, Pippa. These letters are authentic and, frankly, upsetting."

She placed a hand on his arm. "I know it can't be easy, having everything you believed about your grandparents upended like this."

He heaved out a breath. "It's like the whole foundation of our family has crumbled. I can only imagine how Dad is going to feel when he hears his own father fed him a bunch of lies."

"I'm thinking we should probably look through the rest of these things before you call him," Pippa said. "There might be more here than just these letters. And you're right. There had to be a reason Scarlett had them in her possession."

"Do you think Debra had any idea her mother kept all this?"

Pippa shook her head. "No. She was the sort who would absolutely follow her mother's wishes and not open anything until her death. Unfortunately, in this case, Scarlett has outlived her eldest daughter."

"Well, let's go through the remainder of this stuff and then I'll call Dad," he told her.

For the next few minutes, they scanned through the last of the letters without learning much except that by 1968 Cedric had entered a nursing home while Elizabeth continued to do her best to live alone on the farm.

Once Pippa placed all the envelopes safely back into the large manila package, she dug into the tote to see what remained of the contents of the deposit box.

When she pulled out a green-bound leather book tied securely with hemp twine, Flint practically froze.

"What is that? A journal?"

"I'm thinking it's something like a journal or diary." She handed it to him. "The note on top has the same instructions as the other envelope. Not to open until after Scarlett's death."

"After all we've discovered, I'm afraid to think what might be inside this thing," he said in a strained voice.

She gave his forearm an encouraging squeeze. In that moment Flint realized the only thing holding him together was her strong and steady presence.

"Flint, you're a brave man. You'd have to be in your line of work."

"Work is different. This is personal. And..."

When his words trailed off, Pippa said, "It's possible you could discover something good between those pages. Something that might help give context to your grandfather's deceptions."

Groaning, he wiped a hand over his eyes. "It's going to take a hell of a lot to excuse his lies. But I'd welcome anything that might be on a positive note right now."

She gave him a gentle smile and as he looked into her

soft gray eyes, he was taken back to last night and how she'd looked as she'd kissed him and made love to him. He had to believe her feelings were genuine. If she proved to be insincere, his trust in anyone or anything would be lost.

He removed the twine on the leather-bound notebook and as soon as he opened it to the first page, he could see he was holding a journal of sorts rather than daily entries of a diary. It appeared as though Scarlett had begun writing down her thoughts in 1968, the year after her last son, Barton, was born.

Flint said to Pippa, "Listen to this. '*My sons are growing strong. Hadley is six years old now. Wade isn't far behind at four. And little Barton turned one last week. He's beginning to walk on steady feet now and his newfound mobility thrills him. I am so proud of my sons and I can't imagine loving anything more than I love my babies. Unless it would be Lionel. How could I not love my handsome prince of a husband?*'"

"Dear heaven, what could've gone wrong?" Pippa murmured.

A sick feeling began to swim in the pit of Flint's stomach. "Something bad—that's what," he said grimly. "I'll read further and hopefully her words will tell us."

Through the next few pages of the journal, Scarlett had noted down various pieces of news pertaining to the Beaver City area. There was also the mention of friends planning to visit Stone Creek Ranch in the coming months and that Lionel was intent on moving the working ranch yard to a spot over the hill because he hated the pall of dust that hung over the house.

"Hell, and all those years he led his family to believe he'd moved the ranch yard because of Scarlett's demands."

He glanced at Pippa. "I'm beginning to see a pattern forming here."

"About your grandfather?"

He nodded ruefully. "He clearly wasn't the man we thought. How could we not have seen through him?"

She shook her head. "Because he was your grandfather. Because you loved him. And when you love someone, it's easy to let yourself be deceived."

The reality of what she was saying struck him hard. Yes, love made a person vulnerable to deception and heartbreak. But on the other hand, there wasn't much point to life without love.

"Yeah, very easy." Turning his attention back to the journal, he flipped over to the latter pages and, after reading through a few passages, he said, "This is toward the end of 1969. Scarlett says *'I always love getting the ranch house ready for the holidays. The boys adore the decorations and the thought of Santa coming to see them soon. But I fear this holiday isn't going to be cheerful for me. Lionel has been staying gone most nights and not acting like himself. Maybe I no longer look beautiful to him. I try to make it up to him in other ways. But he seems distant.'"*

"Bastard," Flint cursed under his breath.

"It does sound ugly," Pippa agreed. "But you should read on before we assume what happened between your grandparents."

Flint did read on and it was easy to understand from her words that by the time Christmas Eve arrived, Scarlett was resolute about wanting to take the boys and leave Stone Creek. However, she feared Lionel would forcibly stop her. She'd discovered concrete evidence that her husband was seeing a woman in Parowan and possibly others in the area. She'd asked Lionel for a divorce, but he'd refused.

"He must have relented later about the divorce," Pippa mused after listening to Flint read the last entry.

He shook his head. "It seems she forced his hand. Later on, Scarlett tells Lionel if he doesn't give her a divorce, she's going to contact the Hollisters in Arizona and tell them he's Parnell's son!"

"Oh my. What a tangled, vengeful web."

"Let me read the rest and then I'll give you the overview." He glanced at her anxious face. "Is that all right with you?"

"Of course, Flint. But I can see this is twisting you up inside. Are you okay to go on with this right now?"

He reached over and squeezed her hand. "You're here with me, Pippa. I can go on."

Ten minutes later, Flint closed the book and pressed a hand over his burning eyes.

Leaning closer, Pippa placed a steadying hand on his shoulder. "Did you learn any more?"

"Oh yes. It's incredible, but all obviously true. Because now, with what I've learned from Grandmother's journal, it's all falling into place and making sense. Once Scarlett threatened to expose Lionel's birth father to the Arizona Hollisters, he went sort of ballistic. He kicked her out of the ranch house, told her he was divorcing her, and demanded she leave the boys with him. Leaving her children was hardly what Scarlett wanted, but Lionel had the money and means to ensure he got full custody, and she had no way to fight him."

"I can understand that. She was totally dependent on

him. So what about these letters and his birth certificate? How and why did she end up with those?"

"While she was packing to leave, Lionel left the house and went over to the ranch yard. With him gone, she grabbed the papers from a box in the closet and hid them among her things. She took them, thinking she could somehow use the evidence later as leverage to gain custody of the boys. And eventually she did try hard to get her sons back, but Lionel threatened to drag her through an ugly court scene if she ever showed her face to them. And in the end, Grandmother decided she didn't want her young boys to be scarred by such ugliness. She sacrificed her happiness for theirs."

"Oh, Flint. That's so horribly, horribly sad." She blinked her eyes as tears began to spill onto her cheeks. "I'm so sorry for you and your whole family. I realize this happened a long time ago, but it's obviously still affecting your father and you and your siblings. Maybe now that you know the truth, you can begin to get some closure on this whole thing."

He leaned over and drew her into his arms. "Don't cry, sweet Pippa," he said, his cheek pressed against the side of her silky hair. "What's done is done. And as you can read in the journal, Scarlett went on to find true and lasting love with Ode. I'm glad for that much."

"Yes, I am, too," she murmured then, easing her head back, she gave him a wan smile. "I've noticed something about you."

He groaned. "Probably that I look white or green around the gills. To tell you the truth, I feel like I've been on a roller-coaster without any brakes to stop it."

Her fingers reached up to caress his cheek. "No. You don't look white or green. Tired maybe."

His lips slanted to a wry grin. "That is thanks to you keeping me up most of the night. So what else did you notice, other than fatigue?"

"You called Scarlett 'Grandmother.' I've never heard you do that before."

He shrugged. "I never felt like she was my grandmother. Until today. Until learning the real reason for her disappearance."

"Does that mean you're going to go see her? We're only a couple of blocks away from the Neighbors Place where she lives. She won't have the slightest notion of who you are. But I don't think that matters now. *You* know who *she* is."

He moved his head just enough to press a row of kisses over her cheek. "Yes, I'm going to go see her. You will go with me, won't you?"

"I'll be right by your side," she promised.

It wasn't until much later that afternoon, after they'd eaten at a little café on the edge of town, that Flint and Pippa started the drive home to the Bell. The day had been long and exhausting for both of them, especially for Flint. He'd been stunned and angry when he'd discovered what had actually happened to his grandparents' marriage. He'd also been confused and hurt by it all.

Just seeing the pain on his face as he'd read Scarlett's journal had made Pippa want to gather him into her arms and never let go. But she'd understood that he needed to digest what had occurred in his family history before he could move on from the awful truth of the matter.

Before they'd left the park to go to the Neighbors Place,

Flint had called his father and explained everything he and Pippa had uncovered in Lionel's letters, along with Scarlett's journal. Even though she couldn't overhear anything Hadley was saying, she didn't have to ask to know he must have been crushed by the reality of what had happened to his mother. Not only that, now he had to come to terms with his father's infidelity and deceit. But judging from the things Flint had told her about his father, she had no doubt he was a very strong man and would deal with the news accordingly.

After Flint had ended the lengthy phone call with his father, he and Pippa had climbed out of the truck and walked over the footpaths winding through the trees and hedges of the little park. The cold wind and exercise had helped to clear their minds by the time they reached the Neighbors Place to visit Scarlett in her modest little apartment.

Sadly, the elderly woman hadn't recognized Pippa, even though she'd seen her on the several occasions she'd accompanied Debra for a visit with her mother. As for Flint, Scarlett had kept eyeing him and smiling with approval. And when she'd patted his hand and told him how handsome he was, Pippa could see he'd been overcome with emotion.

Throughout the short visit, Pippa had been deeply touched with the gentle and respectful manner Flint had treated his grandmother. Now, as she studied his strong profile illuminated by the lights on the dashboard, she couldn't pretend that what she felt for him was anything other than love. Her love for him was anchored so deeply inside her that she knew with complete certainty it would never change or fade away. At the same time, she was fairly sure that, even if she found the courage to express her feel-

ings to him, it would have little influence on his decision
to head back to Utah.

Snow began to fall as they approached the outskirts of
Bonners Ferry. By the time Flint finally parked the truck at
the back of the house, the wind had picked up considerably.
As Pippa watched the snow blowing horizontally across the
dark ranch yard, she realized the stormy weather matched
the dismal thoughts swirling through her.

Now that Flint had the information he'd initially traveled to Idaho to search for, there was no longer any need for
him to remain here with her on the Bell. Undoubtedly, the
sheriff's office needed him back on the duty roster and his
family would be expecting him to return home. Compared
to those reasons for him to be Utah bound, she was trivial.

"Since it's already getting late, I'm not going to bother
changing my clothes or boots, I'm going on to the barn to
do the night's chores," Flint told her as he handed her down
from the truck cab. "You have to be tired. Why don't you
go to the house? I can handle this."

She realized he was trying to be kind to her, but she
didn't want to miss working alongside him. It might be one
of the last times she'd have the chance.

"Thanks, but I'm going to help," she told him. "Together,
we'll get everything finished faster."

He gave her a faint smile. "Somehow I knew you'd say
that. Okay, let's go."

Before they reached the barn, all four of the dogs met
them with their tails wagging. Pippa said, "They're not
used to their supper being late. And I'm not used to getting home late."

Flint looked over at her. "I've put you through a hell of

a day," he said with a tone full of regret. "I'm sorry about that, Pippa."

She reached for his hand as a poignant pain made a circle between her breasts. "I spent the day with you, Flint. That made it special for me. So don't be apologizing."

He squeezed her fingers. "I couldn't have made it through without you."

The tenderness brought a sting of moisture to the backs of her eyes and because she feared she might break into tears, she tried to lighten the moment. "Of course you couldn't have made it," she said with a bright smile. "I was the only one who could open the safety-deposit box."

He didn't chuckle. In fact, he didn't even smile as he glanced over at her. "That's not what I meant."

It felt as if something strong and real was flowing from his hand to hers and even if her life had depended on it, she couldn't have looked away from him or pulled her hand from his.

"I know what you meant," she said. "And I'm glad I was there—with you."

He didn't say more and once they stepped into the barn and switched on the lights, they went to work feeding, haying and checking water troughs.

Much later, when they finally entered the house through the kitchen, Pippa removed her coat and gloves then started toward the living room. "I'll see if there are enough hot coals left to start a fire," she told him.

"Wait a minute."

Pausing, she glanced over her shoulder to see he was hanging his coat and hat on a row of pegs by the door. Once he finished the task, he strode over to where she was standing and pulled her into his arms.

"Let's not bother with a fire tonight," he said huskily. "Or coffee, or anything else. Let's just concentrate on me and you—in bed. I need you Pippa. So very, very much."

She breathed his name before she wrapped her arms around his neck and tilted her lips up to his. At the same time, she felt his hands spreading strong and warm against her back. And as desire surged through her, she blocked out all thought of the coming days. For tonight they'd be together. Tonight he'd be making sweet, delicious love to her. She couldn't ask him for anything more.

Chapter Fourteen

The next morning, when they returned from feeding the sheep, snow had begun to fall in earnest and Pippa silently wondered if the weather might affect Flint's plans to head south to Utah. He'd still not mentioned anything about going home or concerns about traveling conditions. But if a blizzard set in, it could possibly be days before the highways were safe to travel.

Last night, after they'd made love, she'd come close to asking him point-blank about his future plans. But she'd not wanted to ruin the precious time she had left with him. Instead, she'd pushed her doubts and questions aside and drifted off to sleep in the warmth of his arms. This morning over breakfast, she'd expected him to say something on the subject of Utah, but he'd only talked about things that needed be done on the Bell. A barbed-wire fence needed restretching. The tractor needed a battery and the roof of the barn could use another coat of aluminum paint. And he figured low gear was about to go completely out on the Ford.

So what else was new? He already understood she didn't have the money to take care of those things. And, frankly, she had no idea why he was even bringing any of it up now.

But in spite of her frustration, she remained quiet as she listened to his suggestions and agreed in all the right places.

Now, as Flint braked the old Ford to a halt outside the corral fence, Pippa decided she couldn't keep the loaded question to herself any longer. Maybe he found it too awkward to bring up the subject of his going home, but to avoid it was only making everything harder for her.

"Flint, I'd like to talk to you for a minute."

He switched off the motor and pocketed the key then turned slightly in the seat so that he was facing her. The sexy smile he gave her very nearly made her weep with longing.

"Okay," he said. "Talk away."

She gave her lips a nervous lick then tugged the old hat she was wearing down lower on her ears. "I—I've been thinking you'll probably be going back to Utah, soon."

His expression suddenly turned blank—a poker face that she didn't know how to read. "That's right. You know I have to go back. I have things to tend to there."

She felt sick and hollow at the same time. "Yes, I understand you have to go. I was just wondering—when."

He looked away from her. "I've not made up my mind about that yet. It depends on a few things."

"Oh. Well, I'm going to miss you," she said in a small voice.

He didn't say anything to that, but she did hear him release a heavy breath that sounded frustrated. At her? She couldn't be sure.

Finally, he said, "Actually, I need to drive into town this morning and take care of some things. Would you mind terribly if I made the trip alone?"

A short, dry laugh rushed past her lips. "I'm not a town

girl, Flint. Two visits a month are plenty enough for me. I won't mind staying here."

He looked at her and smiled. "Thanks, Pippa. I promise not to be too long. And then we'll have a real talk about Utah. Okay?"

Her heart heavier than a stone, she nodded. "No worries, I have plenty to keep me busy. And I need to call Taylor and relay everything we found out yesterday about her mother. To tell you the truth, I'm sort of dreading the call."

"Yeah, the same way I dreaded giving Dad the news." He reached over and squeezed her shoulder. "But I know you, Pippa, you'll do it as tactfully as possible."

Fifteen minutes later, she watched Flint drive away from the ranch. Once he was completely out of view, she went to the laundry room and began stuffing muddy work clothes into the washer. After she had that chore underway, she finished cleaning up their breakfast leftovers. Soon, she wouldn't have extra laundry to do or added dishes to wash, she thought. She wouldn't have nearly as much food in the fridge or the pantry. Nor would she have him working at her side or lying next to her in bed.

No, without Flint, the ranch was going to feel very different. She'd never again see the Bell as it was before he'd arrived. Yes, it would still remain the most beautiful place in the world to her, but there would be a piece of it missing with him gone. But then, the change in the Bell was nothing to the upheaval he'd caused in her heart. He'd be taking a part of it with him and she was going to have to learn how to get along without the missing piece.

She waited until noon to call Taylor and was relieved to find her on lunch break. Pippa explained what she and

Flint had discovered about Scarlett and her first husband. And, as expected, Taylor was stunned to hear the tragedy her mother had gone through in her first marriage.

"It's no wonder she never discussed anything about Lionel," Taylor said sadly. "Debra and I had always picked up on the fact that the divorce had been nasty. But we never pressed her with questions about it. Actually, we wanted her to forget it."

"Once you read her journal, Taylor, you'll realize how Ode changed her life for the better. She loved him very much."

"Yes. That's something to feel good about," she said then asked, "So, I expect this means Flint will be going home soon?"

Pippa squeezed her eyes tightly shut. If she didn't, she feared tears would begin to flow everywhere. What in the world had happened to her? Was this what falling in love with a man did to a woman? When Dale had walked out of her life, she'd never shed a tear because she'd had sense enough to realize he wasn't worth crying over. But was Flint worth the pain she was feeling now? Her heart seemed to think so.

Pippa said, "He's not yet decided what day he'll be leaving. Soon, I'm sure."

"And I'm sure you'll miss him terribly," Taylor replied.

Drawing in a bracing breath, Pippa asked, "What makes you think so?"

There was a pause before Taylor finally answered. "I can tell you've grown close to him. I can hear it in your voice when you speak his name and talk about the things you two have done together. Am I right?"

Pippa blew out the breath she'd been holding. "Yes,

you're right. But some things aren't meant to be, Taylor. And I need to go. I hear the dogs barking."

"Yes, my lunch hour is over, too. Thank you for calling with the news, sweetie. We'll talk soon, okay?"

"Of course."

The two women said their goodbyes and once Pippa had ended the connection and put her phone away, she pulled on her coat and hat and headed out the back door.

Snow or not, she had to get out of the house and get her mind busy with the things she was accustomed to doing. And that was ranching chores; not mooning over a good-looking man.

Two hours later, she was pushing a wheelbarrow full of dirty wood shavings and manure out of the barn and over to a compost pile, when she spotted Flint's truck approaching the ranch yard.

Lowering the back of the cart to the ground, she stood where she was and waited for him to park the truck and join her.

"Hey, girl, don't you know it's snowing down on your head?" he called to her.

A big smile was on his face and Pippa could only think he was thrilled that his obligations here were finally coming to an end.

Raising her voice enough to carry over the wind, she said, "A little snow never hurt me."

When he reached her side, he hooked an arm around her shoulders and squeezed her close to his side. "I haven't forgotten how sick you were. Come on, let's go in the house."

"I've not finished mucking out the horse stalls," she told him. "And why do you want to go into the house? Are you hungry? I thought you'd probably eat lunch while you were in town."

"Without you? No way."

Her lips parted. "What have you been doing all this time? It's midafternoon!"

"I had a long list of things to take care of," he told her, his grin on the verge of being sheepish. "Don't get angry with me, but I bought a battery for the tractor. With this snow setting back in, I thought we'd be needing it."

Her brows shot up and disappeared beneath the battered cowboy hat she was wearing. "'We'? I thought you were leaving soon."

The grin remained on his face and she stared at him as she tried to make sense of his attitude.

"I am," he said. "But not without you."

His comment was so outlandish it took a moment for her to catch what he'd actually said. "Without me? Flint, don't even say it. I'll never leave the Bell. It's my ranch. My home. I don't care how handsome and wonderful you are. My roots are here and they're down deep. Too deep for you to pull out!"

"Handsome? Wonderful? I like the sound of that." Laughing, he urged her over to the barn and through the small side door. "Okay. This isn't quite how I pictured it, but since you're such a ranch girl, the barn is as good a place as any for what I'm about to say to you."

Once they were inside and out of the wind, she turned to him and suddenly her heart jumped into high gear. The expression in his eyes was so warm and tender it looked incredibly like love. Was she hallucinating?

"What are you about to say? I don't understand, Flint."

Taking her gloved hand in his, he drew her close enough

that the front of their coats pressed together. "I'm saying I love you, Pippa. I'm saying more than anything I want to marry you."

Her head swung back and forth in disbelief. "No! You can't love me!"

A mixture of amusement and confusion crossed his face. "Why not?"

She groaned with misgivings. "Because I'm me—just Pippa Shanahan. A girl who had no parents. Who was bounced around from one family to the next—trying to find a home and someone to love her. That's not the kind of woman you deserve, Flint."

His expression turned resolute. "I happen to think you're exactly the kind of woman I deserve—if I ever expect to be happy. And you make me very happy, Pippa. Even when you fuss at me for buying things. But you know what? You'd better get used to it. Because I'm going to be doing a lot of buying for you and the Bell. We're going to turn this ranch into something big and profitable. Something we'll be proud to hand down to our children when we're too old to climb the ladder to the hay loft anymore."

"Build up the Bell? Hand it to our children? I realize I sound like a parrot, Flint, but you're going way too fast for me to follow what you're talking about. Only a few minutes ago, you said you were going back to Utah!"

"My darling Pippa, come here and sit down." He guided her over to a wooden bench situated against the wall of the tack room. Once they were sitting together with their knees touching, he reached for both her hands. "I guess I am going a little fast. But it's just because I'm excited about my life now. Mine and yours—together. When I said I was going back to Utah, I meant the two of us together and only for a few days so I can give notice at the sheriff's office and pack up all my things at the ranch. And during that time, you can meet all my family and see the ranch where I used to live."

"'Used to'?"

His crooked grin was full of hope and love. "I'm hoping you'll let me make my home here on the Bell. I've gotten mighty attached to the place."

Pippa didn't know whether to laugh or cry. "But, Flint, you told me that after the ordeal you went through with Rachel, you didn't want any part of love and marriage. Am I supposed to believe you've simply flipped a switch and had a complete change of heart?"

"Sweet Pippa, when I first arrived on the Bell, my whole mind was closed to anything like love or marriage. Then you walked up with your pretty little face surrounded by fake fur and I was rattled."

Rolling her eyes, she asked, "Because you saw a woman in a ten-year-old coat?"

He chuckled. "Only ten? I thought it was more like fifteen years old," he teased and then his expression grew serious. "I was rattled because I realized I was seeing a real woman. A woman with substance, who was facing life head-on. And then when I began to know you, I began to see things about family and love and even ranching in a whole different way."

"In what way?" she asked softly. "You've always had family to love and support you—a ranch the likes of which most people could only dream about living and working on. What did you need to see differently?"

He pulled off his gloves before cupping his hands around her face. "It's hard to explain. But I'd never felt as though I was really needed by anyone before. Yes, my family loves me and my friends and coworkers like me, but to feel really needed is different. Then you were suddenly too sick to care for yourself or anything on the ranch. I knew I had to handle things for you. And as I started taking care of you and the ranch, I began to see that there really was a place for me here, and the realization opened my eyes. You needed me and I need you. We need each other."

"And what about Rachel? Didn't you need her?"

His smile was wry. "No, I didn't. I liked her, but that was as far as it went. I didn't need her, or it wouldn't have been so easy to move on after she was gone. A long time ago, it became clear to me that I never loved her. She squashed my ego and, after her, I was afraid to risk the chance of a woman humiliating me a second time. But since I met you, I've learned that love isn't having a woman in a sparkly dress batting her eyelashes at me. It's an invisible bond that's infinitely stronger than any steel chain. It's too bad my grandfather ruined the love he and my grandmother had for each other."

Leaning forward, she buried her face in the crook of his shoulder. "Oh, Flint, I love you. But I never dreamed you'd ever love me back. After Dale, I wouldn't let myself believe any man would want me."

His arms tightened around her as he pressed his cheek against hers. "He was a fool. You know that, don't you?"

"Yes, I do. And I also know you're the man I'm going to love for the rest of my life," she said huskily.

He eased her head back from his shoulder and gave her a happy smile. "I've been praying you'd say those words to me. Now, let me get to the good part, I bought you something while I was in town."

She chuckled. "You already told me, remember? You bought a battery for the tractor."

"I have something else for you. Something that isn't quite as practical as a battery or five ton of alfalfa hay."

"Oh. You must have found a cheap mechanic to fix the transmission in the old Ford."

He laughed and then reached into his coat pocket. When he pulled out a square velvet box, Pippa's heart turned over.

"Jewelry? Flint, what—"

Before she could finish, he popped open the lid to expose an oval solitaire diamond set on a plain platinum band.

"This is to show the world you're going to be my beautiful wife," he said. "Do you like it? I wanted the stone to be a little bigger, but the jeweler said anything larger than three carats would have to be ordered, and I didn't want to wait."

"Larger!" She choked out the words as tears of joy were suddenly streaming down her face. "Oh, Flint! It's so gorgeous!"

"Let me put it on and see if it fits," he said. "I found a little birthstone ring of yours in your jewelry box and used it for size."

Pippa jerked off her glove and stuck out her left hand. "Broken nails, calluses and all," she said through her happy tears.

"I happen to think it's a beautiful hand," he said as he slipped the ring on her finger.

It was a perfect fit and she gazed at the symbol of his love for only a few seconds before she flung her arms around his neck and smattered his face with kisses.

Holding her tight, he asked, "I take it this means a yes to my proposal?"

"Yes! Yes!" She leaned her head back and smiled at him

with all the love she had in her. "Uh, before we finalize this engagement, I have a question for you. Do you like to fish?"

He shot her a quizzical look. "I'm not much on the sport, but I've done it occasionally. Why?"

Her eyes were dreamy as she scanned the face of her soon-to-be husband. "When spring comes to the Bell and the creeks are running, you can always catch trout. In case you don't have enough around here on the ranch to keep you occupied. I don't want you to become bored."

He let out a hearty laugh and then his lips were on hers, kissing her with a promise of never-ending love.

Epilogue

Two weeks later, Flint and Pippa were sitting with his family around the long dining table in the Stone Creek Ranch house. Because it was their last evening on the ranch before heading back to Idaho, Hadley had hired caterers to supply an elaborate dinner for the newly engaged couple.

Except for Beatrice, who now lived in Idaho with husband, Kipp, and Hunter, who was on the rodeo trail with his wife, Willow, the whole Hollister family was present for the meal. Jack, the manager of the ranch, his wife and their son, Little Jack, were sitting together to the left of Flint and Pippa. Across from them, Cordell, the foreman of the ranch sat with his wife, Maggie, and situated in a high chair between her parents was their two-year-old daughter, Bridget. Then there was Flint's younger brother Quint and his pregnant wife, Clementine. And directly across from them, Grace and her husband, Mack, sat with their two children, Kitty and Ross. On toward the end of the table, Bonnie sat angled to Hadley's left, while his wife and mother of their eight children sat next to her husband's right elbow.

A week ago, when Flint and Pippa had first arrived on Stone Creek Ranch, she'd been a bit overwhelmed by the size of his family. But they'd quickly made her feel as though she was a part of them and these past few days she'd been soaking up their affection like a sponge. Along with the huge family, she'd been totally awed by the massive size and scope of Stone Creek Ranch. Not to mention the beauty of the wide, sweeping valleys and distant mountains, the thousands of heads of cattle and sheep.

At first, seeing the majesty of the ranch had worried Pippa. How could Flint ever settle for the Bell when he rightfully belonged somewhere as grand as Stone Creek? But each time he took her into his arms and kissed her, she remembered he wasn't marrying her for the Bell, he was marrying her because he loved her and wanted the two of them to build a family and home of their own together.

Pippa's thoughts were suddenly interrupted when Quint spoke up. "After Clementine has the baby and gets back in full swing, we were thinking we'd bring a few lambs up to the Bell for a wedding present for you two," he said. "That is, if you have room for the extra lambs."

Flint and Pippa exchanged awed glances before he looked down the table to his younger brother.

"Well, sure we could use them, Quint! I can assure you that Pippa is like Clem. The lambs will be pampered."

"That's an awfully large wedding gift," Pippa said, her gaze encompassing both Quint and Clementine. "Are you sure you want to give us that much?"

Quint laughed. "Well, we didn't figure you two would have much use for a salad bowl set."

The group around the table chuckled and then Clementine said, "The merinos do really well in cold weather. I used to herd them when I lived in southern Idaho. And we know you'll take great care of them."

Cordell looked to where his father was seated at the head

of the table. "Dad, have you stopped to realize you're now going to have two daughters-in-law from Idaho? What's are the odds of that happening?"

Across from Flint, Jack laughed. "What were the odds of Flint finding a woman like Pippa? Slim to none. But somehow he pulled it off and persuaded her to marry him. Wonder of wonders," he teased.

Flint chuckled. "Surprised you, did I, brother?"

Jack grinned. "Pleasantly so. And, Pippa, you're a great addition to the Hollister family."

"Thank you, Jack," she said then glanced gratefully around the table at the rest of the family. "And thanks all of you for graciously welcoming me into your home."

Clearing his throat, Hadley reached for his wineglass. "This will always be yours and Flint's home, too. Anytime you want to show up, you'll always be welcome. And I'm sure you already know Claire is planning a huge wedding for you two here on the ranch. Since Flint is our last son to get married, she wants to have her hand in the ceremony."

"Have you two set the date yet?" Grace asked then bestowed a conspiring wink at her husband.

"Tomorrow," Flint answered without hesitation.

After the chuckling and ribbing died down, Pippa said, "We thought in early May, before all of us started spring roundup. And that might give Beatrice time to design a dress for me. If she's willing."

Bonnie said, "No worries, Pippa. She'll be honored and thrilled to take on the job."

Claire reached over and placed a hand on her husband's arm. "Darling, I know you've always been the big boss around here and I've always let you be."

Her remark caused a ripple of chuckles to travel around the dining table.

"Thanks, honey, for letting me in on something I've known for forty-some years," Hadley told her.

"But I have to say if you ever try to send another one of our children to Idaho, you're going to have a fight on your hands," she told him.

"Why? You have something against the state?" he asked.

"No. It's a lovely state. It's just that the last two children you've sent up to Idaho are staying there. First Beatrice married Kipp and now Flint is marrying Pippa and making his home less than twenty miles from the Canadian border. You send our last single child up there and she might end up completely out of the country!"

Everyone laughed while Hadley shook his head. "You're worrying for nothing, Claire. I'm not sending Bonnie to Idaho. Flint and Pippa have already gathered all the information we needed there. However," he added, turning to address the rest of the group, "now that the truth has come out, Claire and I are planning to drive up to Coeur d'Alene to visit my mother. I can't make up for the loss she endured— that all of us have experienced—but it's a beginning."

Claire rose from her chair and went around the table to plant a kiss on Hadley's cheek. "I'm glad we're going to see Scarlett. I'm also relieved you're not sending Bonnie off to Idaho."

He sipped his wine and directed a coy smile at his daughter. "I've decided Bonnie needs to go the opposite direction," he said. "South. Down to Three Rivers Ranch where she and Maureen can put their heads together and figure out this whole story about Parnell. He was my grandfather. I'd

like to know more about him and try to understand what
caused him to split away from the family."

Pippa glanced down the table just in time to see Bonnie's jaw drop.

"Dad! Are you serious? I don't want to go to Arizona!
I don't want to go anywhere!"

Flint nudged Pippa in the rib cage and spoke under his
breath. "Bonnie is a homebody. But the trip will do her
good. Just like my trip to Bonners Ferry did for me."

Hadley said to Bonnie, "You're the one who's been working on this family tree. You're not going to quit until it's
completed. And don't be worrying about who'll look after
the ranch's office. Your mother and I will handle the book-
keeping and anything else that comes up."

Bonnie's mouth closed and after that no more was mentioned about the family tree or the trip to Arizona. Pippa
almost felt sorry for Flint's pretty blond sister. She understood Bonnie didn't want to be pushed out of her comfort
zone. But if Flint hadn't come along and pushed Pippa out
of the lonely walls she'd built around herself, she'd never
have known the happiness she was feeling now.

After the meal ended and coffee was served in the den,
Flint and Pippa walked out to the patio to have a moment
alone. As they stood close together, gazing out at the moon-
lit night, Pippa could see the tarps covering Lionel's long-
standing rose garden and, for a moment, her heart panged
with sorrow. In many ways, Flint's grandfather had been
misguided and even vengeful, and yet, deep down he must
have felt an abiding love for his mother to have worked so
hard to recreate her garden.

"I'm so glad Hadley called Taylor and the half-siblings
are planning to meet soon. She needs family in her life and

I'm sure your father will love having a sister," she said, then rested her head against his arm. "You know, Flint, if Scarlett was in her right mind, I wonder what she would think if she could see this ranch now. If she could see her sons and grandchildren. Do you think it would make her happy?"

He let out a long breath. "Happy or sad. Who's to say? We'll never know, will we? She was lost to us and we were lost to her. The only thing we can be sure of now is that she'll live on in us and our children."

"Yes. That's a comforting thought."

Drawing her into the circle of his arms, he placed a promising kiss on her lips. "We'd better go back in and show our smiling faces. It's our last night here."

"Yes, and tomorrow is the beginning of the rest of our lives," she said.

"Our life together on the Bell."

He kissed her again and then, with their arms entwined, they walked back into the house to join the family.

* * * * *